All that was PROMISED

All that was PROMISED

VICKIE HALL

BONNEVILLE BOOKS
SPRINGVILLE, UT

No part of this book may be reproduced in any form whatsoever, whether by graphic, visual, electronic, film, microfilm, tape recording, or any other means, without prior written permission of the publisher, except in the case of brief passages embodied in critical reviews and articles.

The views expressed within this work are the sole responsibility of the author and do not necessarily reflect the position of Cedar Fort, Inc., or any other entity.

This is a work of fiction. The characters, names, incidents, places, and dialogue are products of the author's imagination and are not to be construed as real.

ISBN 13: 978-1-59955-479-2

Published by Bonneviille Books, an imprint of Cedar Fort, Inc., 2373 W. 700 S., Springville, UT 84663

Distributed by Cedar Fort, Inc., www.cedarfort.com

LIBRARY OF CONGRESS CATALOGING-IN-PUBLICATION DATA
Hall, Vickie, 1957-
  All that was promised / Vickie Hall.
    p. cm.
  Summary: In 1847 young Methodist minister Richard Kenyon converts to Mormonism. Richard's newfound faith is put to the test as he faces down the anger of his former congregation, his wife's indecisiveness, the betrayal of his brother, and the murderous intentions of misinformed villagers.
  ISBN 978-1-59955-479-2
  1. Mormon converts—Wales—Fiction. 2. Methodists—Wales—Fiction. 3. Christian fiction, American. 4. Historical fiction, American. I. Title.

  PS3608.A54824A79 2011
  813'.6—dc22

  2010035563

Cover design by Angela D. Olsen
Cover design © 2010 by Lyle Mortimer
Edited and typeset by Megan E. Welton

Printed in the United States of America

10 9 8 7 6 5 4 3 2 1

Printed on acid-free paper

For my sister Lori, whose love, assistance,
and encouragement helped to make this book a reality.
You have my eternal love and gratitude.

And to my high school English teacher, Mrs. Harvey, who once
asked me, "Have you ever thought of becoming a writer?"

ONE

———— ✦ ————

If there was one thing that made Leah Kenyon proud, it was her husband. She stood dutifully beside him, her arm linked through his. A polite smile crossed her oval face as members of his congregation departed the old Methodist church.

" 'Twas a fine sermon, Reverend Kenyon," said one of the worshippers who paused on the steps leading from the moss-encrusted north side of the church. His wife and children corralled around the portly man as he shook hands with the reverend.

He gave the man a slight nod. " 'Tis a pleasure to see you in church after last week's illness."

"Aye, but not half as glad as your brother'll be to have me workin' again tomorrow," Niall snorted.

Niall's wife glanced over her shoulder to ensure the reverend's brother was not within earshot. "My Niall's hardly missed a day's work in near fifteen year," she rasped beneath her breath. "Yet your brother's over the top of the dishes if he's to miss even one day."

Reverend Kenyon laughed. "Aye, it does sound like Robert—always a bit unreasonable."

Niall placed his hands on either side of his round belly and smiled. "Aye, he's little like your father, God rest his soul," he said with a sigh of reminiscence. "Your father was a gracious and kind

I

man, and you takes after him, Reverend. But I'm not complainin'," he said, waving his hand from side to side. "Your brother treats me well enough, and I'm thankful to be workin' for Kenyon 'n Sons.

Niall's wife nudged him in the side and jabbed her thumb in the direction of his approaching employer. "We're goin' to go then, are we?" she said hurriedly. "The sermon was a fine one, Reverend Kenyon."

Niall reached out to Leah and took her hand. "So good to see you again, Mrs. Kenyon," he said with a pleasant smile. He leaned forward and whispered in her ear. "You married the better brother."

Leah couldn't help but smile. She had a fondness for the man who had known the Kenyon brothers since they were boys. She often found Niall's tales of her husband's childhood charming and delightful, despite Richard's insistence that Niall's stories were great exaggerations. " 'Tis a pleasure to see you too, Niall," she said, happy to keep their whispered secret between them.

Niall ushered his family down the steps as Richard gave his wife a fleeting glance. He smiled at her and gave her hand a squeeze before his older brother approached. "Robert," he greeted. "How did you find the sermon today?"

Robert Kenyon looked much like his brother; both men were tall, with black hair and striking dark eyes. Robert peered at Richard a moment before responding. "As sermons go, I suppose it was satisfactory."

Richard felt a bemused smirk come his lips. "Ah, but not filled with the same satisfaction as say, a good business deal brings, isn't that right?"

Robert gave him a sideways glance. He didn't feel much like sparring with his brother today. Richard's decision to take up the ministry instead of joining the family business had always been a bone of contention between them. Robert found only a cursory use for religion and never understood Richard's devotion to God.

Robert's wife stepped nearer her husband. Abigail Kenyon was a pompous English woman. She oozed an air of superiority as she glared down her long, pointed nose at Richard and Leah. "I thought I might mention we have been invited by some of our dearest friends to attend Reverend Trahern's church. So many of his congregation are among the better classes, and it would be of benefit for Robert to mingle amid them." Then she added quickly, "For business purposes, you understand."

Leah feigned a smile and blinked several times. "I can't think of a better way to choose a church," she charged snidely. Richard snagged her by the arm as if to restrain the escalating temper he sensed within his wife.

Abigail looked at her sister-in-law with some disdain. "Well, Leah, you must admit, there are a number of benefits to being seen with the right people and mingling with those who can help expand my husband's business opportunities."

Richard couldn't help but feel slighted. Yes, his congregation was made up of people with modest incomes; they were hard-working, common people, but people who found comfort in hearing God's word. He had dedicated his ministry to those who were most in need, those with humble piety who did their best to live a Christian life. It was a well-known fact that Reverend Trahern catered to the wealthy business class and government officials in the city of Cardiff. His congregation's offerings kept him well off and comfortable because his sermons did not call out the wicked nor offend the sinner. *Aye,* Richard thought sadly, *perhaps 'tis where Robert belongs, for his heart is rooted in money and not in the Lord.* "If that is where your heart leads you, then of course, you must go. I will not hold it against you."

"Well, I'll rest easy then," Robert replied with a snide smirk. He took Abigail by the elbow and steered her toward the stairs. "Goodbye, Richard," he said over his shoulder. "Leah."

It was only after Robert and Abigail started down the sidewalk that Leah noticed her niece cowering behind the open church door. She looked at the adolescent girl with softened eyes. Leah stretched out her hand toward the girl and smiled. "Amelia," she called quietly.

The fourteen-year-old girl with her father's dark hair and her mother's pale eyes peered from behind the thick wooden door. Without further provocation, she hurried to Leah and threw her arms around her aunt. "I don't want to leave you and Uncle Richard," she cried. "I don't want to go with them."

Leah smoothed back Amelia's raven hair and looked into her face with great affection. "Now don't you worry about that," she soothed.

Richard lifted Amelia's chin with the tips of his fingers. "If they attend Reverend Trahern's church, you must go with them," he said with tempered firmness. "You know that, don't you, Amelia? You know 'tis wicked to disobey your parents."

Amelia buried her face against Leah's chest. "But I don't want to leave you," she sobbed.

Leah looked at her husband for encouragement. He took hold of Amelia's shoulders and turned her toward him. Richard smiled softly at her, his dark brown eyes penetrating her heart. "You won't be leaving us," he assured her. "We'll see each other often, just as we always have. The only difference is we'll not worship together."

"Aye," Leah added, wiping Amelia's tears away with her fingers. "Nothin' else will change."

Amelia looked at her aunt and uncle with a dubious frown. She'd heard her parents arguing when they thought she was asleep. She knew they were planning to limit her exposure to her aunt and uncle because they were poor—an embarrassment to the Kenyon family name. She wanted to believe her aunt that nothing would change, but in her heart, Amelia feared the worst.

Leah's heart ached for her niece. She knew the girl was daily ridiculed by her mother and ignored by her father. Her parent's loveless marriage spilled over into Amelia's life in the most unpleasant ways imaginable, and as an only child, she had no one to share in her misery. She spoke little of the conditions at home to Leah and Richard, but the situation was evident to them as they experienced first-hand Robert and Abigail's treatment of her. They knew how lonely and miserable she was. Amelia became the focus of Leah's maternal feelings, and she showered her niece with the love and affection that was absent from the girl's selfish parents. She was the nearest thing Leah had to a child of her own. In five years of marriage, Leah had experienced several miscarriages and two stillbirths, which had left an aching void in her heart.

Amelia heard her name called aloud as her mother marched back to the church steps. The girl's blood chilled at the sound of her mother's voice. She lifted the hem of her skirts and padded down the walkway without another word to her aunt and uncle. Leah looked at her husband with that familiar pained expression she so often gave him whenever she witnessed the way Amelia seemed to disappear in the presence of her mother. It was as if the girl became nothing, with no light of her own, falling into the darkness of her mother's domineering shadow.

Richard put his arm around his wife's shoulder and kissed her temple. It was difficult for him too. His sermons on love and kindness were lost on his brother and sister-in-law. No amount of preaching ever seemed to touch them, and he couldn't help but sometimes feel as though he had failed his niece by failing to change her parents. The church was empty now, and Richard closed the creaky wooden door. Taking the key from his pocket, he locked the church up tight and then took hold of Leah's arm as they started for home.

<hr />

The afternoon sky darkened as an impending spring storm brewed in the burgeoning clouds overhead. The Kenyon's small stone cottage sat nestled on a small plot of land surrounded by a stacked stone fence built some two centuries earlier. The thickly thatched roof of the little home was in need of replacement, but it was an expense that would have to wait another season.

Leah glanced through the kitchen window's diamond-shaped panes of wavy glass, her paring knife halted between the potato and its brown spotted skin. The air had a damp coolness to it that made her shiver as she studied the blackening horizon. Thoughts of Amelia hovered in her mind as darkly as the approaching storm. She couldn't seem to shake the vision of Amelia cowering behind her mother last Sunday morning and the look of haunting sadness on the young girl's face.

Richard sat at the kitchen table, his shoulders hunched over the sermon he scribbled onto a scrap of paper. Rain began pelting the windows, pinging musically against the panes with sharp resonance. He pulled the candle closer to him as the clouds blotted out the last of the sun, and he muttered something about not being able to see his Bible.

A rapid knock sounded at the door, its urgency sending a chill down Leah's spine. She dropped her knife into the bowl of peelings, wiped her hands on her apron, and opened the door. A deafening rumble of thunder shook the cottage with its powerful force and continued to reverberate across the distant skies until it faded to a muffled groan. She looked down at a young boy, already wet from the pouring rain as he stood in front of her. "Why, Timothy, 'tis rainin' old women and sticks! What are you doin' out?" she asked with concern.

The thin sprig of a boy peered up into her face, his tears mingled with the rain. "Your mam says I should fetch the reverend," he said with a ragged breath. "Hurry!"

The boy spun about and darted up the cobblestone street, disappearing into the dreary storm. Richard was already at the door, his oilskin coat in hand. He looked at Leah, his face filled with dread. "Mary must be in trouble if your mam has sent for me."

Leah nodded, a sense of foreboding shadowing her fears. Her mother, a midwife, had delivered hundreds of babies into the world. Gwendolyn Murdock was capable and experienced after practicing her skills for nearly thirty years. Only when her earthly expertise failed her did she call for spiritual assistance. Timothy's mother was a frail and sickly woman, and Leah swallowed hard against the rising lump in her throat. "I'm comin' with you," she said grabbing her cloak.

The pair raced into the storm, oblivious to the pelting, icy rain. They proceeded toward Beacon Street to a length of row houses. The door to the Williamses' was left ajar. They went inside and dropped their coats beside the door. Young Timothy raced toward Leah and threw his thin arms around her legs, burying his face against her apron.

Owen Williams stood near the fire, his arms hung limply at his sides. His deep-set eyes were hollow and dark with haunting shadows. "Reverend Kenyon," Owen said scarcely above a whisper. "The baban's died, and Mary's failin' . . ."

Richard rested his hand on the man's shoulder, a silent acknowledgment of his breaking heart. He headed to the back room where Mary and Gwendolyn were sequestered through the process of the birth. Reaching for the doorknob, he turned it slowly in his hand and peered inside. "Gwendolyn?"

The small but sturdy woman motioned for him to enter. Her auburn hair was threaded with glints of silver as she raised the lantern from the nightstand. The look on her face revealed more than any words could say as she walked toward him. "The baban was stillborn," she whispered to him as he came closer. "Mary's hemorrhaged so much . . . I can't stop the bleedin' . . ." Gwendolyn's voice cracked, and she turned away from her son-in-law in an effort to maintain her composure.

Richard went to the bed, where Mary lay motionless, her chest barely rising, her skin pale as moonlight. "Mary," he said gently, " 'tis Reverend Kenyon." Richard reached out and took hold of Mary's hand, but she made no effort to clasp it in return. "Can you hear me?"

He waited, the sound of his heartbeat counting off the seconds in his ears. "Mary? Don't be afraid . . . the Lord is with you . . ."

Again, the woman remained unresponsive. Her breathing was scarcely noticeable, and then the smallest gasp of air filled her lungs. As it escaped her lips with a tiny breath, she fell silent. Richard felt her wrist for a pulse and slowly placed her lifeless arm across her chest. "God bless you, Mary Williams," he murmured. "Rest in peace."

He looked at Gwendolyn, whose face was already stained with tears. Richard draped his arm around her drooping shoulders and squeezed her tightly. " 'Tis not your fault, Gwendolyn," he said softly. "You did all you could."

Gwendolyn wrung her hands. So many joyous births in her years of midwifery all melded together in a blur of happy memories. She could scarcely recall one uneventful delivery from another. But births like this one haunted her thoughts for months and even years. She felt helpless to alter the course of these tragedies, which left her feeling impotent and overwhelmed. "I asks her if she'd stepped over a grave or if she'd heard the shriekin' o' the hag o' the mist," she said absently, straining to put a reason to the awful tragedy, both events known to cause imminent death.

The hag of the mist, he retorted to himself. As if she even existed, much less had the power to bring about death by merely hearing her voice. And stepping over a grave . . . He had neither the desire nor will to correct his mother-in-law during the present circumstance and dismissed the nonsense of the folklore without a second thought. Gwendolyn's superstitions were common to many of the Welsh, with one foot set firmly in the old ways, still believing in legends and wives' tales, while the other was planted in the more straightforward belief in Christianity, which was meant to dispel such ancient traditions. "I'll tell Owen," he offered with a heavy sigh.

"I hears Leah's voice when you come in," Gwendolyn said as she turned toward the bed. "Send her to me so she can help me prepare Mary and the baban for the family."

Richard nodded and left the bedroom, his feet reluctant to carry him to his destination. As he emerged from the back of the house, he motioned for Leah to join her mother and then turned to face Owen. Richard put his hand on Owen's narrow shoulder, but the man remained unmoving. "Gwendolyn did all she could for Mary. Your wife was a good woman, but she's in God's hands now," he consoled. "I'm so sorry, Owen."

Owen's face hardened as he glared at the minister, his emotions swelling within him. "And you, Reverend? Did you do all you could, then?"

Richard recognized Owen's harsh accusation as that of a man's grief-stricken heart crying out for understanding. " 'Twas God's will."

Owen narrowed his eyes and glowered at Richard. "God's will?" he spat, his slim form becoming agitated with anger. "Why is that? What makes him decide to take my Mary away from me? Why don't he take you or your wife, Reverend? Why my Mary? Why our little baban?"

Richard felt himself grappling for answers he didn't possess. There was no other explanation, no trite words of wisdom he could offer that would satisfy Owen's pain-filled questions. For a moment, he wished the deaths had been caused by Mary's stepping over a grave or having heard a shriek from the hag of the mist. Perhaps there was something understandable about those reasons. But God's will was far less comforting. "Owen," he said softly, "I know 'tis hard to understand . . ."

Owen's face reddened as he clenched his fists, the raw emotions now boiling over his ability to contain them. "You're right about that!" he hissed. "I don't understand a God who'd be so cruel, a God who'd take away the only decent thing . . ." His voice choked with emotion. "The only woman . . . I ever loved . . ."

Richard struggled within himself for a way to reach this man. How could he make him understand that God's will was not to be questioned? How could he reconcile this man's loss with the omnipotent mind of God? He couldn't. No matter how he tried, he couldn't find an answer that would suffice. "Owen," he began tenuously, feeling his way through a response, "you mustn't doubt God's wisdom. He alone decides these matters, just as he chooses who will receive salvation."

Owen took a threatening step toward him. "And that's another thing," he hissed, his bony finger pointing at Richard. "When I was sittin' in your pews and listenin' to you preach about salvation comin' only to a few God would choose, I swallows it, thinkin' you're the preacher, you know best. But not no more." He shook his head as if to drive the thoughts from his mind. "There isn't—" he stopped himself and gritted his teeth against a rising flood of tears, "—there wasn't a finer Christian woman than my Mary. She gave to everyone 'round her, took care of her neighbors when they was sick, went to church every Sunday—your church, Reverend Kenyon—and if she isn't worthy of salvation, then no one is!"

Richard swallowed hard. Suddenly his own words slapped him in the face with a cruel realization. His Calvinist-Methodist doctrine taught predestination, that it was God's choosing alone who would be saved and who would not, thus the encouragement for all to live righteously. Owen had voiced the doubts that had silently plagued Richard's own conscience, despite efforts to quell them as diversions from his faith. Yet if only an elect few were to be saved, then what was to become of the rest of mankind? These thoughts tormented him even as he spouted the words from the pulpit. But who was he to question God? How could he doubt in all that he believed, all that he taught to others?

His heart went out to Owen. He saw the suffering in his eyes, the violent struggle within himself to accept his wife's death. If only he had the words to comfort him, words that would help Owen rise above this tragedy. Richard felt his capacity to comfort this man drain away, leaving him an empty vessel. "Please, Owen, I beg of you. Don't turn away from God—," Richard's words sounded hollow as they echoed in his ears.

"Spare me your sermons, Reverend," Owen spat bitterly, his palm extended toward Richard. "They're no use to me now."

Richard took a step toward Owen, but the man's posture became even more defensive as he shunned any further efforts to be consoled. Leah exited the bedroom, drawn by the raised sound of Owen's agitation. She saw Timothy curled up in a ball as he sat in his mother's rocking chair with her shawl wrapped about him, sobbing against the paisley woolen wrap. She moved beside her husband with a questioning look in her emerald green eyes. "Is everything all right?" she asked glancing back and forth between the two men.

Owen spun on his heel, his eyes lit with fire. "No, Mrs. Kenyon, nothin' is right!" Owen hollered, his hands clenched into threatening fists. "You'd best take the reverend and his religion and leave my house before . . ."

Leah was shocked. She'd never seen Owen so much as swat at a fly and now he was threatening bodily harm to his own minister. "Owen, I can see you're very upset, and rightfully so, but you don't mean what you're sayin'—"

"I means it!" he charged. Owen suddenly bolted for the door and flung it wide, the cold rain splattering against the threshold. "Get out!"

Richard and Leah took up their coats and stepped into the bone-chilling storm without looking back as Owen slammed the door behind them. The distance to their cottage was covered in quick, hurried steps accompanied by the silence of their thoughts. Throughout the remainder of the evening, Richard remained sullen, his face buried in the Bible, searching for his own solace, his own redemption for doubting his faith. Leah kept her distance, sensing her husband's inner pain but not knowing how to help him. As they prepared for bed, she could stand the silence between them no longer.

"Richard," she said quietly as she turned down the covers. "You're a good man, a faithful servant of the Lord." She walked around the bed and stood in front of him. The softened light of the single candle on the nightstand flickered in warm golden hues against his handsome face. Leah reached up and caressed his cheek. "I'm so blessed to be your wife," she whispered.

Richard placed his hand over hers, brought it to his lips, and kissed her palm. His self-doubt seemed to dissipate with her touch. He tangled his fingers in her auburn hair and pulled her closer to him. "Aye, but you're beautiful," he murmured.

Leah found herself lost in his embrace as their lips met. Everything else fell away from their thoughts until there was only the two of them, drowned in one another's desires. The rain had stopped, and she could hear her heart beating wildly in her chest. How she loved him, and how it pained her to see him brooding over Owen. She prayed she could help him forget.

❦

Richard shoved his arm into the sleeve of his coat and shrugged it over his shoulders until it rested properly across his back. He buttoned a single button in the center of the dark brown overcoat and took his hat into his hands. "I'll be back in a couple of hours," he said to Leah as she finished clearing the breakfast dishes from the table.

She paused in her work and wiped her hands in her apron. "Be patient with Owen," she gently urged. "The sun always comes to the hill."

Richard crossed the room and kissed her. "Ever an optimist," he teased.

Leah pushed back a lock of his black hair and gazed into his deep brown eyes. "Aye, that I am."

He kissed her again and turned to leave. As he opened the door, he was struck by a cold wind that set the last of the morning fog rolling in billowy swirls. The sun was already hard at work clearing the way for a fair but cool day. Richard put on his hat, waved at Leah, and closed the door behind him.

The great city of Cardiff was already busy for market day. Carts, wagons, horses, and people on foot surrounded him, each burdened with their wares for sale in the city. Tinsmiths, coopers, weavers, cheese makers, seamstresses, and all varieties of tradespeople converged on market day. An older man struggled to balance two rolls of his own homespun flannel over his stooped shoulders, while all about him villagers engaged in animated conversations.

Cardiff was nestled in the lower south-east portion of Wales and had grown from a small village of 1,800 souls in 1801 to a small township of 11,400 by 1841. The port city had become a major player in the Industrial Revolution, receiving tons of coal from further north, first by barge through a system of cleverly designed canals, and then by rail as the steam locomotive became the preferred mode of transportation. From Cardiff Bay, the millions of tons of coal were loaded onto ships and sent throughout the world.

He glanced up to his left at Cardiff Castle, rising on a grassy hill and built on a medieval Norman foundation by the first Marquess of Bute, a generous benefactor to the city. The castle was flanked on the west side by a massive octagonal tower that could be seen for some distance. The historically rich setting conjured to his mind the long-held Welsh tradition that the wise and gracious King Arthur held court in Wales with his stunning queen, Guinevere, and the Knights of the Round Table. He imagined the noble Sir Gawain, Sir Bedivere, Sir Cai, and all the brave knights stationed about their king to defend their country and the rights of the weak. Richard shook himself from his fanciful thoughts and turned his sights to Angel Street as he crossed the cobblestone road to visit his brother.

Kenyon & Sons stood as a prosperous business handling fine imported teas. It was started by Richard's father some forty years previous and had become a well-known establishment. It had even received the honor of providing tea to the royal household. As Richard neared the store, his attention was drawn to a gathering crowd of people across the street. His interest was piqued as he saw a man standing atop a shipping crate, his arms spread wide and an open book in his hand.

He drew nearer and hovered at the edge of the crowd, watching with curiosity. The man was tall and tanned, as if he spent a great deal of time outdoors. Richard guessed he was near thirty years old. His clothes showed obvious signs of wear but were still tidy and presentable. His English was spoken with an American accent that Richard found amusing, but the look of intensity on the stranger's face was one of unmistakable confidence. ". . . Then, before the young boy there appeared two distinct personages," the man declared. "God the Father and His son, Jesus Christ, bathed in a white light, hovered above the humble boy."

A murmur rumbled through the crowd, questioning such a statement with astonished gazes. One man yelled at the American before throwing his hands down in disgust as he stormed away from the swarm.

"I testify to you," the American stated emphatically, "that God and Jesus Christ are two separate beings of flesh and bone, just as you and I—"

"Blasphemy!" shouted a man in the crowd. "You speak lies!"

"I speak the truth!" the man insisted. "Mankind has slept in a stupor for centuries. Precious truths have been lost! The gospel of Jesus Christ has been usurped by wicked men. Even well-meaning men are doing their best, but nonetheless, the doctrine has been changed from what it once was."

"Go back to America!" a voice rose from the crowd.

"I testify to you," the man continued undaunted, "that the gospel of Jesus Christ has been restored through the Prophet Joseph Smith. That which was lost has been restored, those precious truths are ours again, and the plan of salvation is declared to all nations!"

Richard couldn't help but feel some undecipherable power emanating from the tall American, something that drew him in, something that tempted him to believe what he heard. The man spoke with such confidence and passion that it made Richard want to know more. He pressed his way further into the crowd to ask a question. Without warning, someone hurled a rock toward the man, striking him in the forehead, and causing a nasty gash that began to spurt blood immediately. The man stumbled from the shipping crate but managed to keep himself upright.

"Serves you right!" growled one of the on-lookers.

"He deserves worse'n that!" yelled another as the crowd dispersed, satisfied they had put a stop to the unwelcome preacher.

Several in the crowd laughed and took part in deriding the wounded man as he staggered forward, clasping his bleeding brow. Richard pushed his way toward the assaulted man, reaching for his arm to steady him as he began to waver from the unexpected blow.

"Let me help you," Richard said, taking a handkerchief from his pocket and placing it to the man's cut.

The stranger weaved a bit more before shaking off the dizziness he felt. "I'm all right," he said, trying to focus on Richard's concerned face.

"Here, sit for a minute," Richard said, steering the man to the upturned crate. Richard picked up the book that had dropped from the man's hand during the attack and dusted off the cover.

"Thank you for your kindness," the man said, blotting the bloody wound with the handkerchief.

"Let me take a look at that," he said, gently pulling the man's hand from his forehead. "What barbarians," Richard scoffed, voicing his assessment of the crowd as he inspected the injury. "And they profess to be Christians. What's your name, friend?"

"Ben Lachlan," the man said, extending his hand.

Richard took hold of the man's hand and shook it earnestly. "Richard Kenyon," he replied. "Your wound needs tending, Mr. Lachlan," Richard insisted. "I live just a few streets from here. Come with me."

Ben's head pounded as he stood at Richard's urging. "I don't want to be any trouble to you, Mr. Kenyon," he mildly protested.

" 'Tis no trouble," Richard assured him. He handed Ben his book, and they started back to Richard's house.

There was something about Ben that Richard couldn't quite pinpoint. He felt an inexplicable sense of trust in Ben, without cause or even reason. One thing was for certain, Ben Lachlan had stated some outlandish beliefs but some that struck a chord of resonance within Richard. He found himself in an uncomfortable position. Doubting his own faith demanded resolution but so did the validity of the stranger's claims.

Richard said little as they approached the house. He reached for the latch and pushed open the door. "Leah," he called. "*Cariad*?[1]"

Leah turned from the rear of the house at the sound of her husband's voice. "Did Owen throw you out again?" she teased as she came toward the door. She was surprised to see the stranger standing beside Richard. "What's happened?" she asked with concern, noting

---

1 Welsh for "My love" or "Dear one"

the blood-soaked handkerchief above the stranger's eye.

Richard took Ben by the elbow and led him to a kitchen chair. "This is Ben Lachlan," he said. "Someone threw a rock."

Leah instinctively drew Ben's hand away from the wound and inspected it with a keen eye. " 'Tis not too serious, Mr. Lachlan," she commented. "I'll gather a few things and be right back."

"Thank you, Mrs. Kenyon," he replied with an appreciative smile.

Richard took a seat across from Ben at the table. His mind was racing with questions and a curiosity about this man's discourses. "I want to hear more of your teachings," he began, trying to rein in his curiosity. Leah returned and Richard reached toward her. "Leah, you must listen to Mr. Lachlan. I know you'll be interested too."

"Interested in what?" Leah asked as she set down a basin of water and fresh towels.

"Mr. Lachlan is from America, and he was preaching about the most incredible things—" He stopped himself and looked at Ben. "You tell her," he encouraged. "Start at the beginning."

Leah observed her husband's intense demeanor and thought it odd. What had this stranger said that so intrigued Richard? "Is that how a rock came to meet with your forehead?" she asked with a wry grin. "Was it your preachin' that got you into trouble?"

Ben couldn't help but smile. "It was indeed, Mrs. Kenyon."

Leah dipped a towel into the basin of water and wrung it out. She carefully blotted away the coagulating blood surrounding the cut. "Well, I've no rocks in my pocket. Speak freely."

Ben liked Mrs. Kenyon, and Richard too, for that matter. As he revealed the restored gospel of Jesus Christ, Richard listened with interest, stopping Ben on particular points that didn't fit well with his own beliefs. The men carried on for several minutes as Leah cleaned Ben's injury and offered him a clean cotton cloth to hold over the throbbing site. She listened quietly as she cleared away her supplies, her eyes flicking between Richard's concentrated expression and Ben's glowing appearance. She watched the intensity in Richard's eyes as Ben's amazing claims came to light, one by one. It frightened her to see Richard so open to Ben's outlandish tales. It called into question everything Richard had ever preached to his congregation, everything he'd ever believed. Ben related tales of angels and golden plates, of prophets and temples. It sounded more like some story from the Old Testament than a current-day event. Leah was dubious and skeptical of the whole exchange.

The minutes grew into hours, and Leah sat quietly in the parlor sewing as she listened to the men's discussion. As it neared supper-time, she went to the kitchen to begin preparing their meal. She decided on simple fare—*crempog*, a Welsh pancake smothered in butter. She didn't interrupt them as they continued, still in their deep conversation. Only when she presented each of them a plate of food did they stop long enough to take notice.

The pendulum wall clock, a wedding gift from Leah's mother, chimed nine times. Leah set her sewing aside, her eyes tired from straining to see by the dim light of the candle. She walked to the kitchen table and for the first time broke into the men's discussion. "Begging your pardon," she interrupted. "Could I offer you some tea before I retire?"

Ben suddenly blanched with the realization of the time and then quickly blushed with embarrassment as he came to his feet. "Oh, Mrs. Kenyon, please forgive me. I've monopolized your home far too long. How very inconsiderate of me."

Leah glanced at Richard as if to place a portion of the blame on him. "Not at all, Mr. Lachlan," she said. "I've been listenin' with great interest to your unusual beliefs and've been most entertained by them."

Richard stood beside his wife and placed his arm around her shoulder. "I guess time just got away from us." He grinned sheep-ishly. He reached for Ben's hand. "Will you come back tomorrow?"

Ben smiled and shook Richard's hand. "Certainly," he replied. "I'll bring you a copy of the Book of Mormon—it's just two shil-lings. Much as I'd like to give them away, we simply don't have the funds to do so."

"Aye, I'd be very happy to buy a copy from you," he agreed eagerly.

Ben extended his hand to Leah. "Thank you for your kindness and for the lovely meal, Mrs. Kenyon. You have been a most gener-ous hostess, and I promise not to take all of your husband's time tomorrow." Leah managed a smile. She liked Mr. Lachlan, despite his strange religion. "I'll hold you to that."

Richard closed the door after Ben and faced his wife. His eyes gleamed with excitement. "How remarkable," he breathed. "Isn't it amazing?"

Leah studied her husband for a moment and then frowned. "Don't tell me you believed him?"

He seemed stunned by her question. Most of what Ben had taught him appeared to make sense. There was a resonance to it he found difficult to deny. He felt crestfallen as he peered into Leah's doubting eyes. "I do believe him. Don't you see it? 'Tis as though I've been lifted from my doubts. I see now how corrupted man's religion has become."

"Man's religion," she countered. "I thought you preached God's religion, Richard. I thought you were a minister of God's truth, not man's.

He took a firm hold of her arms. "I've been wrong, Leah. Christ's church has been corrupted by man. So many things make sense to me now."

Leah struggled with her feelings. Her husband was a minister, a man who had dedicated his life to teaching the word of God through the enlightened inspiration of Calvin and Wesley. He had worked hard to shepherd his small congregation of followers, despite their meager offerings being scarcely enough to sustain them. It was all he knew, all he had ever wanted of life: to teach and to serve others. How could he jeopardize that future by believing in the incredible claims of a complete stranger?

Her face grew sullen. "It makes no sense to me, Richard. I listened to every word Mr. Lachlan had to say and found no truth in it. Don't let yourself be deceived by his lies."

Richard's heart plummeted into the pit of his stomach. How had he and his wife both heard the same words and the testimony of Ben's convictions and have come to such opposing viewpoints? How was it possible for him to feel such truth and she such deception? He couldn't deny what he felt, couldn't believe what he'd heard were lies, he just couldn't. It touched him too deeply, resonated too clearly in his soul that what he had heard was absolute truth.

Leah put out the candle on the kitchen table and took up the candlestick beside her chair. "Are you comin' to bed?"

Richard nodded. He couldn't bring himself to question her feelings. Instead he felt impressed to pray for her. He turned and followed her silently into the bedroom and closed the door.

TWO

———— ✦ ————

Robert Kenyon sat in the parlor of his stately home, a glass of whiskey in his hand. He swirled the amber liquid around in the glass, allowing his eyes to become glazed and unfocused. He'd already downed two drinks and was feeling quite contented when he heard his wife's shrill voice pierce his comfortable silence. His shoulders involuntarily hunched up at the sound of her voice, and he winced with displeasure.

"Did you hear me, Robert?" she screeched again as she entered the parlor with her heavy footsteps.

Robert slugged back the glass of whiskey and swallowed hard. "I heard you," he grumbled into the empty glass.

Abigail stood in front of him, her hands poised at her waist with disgust. "You're drinking this early in the morning?" she harped.

Robert raised his eyes toward her without lifting his face. "What of it?" he snarled. "I've got to do something to be able to tolerate your presence."

She appeared unaffected by his ugly remark. "I see," she sneered. "Obviously you plan to make a marvelous first impression on Reverend Trahern: the fine and noble Mr. Kenyon arriving drunk on the Sabbath."

Robert glared at Abigail. He'd never loved her. He'd married the Englishwoman because she had money, and he thought she could help him rise in his station and offer him some counterweight against being Welsh. He'd always felt uncomfortable in his Welsh skin. The English impugned his native country as being stocked with a lazy and low-class group of people.

Abigail had provided the connections and the status he so desperately wanted. He had more ambition than being a mere merchant as his father had been. He wanted his name to be known among all of Britain as a highly successful and noted businessman, perhaps even one day obtaining a seat in the House of Commons. With his constant effort and Abigail's social contacts, he'd been able to bring his finest tea to the attention of the royal household and was duly proud of his accomplishment. He remembered the day he had the sign over the shop to read Kenyon & Sons : Purveyors of Fine Teas to HRM.

But it had all come at a hefty price and one on which he'd never bargained. He hadn't counted on his initial tolerance of Abigail at the start of their marriage transforming into contempt and scorn and eventually despising everything she said and did. He hadn't planned on losing control of his life to the hands of his manipulative wife, nor did he expect to be swallowed up by the feelings of despair and self-loathing he now experienced.

Robert pulled himself out of his comfortable chair and slammed the empty glass on the side table. "I am not drunk," he stated flatly. "Though I wish to God I were."

Abigail glared hotly at him, her quick-fired temper easily triggered. "I've planned this move to Reverend Trahern's congregation for weeks. After all, do you expect me to be content being married to a mere merchant? Once you are accepted among those men, doors will open, Robert. Associations will be formed that will allow you to consort with the most influential men in Cardiff, perhaps in all of Wales. It's taken years to smooth the way for this transition, and this is how you thank me? You sit here, numbed by alcohol so that you can act the fool in front of everyone?"

"Oh, I thank you, Abigail," he said sarcastically. "Believe me. I reap my just rewards for your fine efforts on my behalf each and every day."

Abigail narrowed her empty eyes and stared at him. "Change your tie. It's too garish."

Robert seethed inside, hating himself for what he'd become. As he moved from the parlor, he noticed his daughter coming down the large, winding staircase, her eyes cast downward, as usual. Amelia was his only child, conceived in a moment of lustful weakness. She began life a delightful infant and grew to be a precocious toddler, curious and adventurous. She smiled easily, even as a baby, and loved to sing songs she composed herself. Those early years were the happiest for Robert as he found some small redeeming grace from his disastrous marriage in the love of his daughter. But Abigail gradually broke the little girl's spirit with constant criticism and ridicule, destroying her enthusiasm until the child was as miserable as her own mother. Robert hated that he'd been unable to counter the destructive stranglehold Abigail had on Amelia as she gradually choked all joy from the girl's life.

"That's a lovely dress," he commented as Amelia continued toward him.

Amelia kept her eyes lowered and displayed the pale blue skirt between her gloved hands. "It's one of my favorites," she replied softly.

"Get back upstairs and change that dress this instant!" Abigail charged, bolting her way into the large foyer. "I told you to wear the green."

Robert spun on his heel and faced Abigail, his jaw set firmly. "There's nothing wrong with the dress she has on."

She gave her husband a smoldering look. "That dress is nearly the same color as mine. I had this dress especially made for our first Sunday at Reverend Trahern's church. She must change it!" Abigail stomped her foot for emphasis.

Robert felt especially bold. Perhaps it was the whiskey that gave him a greater sense of courage. He leaned into his wife as his gaze penetrated her stubbornness. "She will wear the dress she has on," he hissed through his clenched teeth.

"We'll see about that," she muttered beneath her breath. Abigail held out her hand and commanded her daughter to come forward.

Amelia stood frozen on the stairs, the color draining from her face as her mother pointed to the floor and ordered her again. She felt her feet betray her desire to stay put and walked the few steps to stand before her mother. Abigail reached out and cupped Amelia's face in a tender gesture. "You may wear the dress," she said, and then, without warning, she grabbed hold of the sleeve and ripped it from the bodice of the dress, "to the rag heap!"

Amelia burst into tears and ran upstairs, sobbing helplessly. Something in Robert snapped. He reared back his hand and struck Abigail sharply across the face. "You vindictive, evil witch!"

Abigail gasped with surprise and placed her fingers over the stinging mark on her cheek as her eyes bored into Robert's soul. "How dare you lay a hand to me," she seethed, her chest heaving in anger. "I can make you pay in ways you never thought possible," she hissed.

Robert was unruffled by her threat. She could do nothing to him that wouldn't affect her as well. For the first time in years, he felt a sense of redress. And it had come through striking her. A swelling vindication settled into his reasoning as though he was justified in his action. He felt a sudden surge of power run through him, electrifying his ego and recharging his impotent manhood. "Hurry and change, Amelia," he called up the stairs. "We don't want to be late for church."

❧

Reverend Trahern leaned heavily against the podium as he stared down upon his congregation. His thick neck and sagging jowls shook as he spoke with emphasis. His finely made suit was covered by a velvet robe with gold braiding embroidered on the edge of the sleeves and down the front. He held a regal countenance, one of superiority, as he gazed upon the people held captive to his preaching. "There is a growing threat infiltrating our very midst," he bellowed with dramatic tones, "a threat so monstrous and shocking that I can no longer in good conscience remain silent on the subject." He paused for effect, allowing his congregation to hang in suspense as they waited for his continuance. "I speak of the lies and falsehoods being spread by the so-called missionaries from America . . . the Mormonites."

Reverend Trahern extended his arm, the full sleeve of the velvet robe billowing as he swept his pointed finger across the horizon.

"These men are evil! These men are of the devil! Their very existence is a blasphemy to Christians everywhere! They go about preaching on street corners and infiltrating small gatherings, spouting their wicked lies about a golden bible and the visitation of angels!"

Some of the congregation nodded in agreement. They had seen and heard of these strangers garnering unsuspecting followers throughout Britain. It was commonly thought that only the foolish and unlearned could be tarnished by the peculiar and bizarre claims of the Mormonites. As Reverend Trahern continued, his voice filled with warning. "I tell you, these men are an abomination in the sight of God! Each of you must be ever watchful that you do not fall prey to their devilish spell and be cast into the bowels of hell for all eternity!"

The reverend leaned forward over the pulpit. His eyes narrowed, piercing the congregation with his admonition. "These Mormonites are dangerous men and are not to be taken lightly. Should they come to your places of business, evict them! Should they come to your houses, reject them! Should they encounter you on the street, spit upon them and treat them as the vile, malevolent creatures they are . . . the spawn of Satan! Perhaps only then will they return to America where they belong!"

He straightened up and took hold of the Bible, raising it above his head. "This is the only scripture there is. This book holds all truths, all we need ever know. God does not speak to us, nor does he send angels to teach us, as these Mormonites claim. I am the only teacher you need! I alone have the training and the knowledge to interpret the word of God to lead and guide you in paths of righteousness! Hold to that thought and do not let yourselves stray from my presence, for only I can bring you to salvation! Amen!"

His voice resonated in the high ceilings of the chapel, echoing as if with the very power of God himself. The congregation was visibly moved by the reverend's powerful sermon, and he could see in their faces their dedication to him, their faith in his leadership. As the worship service came to a close, he remained at the podium as if inspecting his flock as they departed from his presence. He did not mingle with them, nor did he bid them farewell as they passed through the church doors. Instead he remained aloof, committed to his image of superiority.

Amid the departing congregation, Abigail intertwined her arm with Robert's and mingled within her group of friends. They discussed the reverend's sermon with excitement, reiterating the evils of the Mormon missionaries. Robert played the game well, giving the appearance of a happily married man, a doting husband, and a respected businessman as he spoke confidently throughout the conversation.

One of the women in Abigail's circle of friends approached with a man at her side. "Abigail," she called.

Abigail waved and drew Robert with her. "Hello, Tressa!" Abigail looked at her husband and smiled. "Robert, you remember Tressa Garrett?"

He bowed at the waist and took her hand. "Of course, I do," he said, gallantly kissing the back of her hand. "Calvan and I have spoken many times. Where is your husband?"

Tressa Garrett snapped her gloved hand downward and clicked her tongue against the roof of her mouth. "He's away in London on business, the silly man. He decided to stay a few extra days this spring so he wouldn't have to return again until the fall." Tressa took hold of the man's arm that stood beside her. "Robert and Abigail, may I introduce Mr. John Morgan," she said politely. "He is somewhat new to Cardiff and has just moved here from . . ." She peered at the man for help.

"From Birmingham," he stated, his well-groomed mustache a handsome fit for his square face.

Robert shook the man's hand. "Mr. Morgan, it's a pleasure to meet you. What did you think of Reverend Trahern's sermon?"

John Morgan found a wry grin creep to his lips. "I found it most invigorating. In fact I had several encounters with the Mormons in England. There is quite a stronghold of them growing there too, I'm afraid. They are every bit as repugnant as the reverend claimed."

"Is that so?" Mrs. Garrett gasped. "They sound absolutely horrible to me," she complained. "I can't imagine how anyone could be sold such a bill of goods."

"That's not the half of it," Mr. Morgan added. "The Americans sell their Mormon women into slavery down in Cuba. The word is that's why their founder, Joe Smith was killed. Some of the men found out what he was doing and shot him." John looked at each of the faces before him. "Though that's not the story the Mormons tell, of course. Oh, no, they say Smith is a martyr to the cause, a hero, if you will, and that he was killed by an unruly mob of Mormon haters. But the truth of the matter is he was done in by his own people."

Robert studied the man. John Morgan seemed an unsavory sort, suited up to appear respectable and refined. Yet something about Morgan intrigued him. "You seem to know a lot about these Mormons," he commented.

John eyed Robert with a steady gaze. "I should, Mr. Kenyon," he replied with a raised brow. "My sister fell captive to their lies and became one of them. She sailed to America last year. I begged her not to go, but she wouldn't listen. I've not heard from her since."

"How dreadful, Mr. Morgan," Abigail sympathized. "You must be heartsick."

"More than you know," he said with a mix of sadness and anger. "I know it is not the Christian thing to say, but I hate the Mormons for what they did to her."

Robert placed his hand on the man's shoulder as a sign of accordance. "I can't say that I blame you. I think I would react the same way if one of them took hold of my daughter, Amelia."

Mrs. Garrett scanned the dwindling crowd. "Where is Amelia? I thought I saw her with you earlier."

Abigail smiled and gave out a forced laugh. "Oh, I'm sure she's talking with the other young people. She's so popular, you know."

Robert couldn't hold back his brief but telling glance at his wife. Amelia was a virtual outcast among her peers, but that didn't stop Abigail from perpetuating a fantasy life for her daughter. "Speaking of Amelia," he said taking a firm grip on Abigail's arm, "we should probably wrestle her away from all her friends and get along home."

Abigail reached toward John Morgan and smiled. "It was a pleasure meeting you, Mr. Morgan. I hope we shall meet again soon."

John bowed and took her hand. "It would be my greatest pleasure."

Robert shook John's hand. "Stop by the shop," he offered. "Kenyon & Sons sells the finest collection of teas in all of Britain."

"I shall do just that, Mr. Kenyon."

Mrs. Garrett bid the Kenyons good-bye, and they parted company. Robert refused to relinquish his firm hold on Abigail's arm as he steered her back toward the church. "I'm sure we should easily find Amelia," he said with a snide tone in his voice. "After all she is the most popular girl in Cardiff. Just find the giggling group of her admirers. . . ."

Abigail tried to jerk her arm free. "You're not funny, Robert. What would you have me say?" she charged between her teeth. "That Amelia is cowering beside some pillar or hiding in the shadows of some portico? The truth is too embarrassing."

Robert spied his daughter waiting on the bottom step of the church near the building, her hands clasped in front of her, her face cast downward. "But it's what you've made of her," he hissed beneath his breath. "Too bad if you're embarrassed by it."

Leah was busy hanging the wash out to dry, the sun feeling especially welcome on this late spring day. Daffodils were already peering from beneath the gray-brown earth, their vibrant green stalks reaching toward the sky. She heard a familiar voice call her name and turned to smile at her sister.

Claire Phillips was two years younger than Leah. She possessed the same oval face and striking green eyes as Leah, but Claire had received her father's wiry brown hair, which plagued her with its strong, coarse determination. The sisters had always been close, even as children. They seemed to share a bond that united them in spirit and mind.

Their father died when the girls were quite young, and they only held vague memories of his laughing eyes and ready smile. Their mother, Gwendolyn, had been determined to keep her little family together. She would not allow her daughters to suffer the fate of working in the coal mines, as so many Welsh children did. Sentencing her children to a future filled with shriveled limbs, heavy lungs, and an early death was an incomprehensible thought. Instead, the young daughters received six years of education in the Cardiff church schools, where they studied English, history, and mathematics. Gwendolyn taught them to sew, which supplemented her meager income as a midwife and helped the family avoid being sentenced to the poorhouse.

Claire embraced her sister warmly. " 'Tis a beautiful day."

Leah smiled and reached for another piece of wet, cool laundry as she nodded in agreement. "Where are the boys?"

Claire had been blessed with two sons: Caleb, who was four years old, and Isaac, barely three. Claire always felt a bit guilty for having borne two strong, healthy children when Leah had yet to deliver a live birth. "They're with Mam," she replied. "I took some eggs and cheese to Mrs. Jones, who's been ailin', and I thought I'd come see you before I went home."

"Let me just finish with this last piece, and then we'll go in and have a nice cup of tea," Leah said hanging Richard's shirt on the line.

"Mam told me about Mary Williams," Claire said as they walked toward the house. "Poor thing . . . and her baban lost too."

"Aye, Mary was always a frail and sickly woman. 'Tis a wonder she ever had Timothy at all."

"Owen is not handlin' it well, I hear," Claire said, reaching for the back door of the cottage. Leah's thoughts were distracted. She placed the empty laundry basket on the kitchen floor and looked at her sister with a serious face. "What do you know about the Mormons?" she asked plainly.

Claire's brows arched in surprise. "The Mormons? Not much." She shrugged. "Why are you askin'?"

Leah went to the cupboard, took down two of her prized Blue Willow china teacups with matching saucers, and placed them on the kitchen table. The china was a family heirloom, passed down to Leah on her wedding day. Even as a child, she had loved the intricate blue patterns on the delicate white dishes. If pride were a sin, then she was willing to suffer the consequences for loving those dishes as she did.

Turning toward the hearth, Leah poked at the fire, prodding the coals to life as she swung the kettle over the flame. "Richard met one of them. They spent all day yesterday talkin' about his beliefs."

She twisted her lips into a crooked smile. "I'll bet Richard put him in his place with a thought or two," Claire grinned.

Leah turned to her sister, the tin of tea poised in her hand. "You might think so," she said with a note of hesitation. "But 'twas Richard who had all the questions and Mr. Lachlan who seemed to have all the answers."

Claire studied her sister for a moment. She could tell Leah was worried. "What are you sayin'? That Richard did the listenin' while this Mormon did the preachin'?"

Leah's face registered the answer without a word. Claire let out a tiny gasp and grabbed hold of Leah's forearm. "You can't be serious."

"Aye," she nodded gravely. "Mr. Lachlan is comin' again today to talk to Richard."

Claire lowered herself onto a kitchen chair with a thump. "You don't think Richard's takin' it to heart, do you?"

Leah hunched one shoulder and turned her attention to the boiling water. "It seems so."

Claire thought for a moment. She trusted her brother-in-law and his opinions, especially when it came to matters of religion. If he was willing to question his own beliefs in favor of this Mr. Lachlan's, then perhaps there was something to what the man had said. "You know Richard doesn't take such things lightly," she said with a cautionary note. "If he believes there's truth in what Mr. Lachlan teaches, then maybe we should take heed as well."

Leah spun about, her mouth agape. "Are you mad?" she exclaimed. "Richard is a minister of God. Why would he put any stock in some American's wild beliefs?" She leaned forward, her hands planted firmly on the kitchen table. "Honestly, Claire, if you'd heard the far-fetched things bein' said, you'd know what I mean."

Claire remembered the time Richard had suggested Samuel build his own cooperage, which had proven to be wise advice. And the time Richard had pressed her to befriend Mrs. Tatum, who was a member of his congregation, even though she didn't like her. It was after a few visits Claire learned Mrs. Tatum had been abandoned by her husband because she suffered with a cancer. Claire became a valued friend to the woman and offered her help and comfort until the day Mrs. Tatum died. Claire still trusted Richard's instincts despite her sister's insistence to the contrary. "I'd like to hear for myself, then," she said, surprising Leah. "I'll come by to meet this Mr. Lachlan as well."

Leah threw up her hands, letting them fall back to hit her apron-covered skirts. "Oh, I could pull a hair from your nose!"

"I'm serious, Leah," she continued. "I would like to meet Mr. Lachlan and hear what he has to say."

"Of course," she replied sarcastically. "Bring the boys and Samuel as well. We might as well have the entire family led to hell in the same hand basket!"

Claire bit her tongue and then burst out laughing. The longer she laughed, the more incensed Leah became. Claire laughed even harder at her sister's reaction. "I'm sorry . . . I don't mean to make light . . ."

Leah felt a smirk twist the corners of her mouth until she was laughing along with Claire. " 'Tisn't funny . . ."

Claire stood up from the table and went to her sister. She wrapped her arms around Leah and hugged her tightly. "Oh, Leah, I do love you."

Leah's laughter settled to a warm smile. "Claire, my *cariad*, I love you too. But I am serious. I fear Richard is makin' a grave mistake."

Claire took hold of Leah's hands and gazed into her eyes. "You might not be over the moon about it, but try to keep an open mind and trust Richard."

Leah pursed her lips and tried to embrace her sister's advice. It would be a difficult task, but perhaps there was truth in Claire's urging. She had always trusted Richard. Leah decided to put her opinions aside for a bit longer and wait to see what developed. Perhaps nothing more would come of the meetings with Mr. Lachlan. She hoped too that her sister would see for herself the folly of Mr. Lachlan's teachings. Then all of Leah's fears could be put to rest.

❦

The day's earlier warmth gave way to a sudden, chilling wind. Ben Lachlan leaned into it, his hand clamped firmly over his hat to keep it from taking flight. His feet stung with open sores, the soles of his shoes having worn through some time ago. He often placed old newspaper or cloth inside the shoes, but it wasn't long before the cobblestones of Cardiff reduced his attempts to futility. He clenched his worn coat tighter across his chest in a fruitless attempt to shut out the wind. An annoying grumbling stirred in his stomach, reminding him he hadn't eaten since yesterday.

Ben was more than happy to arrive at the Kenyons and knocked purposefully on the front door of the little stone cottage. Richard was quick to answer, excited to continue his discussions with Ben. "Come in," he greeted with an anxious smile. "Please, sit by the fire and warm yourself."

"Thank you, Mr. Kenyon," he replied, fingering the brim of his hat in his cold fingers. He looked at Leah and smiled. "Mrs. Kenyon, I'm so pleased to see you again. I hope you will be willing to participate in our discussion this time. I'm sure you must have some questions."

Leah nodded politely but didn't reply directly. "Please, have a seat, Mr. Lachlan," she indicated with a graceful gesture. She went to the kitchen and continued with her earlier preparation of tea and scones.

Richard sat across from Ben, his eyes lit with eagerness. "I've been doing a great deal of thinking," he began, "and what you've taught me sets well with my heart."

Ben smiled and took the promised copy of the Book of Mormon from his coat pocket and handed it to Richard. "I'm very happy to hear that," Ben said, tipping the outside of his feet onto the edges to help alleviate the pain. The shoes now displayed the gaping holes worn into the soles and through his socks to reveal bloody sores on the bottoms of his feet. He tried not to think about their painful throbbing as he spoke. "I offer you my testimony of the truthfulness of the Book of Mormon. I know this is an inspired book written by prophets of God. The Spirit has witnessed that to me, and I know He will do the same for you if you ponder and pray about it."

Richard took the book into his hands and ran his fingers along the cover. He thought about his church, his congregation, and the many years of preaching he had done. He was challenging all he'd ever known by accepting this book. There was a moment of doubt that centered in his heart. Yet his reservations needed answering. If what Ben had told him was true, he needed to know for himself. "I will read every word," he pledged sincerely.

Leah entered the parlor with a tray of tea and scones. She bent down to place it on the table between the men and noticed the raw sores on the exposed portion of Ben's aching feet. Her eyes widened with dismay, and she returned immediately to the kitchen without a word.

When Leah came back, and without asking permission, she knelt down in front of Ben with a basin and towels. She reached for his left foot. "Let me see, please," she said softly.

Ben flushed with embarrassment. "Mrs. Kenyon, please get up. It's not necessary—"

She gently removed his shoe and worn sock and placed his bare foot into the basin. The warm water stung the open wounds, but Ben was grateful for her tender concern. He reached toward his other shoe. "Here, let me," he said.

Richard had not noticed Ben's poor condition at first, and his admiration toward the dedicated missionary grew. "How long have your feet been like this?" he asked.

Ben was embarrassed to tell him it had been several weeks. "I've tried to fill the holes as best I can," Ben said, avoiding a direct answer, "but with the amount of walking I do, the fix doesn't last long." Leah gingerly washed his feet, cleansing the raw sores. Her heart went out to him, wondering how he was able to continue each day without complaint. "Richard, hand me the camphor cake."

Richard's eyes widened. He knew the camphor would be a stringent and painful treatment. "Are you certain?"

Leah looked up into Ben's trusting face. "The camphor will cause some pain, Mr. Lachlan, but it will help seal the wounds and ward off infection."

Ben nodded, accepting the sentence. He braced himself as Richard handed his wife the camphor cake. Leah broke off a small piece and crushed it into the water, swirling her hand about the basin to disperse the strong-smelling remedy. Ben gasped audibly as the potent extract burned and stung his open wounds. He tried to remain silent despite the fact that the pain of the camphor water was more caustic than the pain of the wounds themselves. His knuckles turned white as he gripped the arms of the chair, and he prayed the treatment would soon be over.

Scooping the warm solution up with her hands, Leah continued to bathe the man's battered feet. Finally, she raised his right foot from the bath and dried it carefully. She repeated the action with the left foot and allowed Ben's feet to rest on a clean towel she'd spread out on the floor.

"Richard," she said looking up at her husband, "please bring me a pair of your woolen socks and your Sunday shoes."

"Mrs. Kenyon," Ben protested, "please, you've done so much already. I can't take Mr. Kenyon's shoes—"

"Richard," she quietly ordered, motioning toward the bedroom.

Richard smiled at Ben. " 'Tis best not to argue with my wife," he grinned. "She can be a very determined woman."

Leah completed the task of bandaging Ben's feet with clean strips of muslin cloth and a dressing of glycerin mixed with wool fat to help soothe his raw flesh. She took the clean socks from Richard and carefully fitted them over Ben's bandaged feet. Satisfied she had done all that she could, Leah came to her feet and gathered the basin and towels from the floor.

"You come by each day for a change of dressin', Mr. Lachlan," she smiled gently. "We'll have those feet healed in no time."

Ben found his eyes moistened with grateful tears, though he struggled to keep them hidden. He couldn't help but feel indebted for her loving compassion. "I cannot thank you enough for your kindness, Mrs. Kenyon."

Richard handed Ben his second pair of shoes, the ones he wore on Sundays, believing them to be a reasonable fit. He was happy for Ben to have them and knew they would serve him well. "Wear them in good health," he said, taking his seat once again and turning his attention to the purpose of Ben's visit. "I always felt a bit guilty owning a second pair of shoes. It was my mother-in-law who gave them to me. She always said a minister should have a good pair of shoes to wear on Sunday so when he kicks the devil in the seat of the pants he knows who's done it."

Ben's expression registered his surprise. "You're a minister?" he asked curiously.

Richard cleared his throat as a telling grin twisted his mouth. "Aye, that I am."

Ben nodded and smiled. Nothing surprised him about the

resonating power of the restored gospel of Jesus Christ. "Ah, a minister," he acknowledged.

Leah returned to the compact parlor and gave Mr. Lachlan a scant glance. "Do you find that amusin', Mr. Lachlan?"

"No, not at all," he replied sincerely. "People from all walks of life recognize the truth of the gospel."

Leah wasn't sure how to respond to Ben. She simply stood beside the men and tried to hold her tongue. Richard focused on Ben and waited until he had his attention once again. His thoughts went to Mary Williams and her baby girl. "Has the prophet spoken about infant death?" Richard asked intently. "Are they saved?"

"One of our articles of faith," Ben began, "declares that we believe that man will be punished for his own sins, and not for Adam's transgressions. Children are not held accountable until the age of eight years, so those who die at birth are returned to our Father in Heaven just as they were when they left him—innocent, pure, and sinless."

Leah found it impossible to maintain her silence. She stood beside Ben's chair and folded her arms. "Then what would be the purpose of them bein' born at all if they're turned right back to God?" Leah found the words escaping her lips before she could bridle her thoughts.

"We are in an eternal state of progression, Mrs. Kenyon. It's necessary for us to receive a mortal body, even if only for a brief moment."

Leah had cause to wonder about that. After two stillborn children, there had never been an acceptable answer that could satisfy her understanding of such a tragedy.

Richard glanced at his wife. His mind opened with perception for the first time. "I see," said Richard, his hand poised in mid-air. "So are you saying that infants who die soon after birth, having gained their mortal bodies, then return to God?"

"Exactly," Ben replied. "And those little babies are most special because they have returned without sin, spared a life of mortal grief and agony, waiting for the opportunity to continue their learning and progression on the other side."

Leah's frustration grew as she witnessed Richard's easy acceptance of these teachings. She felt her anger mounting with Richard's perceptible betrayal of his own convictions and knowledge. What would his congregation think if they knew he was entertaining a Mormon missionary? She couldn't hear any more. It was too difficult to stand by and watch her husband throw away his life's work. Leah walked toward the door and took her cloak from off the peg.

Richard looked up, stunned. "Leah? Where are you going?"

Just then a knock sounded at the door, and Leah opened it with a quick jerk, her frustration getting the better of her. It was Claire and her husband, Samuel. "I suppose you've come to see Mr. Lachlan?" she asked, pursing her lips.

Claire screwed up her face in response to Leah's caustic tone. "I was tellin' Samuel about Richard's interest in the Mormons, and he agreed we should hear for ourselves . . ." Her words trailed with the scornful look on her sister's face.

Samuel smiled as he ushered Claire inside. He was a large man with strong muscular forearms and broad hands acquired from his trade as a cooper. His laughing eyes and full beard gave him the look of a gentle bear. "Aye," he added. "Claire said if Richard thinks it all right, then we ought to as well."

Richard hurried toward them, his beaming smile spreading from ear to ear. "Claire! Samuel! This is wonderful!"

Leah swirled her cloak about her shoulders and stepped outside, glancing back at her husband. "I'll be at Mam's."

"Leah!" Richard called after her. "Please, don't go. Leah . . ." He watched her march up the street and reluctantly closed the door. Claire touched him on the arm. "She'll be all right," she encouraged. "She just needs some time."

"Just time?" he asked dubiously. "She can be so stubborn. . . ."

Samuel chuckled. He knew first-hand the stubbornness that was a family trait of the sisters. "Now think about it, Richard," he echoed in his booming voice. "You're a minister and she's a minister's wife. You're callin' into question everything she's ever believed of you and your ministry."

Richard stroked the side of his face. He hadn't thought of that. Perhaps that would explain her reluctance to embrace the truths he now felt so strongly about. He turned toward Ben and motioned for him to sit back down. "Mr. Lachlan has had a bit of bad luck with his feet, so you'll excuse him for being shoeless."

Ben smiled sheepishly and gratefully took his seat once again. "Thank you for overlooking my poor manners."

Claire noticed the smell of camphor in the air and glanced at his bandaged feet. "Oh, never you mind, Mr. Lachlan," she said moving toward the sofa. "There isn't much worse than painful feet."

Richard introduced his in-laws to Ben and smiled as they sat down. Leah had neglected to inform him of Claire's interest regarding Mr. Lachlan. It tugged at his heartstrings to see Leah so resistant to Ben's message, but he was overjoyed with Claire and Samuel's willingness to listen. He could only pray that Leah would find it in her heart to reconsider her initial rejection.

⁂

John Morgan sat in the Three Bells and swilled several glasses of ale. He propped his feet on top of the table and leaned back in the chair until it teetered precariously on its two back legs. He eyed the barmaid with interest, watching her lithe figure slither between tables and booths as she served the thirsty men. She was petite, perhaps not more than five feet tall, but had a look of fire in her eyes that more than made up for her short stature. Her slender limbs worked constantly, fending off the unwanted advances of the drunken men who took every chance to paw her with their meaty hands.

As he observed her movements, her demeanor, he determined she would do nicely for his plans. She didn't know it yet, but she was about to play a very key role in his devious campaign against the Mormons. He had been successful in Birmingham with his harassment and persecution of those Satanists, as he called them, until he'd been accused of the murder of one of them. His successful escape had led him to Cardiff, where he'd heard the Mormons were just gaining a foothold.

She saw that John's glass was empty and made her way toward him. "Will you have another?" she asked scarcely looking him in the face.

John smiled and fingered his mustache. "What's your name?" he asked.

The woman chucked a hand to her waist. "Just never you mind," she retorted against the often-asked question.

John smiled. He reached into his coat pocket and took out two pounds sterling, then threw them on the table. "Now," he said with a cocked brow, "what's your name?"

She looked at the coins hungrily and then looked back up at him. "You can get a lot more than my name for two quid," she smiled slyly.

John stood up, his mouth curved in a lascivious grin. "That's what I thought," he murmured near her ear. "Meet me at the Cardiff Arms when you're done here," he said, scooping the coins from the table. "Room seven."

She reached out and snagged his arm sharply as she peered into his eyes. " 'Tis Meredith," she said, her sable hair falling loose from its combs and curling about the nape of her neck.

"Well, Meredith," he said as he traced the line of her jaw, "I'll be waiting."

The barman barked Meredith's name and ordered her to see to another table. She obeyed quickly, only glancing back once at the attractive stranger as he left the pub. She thought of the two pounds he was willing to pay, much more than she often received, and was already spending it in her mind. She looked at the clock on the shelf behind the barman and noted she had only three hours to wait until her clandestine meeting. Meredith busied herself in hopes the time would pass quickly. She looked forward to earning her two pounds.

THREE

———— ❦ ————

I'D HOPED YOU'D UNDERSTAND BY NOW," Richard said sadly. Leah lowered her face, her jaw set stubbornly. She paused for a moment, not wanting to answer him in anger. Gradually she lifted her gaze and peered into her husband's handsome face. "Richard, what's to become of us, of your congregation?"

He smiled gently at her and bent down on one knee in front of her chair. Richard took hold of her slender hand and gazed into her eyes. "We will manage, *cariad*. I can work with Robert. I'm not a complete stranger to the business; after all, I practically grew up in it."

"Aye, and how many times have you shunned the family business?" she protested. "And you think Robert will welcome you? After all the years you've turned him away?" she countered, her brows knitted together with concern. "Every time he encouraged you to abandon your callin' and join with him, you told him no, that you were bound to a higher callin'. You think now he'll take you in?"

"I can't say," he replied. "But I believe God has an even greater purpose for me now, so not being a paid minister just means I have a need to provide for us in a different way," he said reassuringly.

Leah sighed heavily and withdrew her hand from his. She turned her eyes toward the dwindling fire and then back to her husband. It all seemed so wrong to her, so incomprehensible. What was it about these Latter-day Saints that had so quickly convinced Richard to give up everything, even his livelihood? She tried to understand his newfound convictions, but it all just seemed like so much nonsense to her. "What can I do, Richard? I have no power over you, or Claire and Samuel, for that matter. If you choose to join this church, I won't stop you."

Richard eye's softened. "I know that," he said quietly. He lifted her chin with his finger and gazed into her beautiful eyes. "I'm not making this decision without careful consideration and an answer to my prayers. I have received answers to my questions. It's like nothing I've ever felt," he said passionately. "And if only you'd open your heart and mind, I know you would feel it too."

Leah's expression grew rigid. "Don't expect me to join your church of lunatics," she spat.

Richard's face fell. He stood up, his arms hanging limply at his sides. *How can I make you see what I see . . . make you feel what I feel?* he thought desperately. How can I help open your eyes? "Will you at least join us for the baptisms?" he asked aloud.

The wounded sound in Richard's voice pierced Leah to the core. She came to her feet, her face now softened by her own feelings of guilt. Leah caressed his face with her delicate hand. "Aye," she said quietly.

Ben's smile was as broad as a split-rail fence. He glowed with excitement when he saw Richard and Leah approach from the road beside the River Taff. He'd brought David Simmons, president of the Cardiff Branch, and his wife, Sarah to witness the baptisms. Claire and Samuel Phillips were already there, waiting with eager enthusiasm to begin their new lives as Latter-day Saints.

Richard waved to Ben as he walked toward an uncertain future. What he had learned was indisputable in his mind, but what he might lose hung heavily on his conscience. Still, he could not turn away, no matter the consequences. He knew he'd be denying the truth if he did.

Claire and Samuel met them partway, exchanging hugs and hearty handshakes. Claire could tell by Leah's expression that she was merely tolerating the situation.

"Richard, Leah," Ben motioned, "I want you to meet President and Sister Simmons."

"Ben has told us all about you, President Simmons," Richard greeted with an extended hand. "And you too, Sister Simmons."

David Simmons smiled and clamped his hand over Richard's shoulder. " 'Tis a day for the king! We're so pleased with your decisions. You'll be blessed from this day forward in ways you never imagined."

Claire felt herself near to tears as she stood beside Leah. How Claire wished her sister was joining them in the waters of baptism. Her fears of Leah's resistance driving a wedge between them weighed heavily on her mind. She looked at her sister, her eyes boring into her soul as if to extract understanding or greater acceptance, or perhaps even encouragement. She was disappointed that Leah seemed to offer none of them.

"I brought blankets," Leah said, feeling awkward now. "You'll be freezin' when you come out of the water."

Claire nodded and thanked her. There seemed nothing more to say between them. President Simmons offered a few thoughts on baptism and of the confirmation to follow when they would have the gift of the Holy Ghost conferred upon them. He spoke of the importance of the decision they had each made and how their lives would be forever changed. He spoke of how pleased Heavenly Father was with their choice to embark on the path leading to His kingdom and of the great blessings they could expect for making the journey. President Simmons then offered a prayer and the small group was ready.

Ben waded into the icy water and waited for Richard. Leah was surprised by the placid appearance of her husband's face, how serene he appeared, how he almost glowed. She observed the unfolding ordinance, not knowing just what to expect. It was simple and over in seconds. Richard rose from the water and broke into a broad smile as he made his way to the river bank.

Leah draped a blanket about Richard's shoulders. He captured her and pulled her close, unaware of his soaking clothes as he held her tight. "Leah," he whispered, "how wonderful I feel, how humbled I am to now belong to the Lord's true church."

She bore the cold embrace without complaint, his dripping shirt transferring its frigid water into the bodice of her dress. "I'm happy for you," she said softly. Leah gently pushed him back and pulled her favorite paisley shawl about her as if to seal out the cold.

He smiled crookedly, conscious now of his wetness. "I'm sorry," he said, "I forgot myself."

Samuel waded into the river. He let out a sharp yelp as the cold took him by surprise, but he continued undaunted. Ben promptly repeated the ordinance, and as Samuel rose from the water he gave out a great shout. He shook his head like a newly bathed dog and flung water through the air in all directions. Samuel jogged toward the river bank as quickly as the water would allow, his face beaming, his arms outstretched to his wife. Claire met him with a joyful embrace and then grasped hold of Ben's hand as he led her into the river.

Ben spoke to Claire, but those standing at the riverbank couldn't hear him. Claire appeared to be laughing as she battled to beat down the air trapped beneath her dress. In a moment, the dress gave up its fight and Ben began. Claire came out of the water smiling, and Samuel rushed to greet his wife, laughing as he hugged her.

Ben gratefully received the blanket Leah offered him. "Are you sure you wouldn't like to make it four baptisms while we're here?" he half-teased. "I'm already wet. Might save us a trip."

Leah shook her head. "No, Mr. Lachlan. I'll be stayin' nice and dry."

Sarah Simmons bore a pleasant smile on her kind, round face. "Now get yourselves changed and come to the house right away," she instructed. "I've a nice *cawl*² on the fire for you after your confirmations."

President Simmons ran his fingers through his thick gray hair and returned his hat to his head. "I know Elder Lachlan gave you the address, so we'll see you soon." A smile broadened his face. "I'm as happy as a dog with two tails!"

Richard pulled the blanket around his shoulders and sidled up beside his wife as they walked home. He kissed her on the cheek and took hold of her hand. "Oh, Leah," he said quietly, "I wish you could

---

2. Cawl—Welsh stew or soup

have felt it . . . what it was like to feel so close to God. It was mystifying and thrilling all at the same time. I know without any doubt this is what God wants of me . . . of both of us," he said without apology. "For the first time in my life, the scales of ignorance have fallen from my eyes, and I see with sharpness and clarity how the restored gospel of Christ has been delivered through the Prophet Joseph Smith."

Leah listened silently to her husband's words. There was something in his voice that touched her. His earnestness and sincerity were evidence that he was a changed man. She had never heard him speak with such solemnity before, not even during his own sermons. "I could see by your face when you came out of the water that you were a different man," she said soberly.

"Could you?" he asked with animation. "Could you really? Because I feel like a different man."

Leah couldn't help but smile at him. He sounded like a little boy filled with awe at the sight of his first swarm of tadpoles. "I hope that's a good thing," she teased.

Richard came to a dead stop and grabbed hold of her arm. His expression intensified as he peered into her eyes. " 'Tis, Leah, I promise you that. The Lord has made me see that I will touch many more lives with the true gospel of Jesus Christ now than ever I could as a minister in my own church. And we will be blessed for it, Leah. You and I, and the family we one day will have. We'll all be blessed beyond measure."

His face was lit with sincerity, and her soul was pierced by his promise. She believed him. She couldn't explain it, but she believed him. Her eyes softened, and she felt compelled to kiss him. "Let's get you home and out of those wet things," she urged. "You look like a hen in the rain."

Everyone gathered at the Simmons' home. The tempting smell of the cawl beckoned their appetites as they sat in the parlor talking. President Simmons had been called to one of the branch member's homes and asked that everyone wait until he returned. Sister Simmons was a gracious hostess and made certain her guests were comfortable and warm with tea and biscuits to ward off their hunger.

"Where are you from, Elder Lachlan?" Claire asked curiously. "In America I mean."

"Ohio, originally," he said. "That's where my wife and I were baptized. I left shortly afterward to serve my first mission."

"Your first mission?" Leah said with surprise. "You mean this isn't your first time away from your family?"

"Oh, no," he laughed. "This is my third mission for the Church. I spent a year in Pennsylvania on my first mission. My son Peter was born while I was away. I didn't even see him until he was six months old."

Leah found herself a bit perplexed. "You mean the Church asked you to leave your wife for a year, and she had her baby while you were gone?"

"Well, it's not as bad as you make it sound, Mrs. Kenyon. But yes, I was away serving the Lord when my son was born. My wife was not alone, however. There were many members of the Church with her."

"You said this was your third mission," Richard said with interest. "So where did you serve the second?"

"England," Ben said, reaching for another biscuit. "I spent two years there. And yes," he grinned at Leah, "you might have guessed—shortly after I left for England, my wife had our second baby, another boy we named Paul."

"So you were away from your family all that time with them alone in Ohio," Leah said, her heart sinking heavily into her chest. She could only imagine the loneliness Ben's wife must be feeling, and Ben as well, being separated by such a distance from his new family. "Well, we were no longer in Ohio. By the time I left for England, we had moved to Illinois. We thought that would be our permanent home, but now, well, my family was driven away from there. They crossed the Mississippi River and are waiting to travel further west."

Richard was astounded. "Your commitment to the Church is inspiring," he said earnestly. "Your family has truly made many sacrifices on your behalf, as have you, Elder Lachlan," Richard commented with deep admiration.

"No more than many, many others," he replied modestly. "We must all do our part to build up the kingdom of God."

Sister Simmons sipped at her tea and rested the cup in its saucer. "I know since David's become the branch president, our lives have been greatly blessed. He's a fine silversmith, you know, and left a very successful business in Merthyr Tydfil. But 'tis no sacrifice, I assure you."

"Merthyr Tydfil?" Samuel repeated. "So you moved here when President Simmons was called to his position?"

"That's right," Sarah nodded. "There was no leadership here in Cardiff when the Church started taking hold. President Jones assigned David to this area. We have two grown sons livin' in Merthyr Tydfil with their wives and children. We scarcely see them now, but we're happy to be servin' the Lord."

Ben's expression grew solemn with intent as he scanned the faces before him. "We serve the Lord gladly and know that He will keep our loved ones in his care until we return." Ben reached into his coat pocket and took out a well-worn page of the *Times and Seasons* dated 1841. "I'd like to share some words from the Prophet Joseph," he said as he unfolded the paper and began to read. " 'Love is one of the chief characteristics of Deity, and ought to be manifested by those who aspire to be the sons of God. A man filled with the love of God, is not content with blessing his family alone, but ranges through the whole world, anxious to bless the whole human race. This has been your feeling, and caused you to forego the pleasures of home, that you might be a blessing to others, who are candidates for immortality, but strangers to truth; and for so doing, I pray that heaven's choicest blessings may rest upon you.' "

Ben smiled for a moment as he refolded the paper and tucked it back into his pocket. "This was part of an address given by the Prophet to the first men called to serve missions in Great Britain."

Richard felt a sensation of warmth swell within him. The words of Joseph Smith seemed to resonate in his heart and mind. "How do you go about serving a mission?" he asked Ben. "I mean, do you volunteer or do you wait to be asked?"

Leah blanched. She stared at Richard with a look of horror on her face. How could he ask such a question?

Just then President Simmons threw open the door with a brusque motion and shook off his hat and coat. "All is well," he announced as he came into the room. "Brother and Sister Yates are on speakin' terms. There's Welsh between them once more."

Sarah smiled and tried to stifle her laugh. "Good, now we can get started," she said coming to her feet. "Is everyone ready?"

David took a chair from beside the lowboy and placed it in the center of the room. Ben motioned for Richard to be seated. Leah watched as the two men placed their hands upon his head. She felt an odd and warm sensation engulf her body, emanating from inside her being and spreading to every extremity. She tried to dismiss the feeling, but it would not leave her. The men bowed their heads, but she could not do likewise, her eyes fixed on their solemn faces, anxious to view this proceeding.

Very simply, the words were spoken, and Richard was bestowed the gift of the Holy Ghost. As President Simmons concluded the confirmation, Richard felt as though he floated above the chair, somehow no longer earthbound, and that only the men's hands resting on his head kept him grounded.

"Brother Kenyon," said President Simmons, shaking Richard's hand vigorously, "the Lord's indeed pleased with you this day."

Richard looked at Leah, his heart so full of aching for her to feel what he felt, to know what he knew about the gospel of Jesus Christ. Instinctively he reached for her. She rose to meet him as he took her in his strong arms. He said nothing, though she sensed the unspoken words in his embrace. Samuel was confirmed and then Claire. Feelings were tender, hearts were full, and cheeks were moistened with grateful tears. As they made their way into the dining room, Leah couldn't deny there was something inexplicable about what she had witnessed today. The expressions on the faces of her family as they rose from the waters of baptism had caused her to consider why they seemed so happy. And now, the confirmations had bestowed them with a serene confidence and sense of humility that was visible to the naked eye. It was all perplexing to her and yet somehow impressive and deeply significant.

❧

John Morgan paused at the shop door of Kenyon & Sons and straightened his tie in the reflection of the window. He thought himself an impressive sight from his tailored suit to his polished shoes. He smoothed the edges of his mustache with his finger and then reached for the door. As he opened it, a little bell was triggered and its tinkling sound brought a clerk running.

Niall Pembroke appeared, obedient to the sound of the bell. His rounded belly was covered by a white shop apron, his thinning hair circled about the sides of his head like a laurel wreath of sorts. He smiled broadly and sincerely. "Good day, sir," he greeted. "May I be of assistance?"

Morgan surveyed the shelves that lined the walls, each filled with varying sizes of tins and containers of teas. A linen-covered table stood in the center of the small room, displaying some of the more exotic teas from Ceylon and Java. Their pungent aromas lingered in the back of his throat as he approached the clerk. "I would like to see Mr. Kenyon," he stated flatly. "He extended an invitation to me last week, and I've come to pay him a visit."

"Very well, sir," Niall said with a slight bow. "May I tell him who's callin'?"

Morgan peered at him with an air of impatience. "John Morgan."

Niall turned and disappeared toward the back of the store for a few moments before reappearing and motioning for Mr. Morgan to follow. "Mr. Kenyon will see you," he said with a smile.

John followed Niall, who was dismissed by Robert with a wave of his hand as they entered the back office. Robert stood from behind his dark and heavy desk, his hand extended toward Morgan. "Good to see you, Mr. Morgan," he said. "How do you like Cardiff by now?"

John shook Robert's hand and took a seat in the chair across from the desk. "Well enough," he replied, crossing his legs as he rested his hat on his knee.

Robert took hold of the decanter that sat on the credenza behind him, poured two drinks, and handed one to his visitor. "So what line of business are you in, Mr. Morgan?"

John fingered his mustache and smiled. "I am of somewhat independent means," he said with an air of superiority.

"Ah, how fortunate for you," Robert said slugging back the amber liquid from his glass. "I am chained to my profession, and it rather feels as though it masters me and not the other way around."

Morgan gave him a sideways smirk. "That is what happens, I hear." He tipped his head back, swallowed the drink in one gulp, and then eyed Robert carefully. "I actually stopped by to offer you a warning of sorts."

Robert frowned, confused by the stranger's odd comment. "A warning?"

Morgan adjusted his position in the chair and leaned forward. "If we allow the Mormons to continue preaching here in Cardiff, it won't be long before they have enough deluded followers to affect your business. You see, they have a way of infiltrating a city with their secret brotherhood, banding together to drive competitors out of business, forming exclusive cooperatives that inhibit trade, and soon their followers will only support businesses that are owned by their membership. Their ultimate goal is to convert every major merchant and city official until they are capable of commanding the entire city."

Robert almost laughed. "You'll excuse me for my skepticism, Mr. Morgan, but I find that a rather outlandish theory."

John narrowed his eyes. "It is no theory, Mr. Kenyon, I promise you. These are a very dangerous and devious group of people who mean only to drive honest men like yourself out of business. I witnessed their attempts firsthand in England, and it has happened repeatedly in America. They settle in a city and virtually take it over, driving the original inhabitants from their very homes, forcing them to abandon farms and stores through intimidation and violence. These people give the appearance of piety and gentleness, but they are evil to the core and will stop at nothing until everything is in their control."

Robert leaned back in his chair and scrutinized Morgan. He had heard several strange accounts regarding these Mormons but had never paid them much heed. It seemed Morgan knew what he was talking about, and, added to the concerns expressed by Reverend Trahern about the Mormons, Robert had to admit there was potential for genuine unease. "And how do you propose to 'handle' these Mormons?" he asked with a raised brow.

John leaned back in his chair and smiled slyly. "Mr. Kenyon, after they virtually kidnapped my sister, I have made it my life's work to disable their preaching to the best of my ability. I will not rest until they have been driven back to America and their movement here dies."

Robert fingered the silver letter opener on his desk. "Obviously, you have ways of disabling them. Of course, you needn't supply the details," he quickly added. "I believe I understand the gist of your methods."

Morgan came to his feet. "Mr. Kenyon, it has truly been a pleasure speaking with you," he said with a confident smile. "I trust I can count on your support, should I require it?"

Robert stood up and offered his hand. "I will reserve my decision at present, Mr. Morgan, but you have genuinely roused my interest."

Morgan shook Robert's hand and turned toward the door. "For the sake of your business, I hope that you have more than just an interest. Good day, Mr. Kenyon. I'll see myself out."

❦

Samuel harnessed two horses to the flatbed wagon in preparation for a trip to the countryside. In the lush green of the Vale of Glamorgan, Samuel placed stores of oak staves to dry on a friend's small farm. This weathering process was critical in retaining the wood's properties as he crafted his barrels, and he visited the farm as often as needed to replenish his supply to the cooperage.

It was an opportunity he often shared with his young family, making the trip into an outing of sorts, with a basket of food to share during their journey. His wife and sons loved to go with him, and he enjoyed their gleeful company. He and Claire had invited Leah and Richard along, and they looked forward to the trip as well. The weather was unusually warm and clear, making the day one of expected pleasure and enjoyment.

Caleb and Isaac watched their father with great anticipation. It was exciting to ride in the wagon. They loved the sound of the horses and the bouncing ride along the rough dirt roads. Claire came out of the house with a basket and handed it to her husband. "That should do us," she said with a smile.

Samuel sniffed at the aromatic basket and winked at her as he placed it on the wagon bed.

" 'Tis Uncle Richard and Aunt Leah!" Caleb squealed, running to meet them as they came up the road.

Richard loved his nephews and scooped them into his arms, twirling them around in circles. "How are my boys today?" he laughed as he spun to a stop.

"More, Uncle Richard!" Caleb begged giggling wildly. "Swirl us again!"

Richard set the boys on their feet. "When we stop for supper," he promised.

Isaac grabbed hold of Leah's leg through her layers of dress and petticoats and looked up into her pretty face with a merry smile. She reached down and touched him on the top of the head and then bent down and kissed him. "There's my Isaac," she cooed.

"Aunt Leah, are you ready?" Caleb called anxiously to her as he ran toward the wagon.

"I'm comin'," she called after him, handing Richard the blanket draped over her arm.

Claire had already placed a folded quilt on the flatbed of the wagon and smiled as Richard handed the second to her. "That should make a fine seat for us," she said patting the quilt with her hand.

Leah gave her sister a smile and a hug. The men assisted them onto the wagon bed, handing up the boys to be seated with the women on the blankets. Samuel and Richard shared the driver's seat, and with all aboard Samuel snapped the reins against the backs of the horses. "The Lord's blessed us with a fine day," he commented as the wagon moved forward. "A fine day, indeed."

The wagon jostled its cargo along the cobblestone streets of Cardiff. They approached the River Taff and the handsome stone bridge of three arches that spanned the breadth of water. As they crossed the great bridge and continued along the rutted road, they soon entered the Vale of Glamorgan, with its rolling hills and sunken valleys. Spring was all around them. The leafing trees and hedges brought life to the last of winter's barren, drab landscape. The stunning young green of the trees stood in sharp contrast against the intense cloudless blue sky.

Samuel glanced over his shoulder. The women were well entertained with their conversation, which was mostly drowned out by the sounds of the horses and the creaking wagon. The road became more rutted and difficult to maneuver. The spring melt and heavy rains had given way to a rough surface. He glanced at his brother-in-law and broke the silence between them. "So are you nervous about givin' your sermon Sunday?"

Richard's face registered his concern. "Not so much nervous as worried," he said. "I'll be disappointing a lot of people, people who have come to trust me and count on me for guidance."

"If they have any belief in you at all, they should be jumpin' at the chance to follow your lead and join with the Latter-day Saints," he said with encouragement. "You have influence, Richard, and I believes many'll follow you."

Richard hoped Samuel was right, but he had serious doubts. He felt the task a daunting one but prayed he would be able to influence his former congregation with his prayerful words of farewell.

Isaac climbed onto his mother's lap happily, pointing at objects that caught his eye. His mother absently responded with an appropriate name. He repeated the name to the best of his ability. Claire and Leah carried on a conversation as they sat in the back of the wagon, trying to ignore the hard wooden floor they sat upon during the rough, jarring ride from Cardiff.

Within moments Isaac squirmed from Claire's lap and leaned over the edge of the wagon's sideless deck, entranced with the view below as he watched the wheels pitch in and out of the ruts, squealing with joy each time the wheel fell back into the channel with a thud. Intrigued by his brother's delight at the rolling view, Caleb leaned over beside Isaac to see for himself while the women fell even deeper into conversation. Caleb, being older and taller than his little brother, could stretch much further over the edge, but his balance was precarious at best as his head and shoulders hung beneath the wagon bed.

The front right wheel of the wagon suddenly plunged into an unavoidable hole in the road, pitching the entire wagon sideways. The action threw Caleb from the wagon to the muddy road below. Claire screamed as she watched her little boy disappear, the rear wheel rolling over the tiny body.

Instinctively, Samuel reined the horses to a stop as Claire

scrambled from the bed of the wagon. "What happened?" Richard called in a panic as he jumped to the ground.

"Caleb fell," Leah sobbed, clinging to Isaac. "He went under the wagon!"

Claire was on her knees, scooping the limp little body into her arms as tears streamed down her face. Her boy was silent and unmoving. "Caleb," she wept, frantically searching for signs of injury. His right arm was bent at an odd angle just below the shoulder. Her eyes widened in horror as she felt the break with her trembling fingers. She pulled up his shirt and saw to her horror a distinct reddened mark diagonally crossing his abdomen ending at the top of the broken arm where the wheel had rolled across him. His abdomen was already beginning to swell, and her heart stopped in fear.

Samuel dropped down and took the boy into his arms. "Father," he prayed, "please, spare our boy." He bolted back toward the wagon, his eyes fierce with determination.

" 'Tis all my fault," Claire wailed, following her husband back to the wagon.

"Get in!" Samuel commanded as he climbed aboard the wagon, his boy cradled protectively in his arms. "Richard, get us to President Simmons' house, now!"

Richard didn't have time to analyze the command, but he didn't question the strong impression he received to proceed to President Simmons' home.

Leah scowled, reaching to help Claire back into the wagon. "Caleb needs a doctor," she argued, furious at her brother-in-law's instruction. "Not some stranger!"

Richard glanced back to ensure everyone was safely in the wagon and turned it back toward Cardiff. "Hang on," he shouted, cracking the reins against the horse's backs again and again until the wagon reached some speed. "We'll have the wind in our fists!" Richard hoped the wagon would withstand the punishment of the rough road as they raced toward Cardiff in an unsafe hurry.

Samuel smoothed back the hair from Caleb's pale face. He was grateful, for the moment at least, that the boy was unconscious and could feel no pain.

The boy's abdomen continued to swell, filling with blood from the damaged internal organs. Samuel felt Isaac's stomach and grimaced. He prayed for a miracle.

The women wept, holding each other, with Isaac wedged between them for protection. " 'Tis all my fault," Claire sobbed. "My little baban . . ."

"I'll hear no more!" Samuel snapped. "There's no blame here. 'Twas an accident."

"I wasn't watchin' him!" she shrieked. "He wouldn't have fallen if I were a better mam—"

Leah shook her sister by the shoulders. "Don't you dare say that!" she cried. "This was not your fault! You couldn't be a better mam."

Claire shook her head and buried her face in her hands, their words providing no comfort. Isaac pressed his tiny form against his mother and cried in fear. The wagon ride was no longer any fun, and the reason for his parent's upset was incomprehensible to him.

Richard continued to pray. He was forced to slow the wagon's pace, encountering more and more traffic as they approached the city. His fears were somewhat assuaged as they reached the Cardiff Bridge, crossed it, and made their way to President Simmons' home on Maryann Street.

Time seemed to stand still as Richard did his best to maintain the quickest speed possible through the city streets. Caleb began to rouse, whimpering slightly as he did so, his small form still limp in his father's arms. His whimpering became moaning, and then, coming into full consciousness, Caleb began crying and thrashing about out of pain. Samuel did his best to quiet the boy, holding him against his chest, trying not to further injure his son with rough restraint.

"Hurry, Richard," Leah implored, anxious about her nephew's condition. She locked her gaze on Samuel. "I'll ask but once more. I beg you, Samuel, take Caleb to a doctor."

Samuel shook his head. "I'm not askin' you to understand," he tried to explain. "But I'm askin' you to trust me. I feels it's the right thing to do."

Claire tried to soothe Isaac's constant crying. "Maybe Leah's right," she said, beseeching her husband.

Samuel's commitment was unyielding. "Have faith, *cariad*. All will be well."

"How can you be sure?" she charged. "This is our son, Samuel!"

"Don't you think I knows that?" he shouted back. "Just trust me, Claire. Trust in the Lord."

Richard turned onto Maryann Street and proceeded to the house. He brought the wagon to a halt, set the brake, and dropped to the ground almost in one fluid motion. Running toward the door of the large house, Richard's heart pounded as he pummeled the door loudly with his closed fist.

The door swung open, revealing Ben Lachlan on the other side. His face registered the surprise he felt. "Richard, we weren't expecting you."

"There's been an accident," he said breathlessly. "Samuel's son was run over by the wagon."

Samuel was already rushing toward the house, Caleb clutched to his chest. Claire followed as Leah took up Isaac and met them inside.

"Where's President Simmons?" Samuel asked his face pale with worry.

"He's not here," Ben replied. "He left to visit a sick brother."

Sister Simmons came from the direction of the parlor, her gentle face reflecting her concern. "What's all the fuss?"

"The boy's been hurt," Ben replied.

"Bring him into the bedroom and place him on the bed," she directed, leading the way.

"But you don't understand," Samuel said, his voice on the verge of panic. "I needs President Simmons! I was told to come here."

Ben placed his hand on the man's shoulder. "And you're here now. Place your son on the bed, Brother Phillips. Let's see where the boy's been hurt."

Samuel swallowed hard and did as he was told. Caleb cried out as he released his hold of the boy and laid him on the bed. "There, there, son," he comforted. "Be a brave boy now. Can you do that for your tad?" Caleb nodded his head, his chin quivering as he did so.

Ben examined the little boy. The protruding belly sent a wave of alarm through him. The grotesque angle of the child's broken arm caused him to swallow hard against the sickening sight. "What's your name, son?" he asked kindly, peering over the boy.

"Caleb," he said in a tiny voice.

"Well, Caleb, I'm going to help you feel better," soothed Ben. "Would that be all right with you?" Caleb nodded. "That's a good boy."

The small group gathered around the bed, helpless to know what to do for the child. Ben seemed the only one calm enough and sure enough to be of any service. Richard watched keenly as Ben placed his hands on the boy's arm. "Please hold him steady," he said grimly. "I'm going to attempt to set this break."

Collectively the family held the boy still. Sister Simmons touched Ben on the shoulder, her brow furrowed with concern. "You've done this before?"

Ben hesitated to answer. He had never performed such a thing in his life, yet the Spirit was strong, and a vision came clearly to his mind. "I know what to do," he said with conviction.

Ben nodded to the family, indicating he was ready to begin. He bent over Caleb and whispered something to him. Ben placed one hand below the shoulder joint and the other at Caleb's elbow. Without further notice, he pulled the boy's arm into place so swiftly and deftly that it took the family by surprise. Little Caleb endured the procedure bravely, making only a single painful cry as the bone in his upper arm came into alignment.

There seemed a momentary sigh of relief among the family, but there was still the matter of the boy's swelling abdomen. Ben placed his gentle hands upon Caleb's head and closed his eyes. He prayed for the child to be made well and for the comfort of his parents. He told the boy that one day he would testify of this healing to the conversion of many. There was a palpable sense of awe among all gathered in the room. Silent tears streamed down every check in gratitude and humility. Samuel was the first to move, offering his hand to Ben. They shook hands, the warmth and power of the Spirit seeming to flow down Ben's arm and into Samuel's hand. He couldn't speak, but Ben perceived the man's thoughts.

"Sister Simmons," Ben said quietly. "Will you see to a splint and bandage for the boy's arm?"

She nodded and disappeared from the room. Claire clung to her husband and wept softly into his shoulder. Relieved of his pain, Caleb slept peacefully, his small frame engulfed in the large bed. Richard put his arm around his wife. The moment was too sacred for words, too awe-inspiring for conversation. They stood motionless, gazing upon the sleeping child, captivated by Ben's beseeching of the Lord.

Ben finally stepped away from the bed. "Perhaps we should let him sleep," he suggested. "We'll be near enough to hear him stir."

Richard followed Ben from the room, his arm still around Leah's shoulders as she cradled Isaac in her arms. Samuel left too, but Claire sat on the edge of the bed, stroking her little boy's forehead as tears flowed down her reddened cheeks.

Leah's thoughts whirled as they gathered in the parlor. She chided herself for having questioned Samuel's inspiration. But how could she have foreseen what was to take place? A doctor would have set Caleb's broken arm, but only Ben held the power of the priesthood to invoke a healing upon the boy. She knew that now.

The mood remained somber for a few moments. Sister Simmons hurried by them on her way to the bedroom with Caleb's bandages. It was Samuel who broke the silence. "How did you happen to be here today?" he asked Ben.

"I had stopped by the house to deliver some missionary tracts just as President Simmons was leaving. He asked if I would join him on a visit to an ailing church member," he explained. "Sister Simmons suggested I stay here and give my feet a rest, and President Simmons agreed."

"So 'twasn't President Simmons I needed so much as 'twas you," Samuel said. "I just felt I should bring Caleb to this house."

Ben smiled shyly. "It wasn't me you sought, Brother Phillips, but the power of the priesthood. It could have just as easily been President Simmons."

"It is well you listened to the prompting of the Spirit, Samuel," Richard offered. "The moment you told me to drive here, I found no reason to doubt your decision."

Leah lowered her gaze as Richard's comments stung her conscience. Questioning Samuel's judgment only proved to illustrate the weakness of her faith, of her trust in God. She wished she felt the sureness Richard and Samuel felt.

Claire came into the parlor and approached her husband. "Caleb wants to see you," she said somberly.

Samuel's face fell. *Was he worse?* he wondered. *Did the blessing fail? Was he going to die?* He entered the bedroom and sat beside his son. "What is it, Caleb?" he asked with a catch in his throat.

The little boy was sitting up, pillows propped behind him. He smiled and reached out for his father to come closer. Samuel leaned over the boy.

"I'm hungry," Caleb whispered.

Samuel laughed, and fresh tears filled his eyes. He looked at his wife and took hold of her hand. She lifted the covers to reveal the boy's torso. The bloating was gone, and even the imbedded track made by the wheel had vanished.

Richard and Leah stood at the entrance to the bedroom, amazed by Caleb's remarkable recovery. Leah could no longer deny she had witnessed a miracle.

"Somethin' to eat . . . did you ever hear of such a thing?" Samuel asked with surprise.

Sister Simmons stood at the perimeter of the room, the remnants of her bandaging efforts still in her hands. A broad smile crossed her round face. "Then somethin' to eat he shall have."

FOUR

RICHARD STOOD BEFORE HIS CONGREGATION, his countenance serene as he prepared to speak. He felt the Holy Ghost
with him and prayed that what he said would somehow be acceptable to the people sitting before him. He knew they were unaware
of how very different this Sunday was to be than any other they'd
encountered.

Leah sat in the back row so she could easily see her husband
instead of her usual place below the podium on the first row. She was
fearful of the congregation's scorn and wrath at losing their minister,
especially to such a controversial religion. She held her breath as he
began.

"My dear friends," he said without smiling, "I have a dubious
duty to perform this day. On one hand, I am elated beyond description, for I have found real truth. Yet, on the other, I am sorrowed
because finding this truth means I must step down as your minister."

Gasps and murmurs swept through the congregation. He held
up his hands as if to qualm their concerns. "I pray that when I am
finished speaking, you will choose to know more of what I have
come to know, choose to discover for yourselves what I have discov-
ered, and find the most compelling revelation of God's truth ever
known to man in modern times."

He could tell the people were holding their breaths, as if waiting
to plunge beneath a pool of water. Richard knew it was time to offer
them some relief, and he grasped the podium firmly in his hands.

"The truth I have found is in the restored gospel of Jesus Christ as revealed to a prophet of God, a man named Joseph Smith."

An audible gasp escaped from the audience, and vocal decries of his statement filtered through the crowd. "Now, I know that many of you have heard untrue things about Joseph Smith, indeed, about the Latter-day Saints as a whole, but I denounce them as the lies they are and tell you that if you will seek for the knowledge and truth as I have, your eyes will be opened to the Lord's only true church upon the face of the earth."

"Traitor!" cried an angry voice. "You are the liar!"

A murmur of agreement rolled through the room, and Richard tried to maintain control of his former flock. "I understand that for some of you this is a hard thing to hear. But as I listened and learned from a missionary called of the Lord, I knew I was hearing the truth! You too can know of the truth of the Book of Mormon and all its implications as to its witness that Jesus is the Christ!"

"No more!" exclaimed an irate man as he bolted from his pew. "You're dancin' on the edge of a cliff, Reverend. I'll hear no more of it!"

Richard prayed that the crowd would not grow into an angry mob. "Please, let me finish," he begged, his hands raised high as if to call down help from heaven. "I pray that your hearts will be open to what I have said today and that you will earnestly seek for this marvelous truth of your own accord. If I have offended you today, then I pray your forgiveness. If I have disappointed you, then I am sorry. But I will not apologize for my testimony of the truthfulness of the gospel of Jesus Christ, for I now know the church as it existed in Christ's day has been restored! I so seal my testimony upon your heads in the name of our Beloved Savior, Jesus Christ. Amen."

Most of the congregation was already out of their seats, waving their hands in disgust as they turned their backs on him. Heavy, angry mutterings tainted the room with ugly claims and malicious comments. Richard wasn't allowed their further attention to explain that the treasury would be refunded to its contributors, or that the lease on the church was only paid until the end of the month, or that he had written an old friend to ask if he would be willing to direct his former congregation. Instead the church emptied quickly, leaving Richard with a sense of failure and remorse. He had betrayed them, betrayed their trust, and had probably done more damage than good. No one would be willing to receive the truth now, a fact that disappointed him most of all.

Leah remained seated in the back pew, her heart aching for her forlorn husband. How dejected and sorrowful he appeared. She was about to go to him when she noticed an elderly couple and a young man moving toward the pulpit. It was Mr. and Mrs. Bryant and Jonah Reese. Her surprise led to curiosity as they moved against the tide of concurrent opinion and looked up at Richard with open expressions. He didn't notice them approaching, his face cast downward as tears clouded his eyes.

"Reverend Kenyon?" Henry Bryant said quietly. "Charlotte and I wants to know more about the Latter-day Saints."

"Aye, me too," added young Jonah.

Richard could scarcely believe his ears. A renewed joy swept through his emotions, erasing all his feelings of failure and betrayal. He beamed as he stepped down from the pulpit and shook their hands. "Mr. and Mrs. Bryant, Jonah, I thank you for your open hearts."

Charlotte smiled and patted Richard's hand. "There's somethin' different about you now, Reverend; we noticed it the minute you stood before us. I says to Henry, look at his face, he seems to be glowin'."

"Aye, she did say that," the old man confirmed.

Seventeen-year-old Jonah looked at Richard square in the eyes. "If you believes what your tellin' us, then I needs to as well," he said sincerely.

"I don't know what to say . . ." Richard found his emotions choking off his words. He shook their hands and finally found his voice. "I want you to meet a missionary," he said, "by the name of Elder Ben Lachlan."

Leah watched the Bryants and Jonah basking in Richard's happiness. A warm sensation engulfed her as she saw the look on his face as he testified to them. *Perhaps it's time I stop allowing my head to overrule my heart,* she thought. *Perhaps it's time to put my resistance aside and embrace the restored gospel of Jesus Christ.*

Meredith Cullen peered into the small gathering of now twenty Saints huddled in a small rented hall in the Tredegar Arms as they prepared to begin their services. President Simmons saw the unknown young woman looking about as she entered the room and went to greet her. "Welcome," he smiled, "to the Church of Jesus Christ of Latter-day Saints."

Meredith smiled in return. "The right place I has, then," she said with satisfaction.

"I'm President Simmons," he said by way of introduction. "Thank you for comin'."

Meredith was a bit nervous. She'd received her instructions from John Morgan, but she was still feeling a little awkward as she scanned the faces in the room. She hoped she wouldn't see anyone who might recognize her and was somewhat relieved when the faces all appeared to be those of strangers. "Meredith Cullen," she replied. "I hears one of your missionaries preachin' some time ago, and my heart hasn't let me rest since."

President Simmons motioned for her to join the small congregation. "We're so pleased to have you with us, Miss Cullen. Let me introduce you to the others." He politely took hold of her elbow and ushered her forward. "As you can see, our numbers are yet few, but through the efforts of many, that will change quickly." *Aye*, she thought, *that's just as John had said. It was best to stamp out these Mormons while they were still a small group and could be handled more easily than after they had grown strong in numbers and resolve.* She took special notice of each person she was introduced to, making mental notes that would be useful to John. As she took a seat beside an elderly couple, she found they were very open and gracious to her, not at all as she expected.

"Now, you was the Bryants?" she asked, rehearsing their names in her mind.

"Aye," Henry said with a genial smile. "I'm Henry, and this is my wife, Charlotte."

"Have you been members long?" she asked.

Charlotte smiled proudly. "We were baptized just yesterday," she replied happily. "We're still wet behind the ears."

Henry laughed, and Meredith felt compelled to join him.

"Congratulations," Meredith said trying to sound genuine. "Are you Cardiffians?"

"Charlotte is," Henry said, "but I was raised in Aberdare."

The old couple was quite pleasant, and Meredith continued to pump them for information without seeming too obvious. "Do you travel far to these meetin's?"

"We're just over on Duke Street," Charlotte volunteered. " 'Tis my family home," she said with a note of pleasure. " 'Tis the only house on the street with large bay windows, somethin' my father insisted be added."

"Bay windows," Meredith said as if making a verbal note. "I never had a house of my own," she said.

President Simmons cleared his throat, and the threesome quieted as he began the meeting. Ben Lachlan sat in a chair beside President Simmons, his expression registering his excitement at seeing the new converts gathered together. It was rewarding to see five new members added to their tiny branch in such a short span of time. And now there was a curious young woman sitting beside the Bryants who might prove to be the next one in line for baptism.

The meeting began with a hymn, one that was not familiar to the newest members, who listened to the words as it was sung.

The Spirit of God like a fire is burning!
The latter-day glory begins to come forth;
The visions and blessings of old are returning,
And angels are coming to visit the earth . . ."

The words of the hymn burned into Richard's soul as he listened with rapt attention. He looked at Leah and instinctively reached for her hand. She eagerly accepted his grasp and returned his gentle smile. "Thank you for coming with me," he whispered to her.

Leah nodded and squeezed his hand.

Ben offered an invocation, and then President Simmons began with a few remarks about Caleb's miraculous healing only a few short days ago. Meredith sat uncomfortably through the meeting, knowing her attendance was merely a pretense. She had not set foot in a church of any kind since she was a small child. In fact, the last time she'd done so was when her mother was still alive. She was eight years old then and had been forced to quit school soon after her mother died. And her father, whoever he was, had abandoned her mother, a loving and kind woman, as soon as Meredith was born.

The words President Simmons spoke made Meredith uneasy too, partly because he spoke of unfamiliar things, but more so because she felt most unworthy to be in a church, even if it was just a rented room. She led no angelic life; after all, she'd been forced to fend for herself after her mother's death. But what did it matter now? *Mr. Morgan pays me well enough,* she thought. *I don't have to believe in it. It's only pretend.*

At the conclusion of the meeting, Meredith lingered, asking questions and trying to convince the others of her interest to learn more. They were so kind to her, treating her with a respect she was seldom shown, and interacting with her as if she were a person of worth. It was unnerving to her, and she wondered how they would treat her if they really knew what sort of woman she was. But soon Meredith began to find a self-assured confidence in her acting, amusing herself with her ability to make them respond favorably to her newly created persona. At times she could scarcely keep from grinning as she manipulated them into accepting her as an equal.

President Simmons took Samuel and Richard aside as the others continued to visit. "Brethren," he said with a pleased smile, "as we discussed after your baptisms, I wish to ordain you both to the Aaronic Priesthood today."

Richard braced himself to receive the priesthood—the very power through which Ben had baptized him and had healed Caleb. He was humbled and anxious.

President Simmons motioned for Ben, and they gathered together near an empty chair. Claire held Isaac in her arms as Leah kept Caleb close beside her, and those remaining sat silently behind them. Samuel sat down, his heart pounding as he waited. Then Ben and President Simmons set their hands on his head and conferred the Aaronic Priesthood upon him. Richard took the chair and the ordinance was repeated, but as the final amen was spoken, President Simmons held Richard in his seat with a firm hand to his shoulder.

"Stay seated just a moment, Brother Kenyon."

President Simmons looked at Ben and the others. His face reflected a solemn look, his voice steady and filled with import as he addressed them. "Brothers and sisters, the Spirit has testified to me that Brother Kenyon has been called to do miraculous things in the buildin' of the kingdom of God upon this earth. Through the power of the Spirit of God, the Lord has instructed me to ordain this brother to the Holy Melchizedek Priesthood directly. All in favor?"

Ben's eyes widened with surprise, and there was an audible gasp from some of the members. Such a thing was not unheard of, but it was most unusual. Yet Ben was confident that if President Simmons was inspired to do such a thing, he could fully support the move. Leah and Claire looked at each other, unsure of what it meant. Those in attendance raised their right hands, and President Simmons nodded. Again President Simmons and Ben placed their hands upon Richard, bowed their heads, and ordained him an elder in the Church.

President Simmons snagged Richard's hand firmly, pumping his arm with joy. "Elder Kenyon," he said with a grin, "I commend to you a strict course of righteousness from this day forward. Marvelous things will happen in your own life and in the lives of those around you."

Richard seemed stunned by the unexpected event. All he could manage was a nod of acknowledgment, all words sticking in his tightened throat.

A rumble of threatening voices clamored outside the room, their tones angered and boisterous. President Simmons recognized the menacing intentions of the gathering crowd immediately. He held out his hands to the others in a reassuring motion. "Brothers and sisters, please remain calm. It appears as though we have visitors again."

A rush of whispers ran through the room, and people got to their feet with pounding hearts. Husbands encircled their wives and children in protective embraces as they nervously stared at the door. Richard sprinted to Leah's side and stood before her as if to shield her from the unidentified threat.

President Simmons moved through the crowd, approaching the door as it flew open to expose a dozen men scowling and hot with anger. "Can I help you, gentlemen?" President Simmons asked, calm beyond reason.

One of the men forced his way further into the hall, his fists balled and his eyes blazing with irrational hatred. "I told you last week, Simmons," he spat, "you isn't welcome here!"

President Simmons displayed little emotion. "And I told you, sir, that we had a legal right to meet in this room and that we would continue to do so."

"Legal or not, we's breakin' up this meetin'!"

A rise of shouts and threats spewed from the angry men, their fists shaking as punctuation marks in the air. Richard came forward, recognizing the leader of the group. Leah grabbed for his arm, but it was too late; he was at President's Simmons' side in a moment.

"Gerald Thornton!" he called out, his voice rising above the shouting. "What is the meaning of this?"

The man stopped, staring incredulously at Richard. "Reverend Kenyon?"

"You know this man?" asked President Simmons skeptically.

Richard nodded. "He came often to my sermons."

"I hopes you're here to talk some sense into these fools, Reverend," Gerald snarled.

"Gerald, I ask that you step back, take your men with you, and depart from this meeting." Richard's voice was level but commanding.

Gerald's eyes narrowed. "Don't tell me you's one of these Joe Smith lovers!"

Richard moved toward Gerald, his gaze steadied on the man's livid face. "Gerald, I believe you are mistaken about the teachings of the Latter-day Saints. Please, step outside and let's discuss this calmly."

Leah's heart lodged in her throat. Richard was deliberately putting himself in harm's way. She started forward but was caught short by Samuel's large hand. He shook his head and held her fast.

"You won't convince me otherwise," Gerald growled. "That you've been taken in by these devils only proves how right I am to be here!"

The men behind Gerald shouted their agreement. Richard was

unyielding. "Gerald, please. Step outside." Richard clamped his hand firmly onto Gerald's shoulder.

The hot red color drained from Gerald's face. He suddenly appeared timid as his intense gaze lowered in submission. He had no idea what had caused him to surrender his fight. He was confused and momentarily unsure of himself. Gerald abruptly jerked away from Richard's hand and refocused his narrowed eyes. "You haven't heard the last of this, Kenyon," he warned. Gerald spun around and motioned for the others to follow.

Leah jerked her arm free from Samuel's grip and pushed her way toward her husband. Others of the congregation had encircled Richard, offering their thanks and gratitude, making it difficult for Leah to break through.

President Simmons shook Richard's hand once again. "Elder Kenyon, thank you for your courage."

"But I did nothing," he argued. "In all my dealings with Gerald Thornton, he has acted with the utmost congenial behavior. I am at a loss to understand the incredible change."

"Opposition in all things," he said. "Satan will not go quietly from the lives of the Saints."

Leah arrived at her husband's side in time to hear President Simmons' remark. She grasped Richard's arm and felt herself breathe again. "What were you thinkin'?" she whispered harshly. "Those men might've hurt you!"

Richard patted her hand reassuringly. "But they didn't."

President Simmons held up his hand. "Brothers and sisters, we will reconvene at six o'clock this evenin'," he announced.

The congregation shuffled from the rented hall, their voices low but still excited by the events they had just witnessed. Leah's heart sank. How could they subject themselves and their safety to yet another meeting? She recalled the rock that had been thrown at Ben by angry onlookers. What other threats awaited these saints of God? "We aren't comin' back, are we?" she asked Richard, her eyes wide with foreboding.

Richard saw the trepidation spread across her face. He smiled softly. "It'll be all right," he said. "We'll be safe."

"But how can you be sure?" she argued.

Richard understood his wife's anxiety. How could he make her understand he felt no concern for their safety? What words could he offer that would allay her fears? He decided there was nothing he could say or do to soothe her distress. "You can stay home, if you wish, while I attend the meeting."

Leah pulled away from him, her jaw falling slack. "You can't be serious, Richard. You intend to come back here knowin' full well that those men could return to do you harm, or even—" She couldn't bring herself to finish the thought.

Richard took his wife's arm and tried to steer her out of the hall. "This is neither the place nor the time for this discussion, Leah."

Leah's green eyes flared with heated fury. She elbowed her way past the last few stragglers exiting the hall and marched down the street, fuming in a mixture of anger and dread.

"I'll meet you later," Richard called to Samuel and Claire as he followed after his wife.

Leah's rapid pace slowed as she blindly walked the street of shops. She had no sense of purpose other than allowing her anger to propel her feet. Her steps faltered as a blaze of hot tears welled in her eyes, quenching the fire that had been there. She staggered to a stop and pressed herself against a wall of coarse brick, smothering her sobs into the crook of her arm.

Richard wasn't far behind, his heart breaking at the sight of her. As he neared, she was unaware of his presence. He touched her back, and she spun around in momentary panic. Richard took Leah into his arms and held her tightly as she sobbed against his chest. He stroked the side of her cheek with the back of his hand, her tears moist against his skin. "Please don't cry," he whispered. "I promise you . . . it will be all right."

She wanted to believe him but couldn't. The possibility of Richard coming to harm was too real. Now that she had seen for herself the impending consequence of his membership in the Church, it was all too transparent that it was only a matter of time.

"How can you believe that?" she cried, wiping the tears from her cheeks. "How can you stand here and pretend you can't be harmed at the hands of those madmen?"

"I didn't say I couldn't be harmed," he corrected gently. "I only said it would be all right." He kissed her softly. "Leah, believe me when I tell you how important faith is in all of this. I have faith all will be well."

Faith. There was that word again. Why was it so elusive to her? Leah felt drained. She had no fight left in her for the time being. Nothing she could say or do would sway Richard from returning to the hall that evening. She sighed heavily and kept her remaining thoughts to herself.

Amelia Kenyon sat at the piano, her hands poised above the keys. Playing the piano was her solace, her only joy in life. She was accomplished at it too, which gave her some satisfaction since her mother could not play a note. It was her secret triumph over her mother, the only thing she knew her mother could not take away from her. In this one thing, Amelia was confident, for she knew she played well. No matter how her mother criticized her music, she was unfazed by it.

Robert Kenyon sat in his study, a drink clasped loosely in his fingers, his eyes closed as he listened to Amelia play. She often chose somber, moving pieces that suited the sadness of the girl's life. Yet despite this knowledge, he felt completely unable to help his daughter. He'd never been a demonstrative sort of man anyway, and it was uncomfortable for him to display affection. It wasn't that he didn't love his daughter; it was his inability to express it. Besides, didn't she have a home, plenty of food, clothing, and every creature comfort he could provide? Surely that was evidence of his love for her.

Robert sank deeper into his chair by the fireplace and traced the pattern of the upholstery with his finger. He reached for the decanter of whiskey and poured himself another drink. His life was miserable, and he was tired of the charade of a loving marriage for his associates when he faced endless bickering with his wife. There were times when he fought the desire to flee, to abandon everything he had worked for, every good thing he had earned, just to be free of his self-imposed wretchedness.

Abigail sauntered into the study unannounced. Robert shot her a heated glare. "What do you want?" he snarled. "I told you not to bother me in my study."

She seemed oblivious to his desires and continued into the room until she stood directly in front of him. "I am planning a large dinner party for our fifteenth wedding anniversary," she said, smoothing down the gold silk front of her dress. "I am not inviting Richard and Leah, so don't mention anything to them."

Robert glared at her. "No, they wouldn't fit in with your class of friends, now would they?"

"Well, of course not," she chided, "you know that. And besides, Reverend Trahern will be there."

"I should think my brother would count himself lucky then," Robert grumbled into his glass.

Abigail placed her hands to her waist. "Is this what you intend to do all evening? Sit here and drink?"

"We're not having this discussion again, are we?"

Abigail moved to the hallway and shouted at Amelia. "Will you stop that playing? I can't hear myself think!"

The room grew silent as Amelia withdrew her hands and closed her music with a sigh. Abigail marched back toward her husband. "We are going to have this discussion again," she insisted. "How do you think it makes me feel to know I have a husband who can't control his appetites?"

"I don't care how it makes you feel. I care how it makes me feel. I'll drink as often and as much as I please!" he shouted, bolting from the chair.

Abigail reached for the decanter, but Robert intercepted her and grabbed her sharply by the wrist. She winced painfully, his grip vise-like as he twisted her arm to the side. "Let go of me," she hissed hotly into his face.

Robert's nostrils flared, his breath coming fast and irritated. "Don't you ever touch my liquor again," he warned.

"You're mad—"

He pulled her closer, his hold on her tightening even more. "Am I?"

"Robert, you're hurting me—"

His mouth contorted into a twisted smile. "Good," he said, releasing her with a violent shove.

Abigail shuffled backward from the push, her feet tangling in the hem of her skirts. She lost her balance and fell to the carpet, her eyes wide with astonishment. Then her face steeled into an icy visage, her pale eyes boring deep into him with vile hatred. She came to her feet and left the study in a raging huff.

Amelia had just entered the foyer from the music room when she saw her mother charge from the study. She froze in place, waiting to see which way her mother was headed. Abigail glared at her daughter with vengeance in her eyes. "What are you still doing up? It's past your bedtime!"

"But it's only half past seven—"

Abigail moved toward her, her hand lifted. Amelia cowered instinctively as her mother's angry hand came down across her face. "Don't argue with me! Go to bed this instant!"

Amelia glared back at her mother, her hatred for her seething inside. She would not give her mother the satisfaction of seeing her cry. Instead Amelia gritted her teeth and raced upstairs to her room, slamming the door behind her.

Abigail's boiling temper overflowed at the sound of the slamming door. She charged up the stairs and reached for Amelia's door. She turned the knob but found the door locked. "Amelia! Open this door at once!" she yelled, rattling the doorknob violently.

Amelia's courage had slipped away as she cringed on her bed, her knees drawn up to her chest. She stared at the locked door, fearful of the wrath she had stirred in her mother.

"Do you hear me?" her mother shouted angrily, her strident voice rising in pitch. "If you don't open this door right now, Amelia, I promise you'll regret it!"

Amelia swallowed hard. She knew it was futile to continue to provoke her mother. Creeping off the bed, she unlocked the door and braced herself for the onslaught. Abigail flung open the door and caught Amelia by the arm so quickly the girl gasped in surprise. In one swift motion, Abigail struck Amelia across the face, leaving a stinging red imprint of her hand on the girl's cheek. She fell backward and stumbled to the floor in a sobbing heap.

Abigail leaned over her weeping child like a ravenous vulture, sneering at her in disgust. "Don't you ever slam this door again," she hissed. "I won't tolerate such ill manners from my own child!" She reared back her hand in a threatening motion. "Do I make myself clear?"

Amelia nodded, rubbing the throbbing welt on her face. Abigail removed the key from the door and used it in a stabbing motion to punctuate her words. "You will remain in this room until I decide otherwise!"

Amelia whimpered as her mother closed and locked the door. The room seemed to engulf her, swallowing her up in a prisonlike doom. She crawled to her bed and pulled herself onto it, her cheek still burning from the heated blow. Her tear-filled eyes were drawn to the window. The pale light of the moon filtered through the glass, giving everything a silvery gray shadow. She realized it was an appropriate color, for it mirrored the grayness she felt inside.

❧

Leah wrestled with her inner turmoil. Between her struggle to believe what Richard believed and her fear of the repercussions of those beliefs, she was torn in a way that seemed insurmountable. Without much forethought, she left the house in search of her mother, the only person she thought could help her.

Gwendolyn knelt at the perimeter of her tiny home, digging at the rich soil surrounding her budding daffodils. She wore much of the traditional Welsh dress, which consisted of a flannel bedgown and voluminous checked skirt, a large red shawl tied about her shoulders, accompanied by a kerchief at the neck. Her head was covered by a ruffled cotton cap upon which rested a tall black silk hat similar to those worn by the men of the day. Leah found the hat somewhat comical looking and never cared to wear one, but her mother embraced the outfit with pride.

Leah called out to her. "Mam!" she exclaimed. "Hello!"

Gwendolyn straightened, waving excitedly at her daughter. "*Cariad!* How good to sees you," she replied, wiping her hands against her apron. "I was just thinkin' of you."

Leah smiled. "How so?" she asked curiously.

Gwendolyn smiled and swept her hand in the direction of a rough wooden bench resting beneath an ancient oak tree. "I was just rememberin' when you and Claire was little girls and how you loved the first sign of daffodils and snowdrops as they come into bloom. Remember? They was a sign of warmer days to come, and you girls couldn't wait for 'em."

"I remember," Leah said, smiling fondly and taking a seat on the old bench.

Gwendolyn smiled with fond recollection. It seemed only days ago her two little girls were getting under foot as their playful laughter filled the house with joy. How she loved to watch them from her kitchen window as they sat beneath the protective oak tree, playing with their dolls.

Gwendolyn sat beside Leah and smiled. "I just come back from a visit with little Caleb. Fit as a fiddle, he was," she said, shaking her head in disbelief. "Claire removed the splint from his arm yesterday. He was complainin' so about it."

"Aye, and just four days after the accident," Leah said. "I wish you'd been there, Mam, to see the miracle. When Elder Lachlan laid his hands on little Caleb and prayed for a healin', 'twas the most amazin' thing I've ever witnessed in my life."

Gwendolyn patted the back of Leah's hand. "Aye, your sister expressed the same. To be sure, Caleb must be one of God's elect."

Leah grew pensive, her brows knitted together in thought. "I've been givin' that some thought," she began. "It was more than that. . . . It was the power of the priesthood. . . . It was a mortal man who acted in God's name to pull down the powers of heaven."

Gwendolyn interlaced her thin fingers and rested them in her lap. She cast her gaze to the western horizon, her eyes tracing the silhouette of trees against the sky. "You're to be baptized as well, are you then?"

The inner struggle rose up to choke off her thoughts. "I . . . oh, Mam! There was an ugly mob on Sunday, but Richard's so convinced . . ." Tears sprang to her eyes with the awful turmoil of her emotions. Leah peered into her mother's face, lined with age and wisdom, as if to find her answer there. "I don't know what to do, Mam. There are times when I think I believe, but then somethin' happens to turn me away."

Gwendolyn tenderly touched Leah's cheek. "Do you recall the story of Gelert the dog?"

Leah nodded with a scowl, not comprehending where her mother was going with the mention of the old folktale. "Wha—"

"Aye, Gelert was a loyal and favorite dog of Prince Llywelyn the Great." Gwendolyn said. "One day, when he returns home, the dog bounds to greet him, his jaws drippin' with blood. The Prince draws a terrible conclusion; could the blood on Gelert's muzzle be that of his tiny son? Racin' to the nursery, he finds the child's upturned cradle and blood spattered on the walls. Prince Llywelyn, mad with grief, plunges his sword into Gelert's heart. As the dog lay dyin' in agony, the Prince hears a cry from beneath the upturned cradle. 'Tis his son, and there beside the child is a wolf, dead, killed by the loyal Gelert."

Leah peered at her mother with a quizzical smirk. "And what has this to do with me?"

Gwendolyn sighed and took hold of her daughter's hand. "I'm just sayin' you should be careful not to jump to false conclusions. Per'aps your waverin' is a sign you shouldn't do this thing." She retrieved her hand and sighed. "But you must do what your heart tells you, *cariad*," she said softly.

"And what does your heart tell you?" Leah returned with a gentle reply.

Gwendolyn came to her feet and adjusted her apron. "About the Mormons, you mean?"

"Aye," she prodded.

Gwendolyn's heart was awash with a confusion of emotion. She failed to comprehend this strange religion and the hold it had taken on her daughter and sons-in-law. She was steeped in her own beliefs and was committed to them as deeply as her family now seemed to be to the Mormons. She worried for her little family. She'd heard of the violence and persecution that seemed to follow this strange new religion wherever it went. It was a hard life they had chosen, she believed, and one that she prayed they would soon abandon. Gwendolyn looked deep into Leah's green eyes, searching for the words that came hesitantly to her voice. "Let the hens roost where they may."

Leah stood up from the bench. "Then you think 'tis a mistake to join Richard."

She held up her palm, stopping Leah short in her urging. " 'Tis a mistake to think the church you've always loved is now your enemy. As for me, I wants no part of the Mormons."

For a moment, the two women fell silent, the dappled sun playing off the color of their disparate hair as they stood beneath the great oak tree. Leah came to her mother's house hoping to find an answer to her dilemma but now seemed even more confused than ever. A shrieking male swallow swooped at some unseen threat to his nest over head. The air was astir with the slight rustling of leaves in the emergent breezes and the silence of their unspoken thoughts.

"It looks as though there might be a storm comin' in," Leah said, feeling compelled to fill the void in their conversation.

"Aye," her mother replied. "Old age doesn't come alone. My bones seem to ache with every little change in the weather nowadays. Mrs. Romney delivered yesterday, she did. A fine boy."

For a few moments, Leah and Gwendolyn exchanged pleasantries, their dialogue hollow with the attempt. Finally Leah ended her visit, inviting her mother to dinner the following evening. She hugged her good-bye and started up the lane leading from her mother's house. The breezes became more brisk as the darkening clouds drew further into the western sky.

As she arrived home, the brewing storm intensified. The sky was no longer bright and sunny, and the temperature had taken a noticeable dip. She closed the door behind her, grateful to be inside. Leah set about rekindling the cozy fire in the hearth. The tinder snapped and popped as it glowed orange beneath the grate, its growing effort soon burning brightly as Leah continued to feed the voracious flames.

She had planned Richard's favorite dish for supper: Welsh rarebit, a simple meal of sliced bread toasted and smothered in a thickened cheese sauce spiced with dry mustard and pepper. It was a good way to use the last of the oldest bread before she baked fresh tomorrow. The dish was easy enough to make, but best of all it was made from available ingredients, the larder somewhat bare with their dwindling income.

Glancing at the wall clock, Leah estimated it would be at least an hour before Richard returned home. He had gone to talk to his brother about working at Kenyon & Sons. It would be a challenging adjustment for her husband to make, but she knew he was committed enough to the gospel to do whatever was necessary to provide for the both of them.

Leah began work on mending a shirt brought to her by Owen Williams. Since Mary's death, he had no one to look after him and his boy. She felt a twinge of pity for the two of them, absent of wife and mother. Owen left the boy alone most of the time. Young Timothy wandered about the city dependent upon the kindness of those who were willing to feed him and let him into their homes for a time.

Leah saw little of Owen. He spent his days working on the Cardiff docks and his nights drinking at the pub, often failing to return home at all. The man seemed a lost soul, aimless and sunken in the depths of depression, even to the exclusion of his own child. Owen was too absorbed in his sorrow to care about the hissing gossip that swirled about him, the wagging fingers, and the condemnation of his actions.

Leah fingered the ragged hole in the shirtsleeve, distressed with sadness toward the poor man's plight. She wished there was a way to comfort him, some way to help him mend the frayed pieces of his life as she did with his garment, so he could live again and be whole.

The clock struck on the hour, and Leah realized it was time to begin preparations for supper. She slid the needle through the fabric a few more times and then neatly tied off the thread. As she entered the kitchen, her thoughts continued to dwell on Owen and Timothy. She trimmed bits of molded cheese away and sliced the remaining block into thin slivers to be melted in warm milk and butter.

The sky darkened with clouds, restricting the light coming through the windows of the cottage. A gloomy shroud of gray crept into the room, deepening shadows and corners with a dreary influence. Finally little taps of rain riddled the windows with droplets of water.

Richard knocked on the large double door of his brother's house. Within moments, the housekeeper, Lucy, answered it, her starched uniform crisp and stiff, just as Abigail demanded. "Good afternoon, Mr. Kenyon," she greeted happily.

"Niall told me Robert was home today," he said coming into the large foyer. "Is he ill?"

Lucy cast her eyes downward, afraid to make much of a comment. She knew her place all too well and kept the Kenyon family secrets without fail. "No sir, I doesn't reckon so. Mr. Kenyon's in the study. Should I announce you?"

"No, that won't be necessary," he said with a smile.

Lucy nodded dutifully and disappeared to continue her household chores. Amelia heard the sound of her uncle's voice and rushed into the foyer to greet him. Her face lit with excitement, and she threw her arms around him, burying her face against his broad chest. "Oh, Uncle Richard," she breathed, "I'm so glad to see you."

He held her for as long as she wanted, knowing how seldom she received any affection. "I've missed you," he said softly.

She finally leaned back but did not remove her arms. Her eyes were pensive and clouded with pain. "It's awful going to Reverend Trahern's church," she said quietly. "He is nothing like you, Uncle Richard. It's as if he has no soul. He preaches hatred and ugliness, and I don't feel God there at all. I wish I could come back to your church."

Richard smiled lovingly at her and cupped her face in his large hand. "I wish you could too, *cariad*, but there's no more church to come back to. I've left the ministry—"

He couldn't finish before Amelia gasped and recoiled from his embrace. "Uncle Richard! You can't mean that!"

Richard smiled disarmingly. "Now, it's not what you're thinking," he said with a teasing grin. "I've found another church, one I believe to be Christ's true church, and so I've joined the Latter-day Saints, the Mormons, some call them."

Amelia's face grew pale. "Oh, Uncle Richard, no! Reverend Trahern says the Mormons are devils!"

Richard shook his head in mild disgust. "I might expect that from the likes of Trahern, but it's not true, Amelia." He gazed into her eyes with a deep sincerity that caused her to focus all her senses on him. "Believe me when I tell you, *cariad*, I would not join another church if I didn't believe it with all my heart. You know that, don't you?" She nodded, her faith in him unwavering. "Reverend Trahern and others like him fear the truth and perpetuate lies to keep people enslaved to them. I have found something wonderful in the restored gospel of Jesus Christ, and nothing anyone can ever say or do will sway me from that testimony."

Amelia hugged him again. "I believe you, Uncle Richard."

Abigail sauntered into the foyer, wearing her usual pinched and discontented expression. "Ah, Richard," she said feigning surprise, "I thought I heard your resonant baritone voice."

Amelia withdrew from her uncle instantly and stood beside him, her face cast downward. "We were just talking," she offered meekly.

"Yes," Abigail said snidely, "I could see that." She bristled at the sight of her daughter on the receiving end of Richard's affection. "Amelia, you haven't yet practiced your piano today."

Amelia turned an eager face toward her uncle. "I'm learning a new piece, Uncle Richard. Will you listen to it before you go?"

Abigail shooed her daughter toward the music room. "I'm sure your uncle has far better things to do than listen to you struggle through some unpracticed song. Now get along."

"I would love to hear it," Richard called after her, belying her mother's attempt to derail his niece's offer.

Amelia cast a smile over her shoulder, disappeared into the music room, and closed the door.

Abigail turned her attention to her brother-in-law. "So what brings you here today?" Her interest was superficial, her voice void of real expression.

"I've come to see Robert," he said. "Niall told me he was home today."

"You'll find him in the study," she said, turning from the foyer as she headed for the parlor.

Richard knew his boyhood home well. His parents had died in the cholera outbreak of 1831. Robert married the following year, and Richard moved out to avoid imposing on the newlyweds even though the house was most accommodating for all of them. Over the years, Abigail had filled the house with superficial things— paintings, sculptures, fine carpets, porcelain figures, silk and damask drapery, excessive amounts of furnishings, all touches that overran the house with a feeling of clutter. He walked directly to the study and knocked on the closed door.

"Go away!" came a sharp answer.

Richard frowned momentarily, cracked the door open, and stuck his head inside. "Robert?"

His brother craned his neck about from his chair by the fireplace. "Oh, Richard, come in. I thought you were Abigail," he said, coming to his feet. "Although I don't know why; she never knocks before entering."

The brothers briefly embraced, and Robert took his seat once again. Richard noticed the decanter of whiskey and a half-empty glass of the stuff beside Robert's chair as he sat opposite his brother. "So what brings you here?" Robert asked dismissing his brother's notice of the liquor.

Richard cleared his throat and leaned forward, his arms resting on his knees. "Well," he began cautiously, "this may come as a surprise, but I've left the ministry and would like to join you at Kenyon & Sons."

Robert's jaw dropped open slightly and then his face registered a pleasant shock. "You mean after all this time, you've finally come to your senses?"

Richard laughed. "Well—"

Robert leapt to his feet, his thoughts reeling. "You have no idea what this means to me," he said with more excitement than he'd felt in years. "I've been yearning to open a shop in London in order to expand the business even more, and now with you on board I can do that!"

"London?" Richard echoed with astonishment.

"Yes, don't you see? You can run the business in Cardiff while I open the office in London. It takes me one step closer to the House of Commons. I need the connections London can afford me, and together we can build Kenyon & Sons into a powerful business."

Richard held up his hand momentarily and shook his head. "Now wait, Robert, you don't understand. I have no desire to dedicate my life to business. I merely need employment now that I am no longer a minister. But I've no intention of building an empire."

"Employment," he said flatly. "Is that all this is to you?"

"Of course. My devotion to God has not changed, nor has my

desire to serve others. My life is still dedicated to God's work."

Robert scowled and paced in front of his chair, his hands clasped behind his back. "Then it doesn't sound as though you've left the ministry at all," he charged.

Richard came to his feet and looked his brother in the eye. "I've found something better, Robert, something more wonderful than I ever imagined." He took hold of his brother by the shoulders. "I've found the true church of the living Christ," he said profoundly, "and it has changed my life forever."

" 'The true church of the living Christ,' " Robert scoffed. He jerked himself free of his brother's grasp. "You haven't changed at all."

"But I have, Robert, and if you'd let me teach you what I now know, it will change your life as well."

Robert reached for his glass of liquor. "My life doesn't need changing," he sneered, swirling the liquid around in the glass before downing it with a gulp. "I have things planned out just the way I want them."

"But are they what God wants?"

Robert threw the empty glass across the room, smashing it against the wall. "What do I care what God wants?" he shouted. "It's what I want that matters!"

Richard felt nothing but sorrow for his brother. How could he have strayed so far from the boy he used to know? "Robert, listen to me," he urged calmly, "I left my ministry to join with the Latter-day Saints, and—"

Robert's face reddened. He looked as though his blood was beginning to boil, threatening to explode from within. "The Latter-day Saints? You mean the Mormons?" he spat distastefully. "How dare you come into my house begging for a job because you've left your only means of support to become one of those contemptible Mormons!"

"It's not what you think," he implored. "The gospel of Jesus Christ has been restored through a prophet—"

Robert's eyes blazed, and the revulsion of his brother's ignorant and misguided choice filled him with rage. He reared back his knotted fist. "Get out of my sight!" he seethed through his clenched teeth.

"Get out, or so help me—"

Richard backed his way toward the door of the study. He had never seen so much hatred on his brother's face, and to know it was directed at him made it all the more painful. "Robert, please—"

"Get out before I kill you!" he threatened irrationally. "And don't ever come back!"

Richard's heart broke as he turned from the brother he loved. As he entered the foyer, Abigail was there listening, a self-satisfied smirk crossing her thin lips. Amelia had cracked open the music room door at the sound of her father's raised voice to listen to the exchange, which had filled the house. Richard silently swept by his sister-in-law and threw open the front door without closing it behind him.

FIVE

R ICHARD SLOUCHED IN THE ROCKING CHAIR, feeling the disappointment from the encounter with his brother the day before. His fingers absently flicked across the pages of his Bible in a rhythmic shuffle, flapping the pages noisily again and again as he stared out the window. Leah watched him from the kitchen as she dried the last of the breakfast dishes. Her own thoughts were swirling as she swallowed hard and searched for a flush of bravery.

"Richard," she said softly as she approached him.

He turned his face toward her and smiled fleetingly as he shifted his position in the chair. "What is it, *cariad*?"

Leah reached for his hand and sat on his lap, pulling his arm around her waist. His eyes melted as she gazed at him, her oval face offering him a look of serenity. "I've been prayin'," she began quietly, "and thinkin' an awful lot."

Richard's pulse quickened as he searched her face, fearing to anticipate what message would come next from her lips. He waited in silence as Leah seemed to be gathering her courage before she continued.

"I've been afraid of change and what it would mean to us," she said, lacing her fingers behind his neck. "I've been stubborn too and tried every way possible to keep from believin', but I can deny it no longer. I believe it, Richard, all of it. . . . My prayers have been answered."

Richard held her tightly. He loved her so very much and was

greatly humbled that she had sought the Lord in prayer for her own answers. "How thankful I am to have a wife who seeks the Lord," he murmured, "and that you have found the truth for yourself."

She peered into Richard's dark eyes as the tears welled in her own. "I know too that the Lord wants me to be baptized. I'm ready for that now, Richard." She kissed him and felt closer to him than she ever believed possible, the bond between them strengthened even further by their love of the gospel of Jesus Christ.

He embraced her and held her for a long time, reluctant to lose the enchantment they shared as tears of gratitude flowed freely down his cheeks. Richard kissed her ardently and swept back the auburn hair from her temples. "I love you more than I can say. . . . You are my joy."

Leah stood at the water's edge, smiling with excitement as Richard took her by the hand and led her into the cool river. Ben Lachlan, Claire and Samuel with their two boys, and President and Sister Simmons were anxious onlookers, watching from the grassy edge of the bank. Richard beamed as he kissed Leah and smiled before raising his right arm to the square. The words Ben had spoken at Richard's own baptism were firmly planted in his mind as he began the sacred ordinance.

Leah's heart raced, yet at the same time, a peace and tranquility warmed her from within. All hesitancy had vanished from her heart, replaced by a conviction of the gospel of Jesus Christ. She embraced her baptism eagerly and absorbed every word that Richard spoke.

As he lifted her from the water, she felt exhilarated and renewed, as though she had truly been reborn. Her smile was infectious as Richard hugged her tightly, and the others waiting for her on the riverbank were radiant in their joy. Richard steered her from the water, his arm encircling her waist until they were once again on firm ground.

Claire wrapped a blanket about Leah's shoulders and hugged her tightly. There were no excuses offered for the tears that streamed freely down their cheeks, no words needed to express their mutual elation.

Caleb screwed up his face and looked up at his father. "Why are they cryin'?" he asked innocently. "Are we supposed to be sad too?"

Samuel chuckled and tousled the boy's hair. "They're cryin' happy tears," he said.

"I never cries happy tears," he said thoughtfully, "I only cries sad tears when I gets hurt."

Samuel knelt down beside his son. "Sometimes," he began, "when you're very, very happy, you're so happy you cry. That's what happy tears are for."

Caleb was quiet a moment, trying to comprehend his father's explanation. "Do happy tears feel different than sad tears?"

Samuel nodded and smiled. "You'll understand some day."

President Simmons approached Leah with a pleased smile. "Welcome, Sister Kenyon. I know the Lord has a special work for you to do. Seek His counsel often, as you do Richard's, and remain a true and faithful servant all of your days."

Leah wiped her tears with the corner of the blanket. "Thank you, President Simmons. I will try my best to do what the Lord expects of me and be acceptin' of His will."

"I know you will," he replied warmly.

"Let's get back to the house," Claire said, "before you both catch your deaths."

Ben and the Simmons departed from the group to meet later for Leah's confirmation. The family began down Castle Street, passing by Cardiff Castle, which rested on a sloping hill, and headed for home. Richard bent down, swept Caleb high onto his wet shoulder, and began singing a lively tune. His rich baritone voice carried on the breeze, and within a few dynamic notes the others soon joined him.

Under yon oaken tree
Whose branches oft me shaded;
Elves and fairies dance with glee,
When day's last beam hath faded
Then while the stars shine brightly,
So airy, gay and sprightly,
'Till Chanticleer tell dawn is near,
They trip it, trip it lightly.

Yet no trace of them is seen,
When morning rays are glancing,
Not one footprint on the green
Shows where the elves were dancing:
Oh! where are they abiding?
In what lone valley hiding?
Come next with me and we will see
The fairies homewards gliding.

They laughed together at the song's conclusion, giddy with their lighthearted mood and the brisk walk home. It seemed their world was perfect, and for this moment in time, it was. Nothing could sway their happiness nor defeat their glad hearts. Bound together with their love for one other and for the gospel of Jesus Christ, they were invincible.

A portly man dressed in a fine suit and wearing a tall hat with a black satin hatband stepped in front of them as they crossed Angel Street, forcing them to come to a halt as he stretched out his arms. "Well, I'd heard it but I couldn't believe it, and now here you are baptizing another faithful convert," he smirked.

Richard's jovial mood was quickly quashed as he peered at Malcolm Trahern. "Please, step aside and let us pass," he said calmly.

"In a moment," Trahern grinned smugly. "I just couldn't let this opportunity pass without begging you to reconsider your horrendous mistake in taking up with the Mormons, Reverend Kenyon. You of all people should recognize the workings of Satan, for he is most surely directing these Mormonites. I beg you, turn away for the sake of your immortal soul and repent for this foolish misstep."

Richard remained remarkably tranquil as he faced Trahern without apology. "I appreciate your concern, Reverend Trahern, but I assure you it is not my immortal soul that is in jeopardy."

Trahern rocked back on his heels and cleared his throat in an effort to maintain his mounting temper. "As a minister of God, I must do everything in my power to prevent others from falling prey to this evil Mormon influence!"

Richard was unruffled and tried to shoulder his way past Trahern but was parried with a like motion. Richard bridled his tongue.

"We have nothing more to say to one another; please let us by."

Trahern's nostrils flared, and his dull eyes became hot with loathing. "The world must know of the evil teachings you espouse and the wicked dealings you have with the devil!"

Richard squared his shoulders and fixed his eyes on Trahern's reddened face. "I am sorry for you, Reverend."

Trahern's mouth gaped open in astonishment, and then his temper rose up to consume him. He pointed his meaty finger at Richard and narrowed his eyes. "I will never pray for you, Kenyon! Never!"

Richard's words were sincere. "That is for you to decide, Reverend Trahern, but I will pray for you."

A momentary lapse in Trahern's bluster offered Richard and Leah the opportunity to step around him and continue on their way. The others followed quickly, keeping pace with Richard's purposeful stride.

"Don't think for a moment you've bested me, Kenyon!" Trahern shouted, spinning about and shaking his fist in the air. "I promise you I won't rest until every last Mormon is driven out of Cardiff!"

Robert Kenyon leaned back in his office chair and circled his finger around the rim of the glass of port on his desk. He glanced absently at the clock and determined John Morgan would arrive any minute. He had not found peace of thought since his brother announced his union with the Mormons. It gnawed at him incessantly, digging into his conscience like a cancer. His growing hatred of the Mormons had taken a personal turn now, and there was something far greater at stake than just despising them. His only focus was to find a way to drive a wedge between his brother and these Mormons in hopes that Richard would abandon this foolishness and return to his senses. Perhaps then Robert could convince his brother to join him in the pursuit of expanding Kenyon & Sons.

Finally there came a knock at the door, and Robert grunted permission to enter. John Morgan smiled congenially and reached to shake Robert's hand. Robert remained motionless, and John gradually withdrew his hand with a look of scorn. "You wished to see me?" John asked.

Robert pointed to the chair across from his desk and John took a seat. "As you may have heard, my brother Richard threw over his own ministry and has become a Mormon."

John nodded, his knowledge of all the activities of the Mormons were well recounted by Meredith, who mingled easily among them. "I was sorry to hear that," he said. "And did you know his wife joined them yesterday?"

Robert raised an eyebrow, and then his face fell into a grimace. "I don't care about her; it's my brother that concerns me."

"As I can well imagine," John commented, waiting for Robert to come to the point. Robert drew in a deep breath and let it out slowly as he peered into John's narrow eyes. "You mentioned in our earlier conversation you had ways of dealing with the Mormons, to . . . discourage them from their membership."

"And you would like me to discourage your brother, I take it?" he surmised from Robert's expression.

"Indeed, you've read me quite well, but I want it done with the utmost discretion. He must never suspect I have a hand in this, Mr. Morgan. Are we clear on that?"

John fingered his mustache and nodded slowly. "I can personally guarantee your brother will never suspect your request."

Robert looked at him. "Out of curiosity, how will you go about it?"

John gave him a little smirk and a sideways glance. "I am not prepared to reveal that, Mr. Kenyon. Let's just say that some people respond to basic intimidation, and some require more . . . extensive means of persuasion."

"The sooner he comes to his senses the better," Robert grumbled. "Use whatever means necessary."

Morgan nodded in understanding. "To start, I will need a hundred pounds—"

Robert shot to his feet, his face reddening like a boiled lobster. "A hundred pounds? Are you out of your mind?"

John chuckled disarmingly. "Mr. Kenyon, you don't think I do these things merely out of the goodness of my heart, do you? I must deal with some of the most nefarious characters in the city to accomplish these means, and their efforts do not come cheaply."

Robert sat back down, his flaring temper cooling with reason. Of course, how could he have assumed there would not be a price to pay for John's services? Robert smiled inwardly. He liked John; he was a shrewd businessman. Any price was worth bringing Richard back to him. He reached for the cash box, counted out a hundred pounds, and handed the money to John. "See that this is accomplished quickly."

Morgan stood up and gathered the money. "That all depends on your brother," he replied, stuffing the cash into his pocket. "But I always succeed one way or another."

Meredith Cullen lived a different life than ever before. John Morgan had taken her away from the daily drudgery of working at the Three Bells, provided her with a small flat of her own, paid her handsomely to garner information on the Saints, and lavished his affections on her. She lived a copious life by comparison to her previous twenty-two years and was not about to do anything to jeopardize it. So she willingly sat in the Sunday meetings and pretended to be interested, socialized with the membership on a regular basis, and furnished John with details about their businesses, their homes, their families, and their means. She never asked what he intended to do with the information, nor did she care. So long as the money flowed, she would seek out tidbits of information to feed his curious appetite.

The one thing she was now required to do in order to complete the ruse of her interest in the Church was to be baptized as one of its members. This would seal her charade and cement her as one of them. She willingly stepped into the River Taff as Ben Lachlan reached for her hand to steady her into the water. It was all meaningless to her, their talk of remission of sin and repentance. None of that mattered to her; she didn't really believe in God.

As she rose from the river, Ben escorted her to the bank where President Simmons stretched out his hand to her. "Welcome, Sister Cullen," he smiled warmly. "You have taken your first step to becomin' a righteous instrument in the Lord's hands."

That's a strange thing to say, she thought. *What's a righteous instrument in the Lord's hands anyway?* She shook it off as just another one of the oddities of this quackery they called a religion and pretended to understand what he'd said.

Brother and Sister Bryant were there to witness the great event. Charlotte especially had become quite fond of Meredith, seeing her as the daughter she'd never had. The Bryants were childless, their feathered nest never filled with chicks of their own. Now there was Meredith, a sweet and gentle young woman all alone in the world. Charlotte couldn't help her maternal feelings toward the girl and made no excuses for it. She wrapped Meredith in a quilt and hugged her tightly. "Now you are a member of Christ's true church," she beamed.

"Aye, and I has your example to thank for it," she replied. "You and Mr. Bryant both."

Henry blushed and gave her a hug. "No, no," he insisted, "we're no examples to follow. We're quite imperfect and still learnin', but 'tis kind of you to say so."

"Let's get to the house so you can change," Charlotte said.

"Thank you for invitin' me to be confirmed in your home," Meredith said as they started from the riverbank. "You're so very kind to me."

"Not at all," Charlotte said, patting her thin hand. "We're happy to do it. It's always been too big for just the two of us. We enjoy fillin' it up with happy people."

President and Sister Simmons followed the Bryants and Meredith as they led the way. The sun was warming and welcome as the beginning of May filled the city with a long-awaited change from the cold, damp weather. As they neared the Bryants' home, a breathless young man raced toward them, his eyes wide with panic. "President Simmons!" he shouted, waving his hands to attract his attention. "President Simmons!"

The procession halted abruptly, and David Simmons caught the boy as he scooted to a stop. "What's the matter?" he asked with grave concern.

" 'Tis my tad," he panted. "He was attacked at his store and beaten. Please, you've got to come!"

David gave his wife a sorrowful look and motioned for Ben to join him. They darted off with the young man, leaving the others aghast at the news. "Poor Brother Yates," Sarah bemoaned. "I hope he's not badly hurt."

"Brother Yates," Meredith said ticking off his profile in her mind, "He's the tinsmith, aye?"

"Aye," Charlotte confirmed, "and such a gentle man. Why would anyone want to harm him?"

Sarah touched Charlotte on the arm. "Why don't you take Meredith on home? I'm goin' to Sister Yates. I'm sure she's beside herself."

"Aye, that'd be best," Henry said, ushering Meredith and Charlotte on toward the house.

They walked a few yards, and Charlotte kept shaking her head. "Poor Brother Yates," she said quietly. "We must pray for him."

"That we will," Henry agreed. "He's such a good man and a fine father, too. I know his wife and son would be devastated if anything serious comes of this."

Meredith felt a mild pang of conscience. She had told John the location of the tinsmith's shop a few weeks ago and where the Yates family lived as well. In the back of her mind, she knew what John intended to do with the information she provided, but she'd been able to push it aside while concentrating on her new clothes and the other niceties his money afforded her. Now there was a tangible connection to the beating of an innocent man with the reports she shared with him. She was slightly uncomfortable but quickly dismissed her concern as frivolous and foolish.

They approached the old house with bay windows. It was in need of minor repairs, but Henry was no longer able to keep up on the routine maintenance, and they were unwilling to spend the money required to hire it done. The interior was quite a surprising sight as Meredith scanned the amazing collection of strange and exotic items displayed throughout the home. African masks, brass Indian gods, Chinese silks draped against the walls, carved ivories, and trinkets of every kind were scattered on nearly every wall and piece of furniture she could see. She was in awe of the spectacle and had never seen anything like it.

A medium-sized dog came bounding toward the foyer at the

sound of Charlotte's voice. "Sailor! Have you been a good boy?" she asked reaching for his furry head. She looked at Meredith and offered a guilty smile. "This is Sailor, and aye, he stays in the house with me."

Meredith smiled. "A dog is a fine companion," she said, extending her hand for the black dog to sniff. She remembered a small brown dog owned by a neighbor when she was growing up. She'd always been found of the thing and mourned the day it was run over by a carriage. "He's very beautiful."

"Henry was at sea so much of the time that I would get lonely," she continued to explain. "Now he's just like family."

Henry chuckled. "He's a dog," he said firmly, "not a member of the family."

Charlotte was undeterred. "He is to me." She returned her eyes to Meredith. Charlotte could tell by Meredith's expression how awestruck the younger woman was by the contents of the house. "These are just a few of the things Henry has collected in his world travels as a sea captain."

"My," Meredith finally said, finding her voice. "I never saw anything like it. Where is that from?" she asked curiously, pointing to one particularly interesting primitive carving.

Charlotte took hold of Meredith by the shoulder. "Never mind that now," she said with authority. "You get out of those wet things, and afterward Henry will take you on a grand tour of the house."

"Really?" she asked, eager to learn of the amazing oddities. "I'd like that!"

"Not nearly as much as Henry will enjoy tellin' you about them," she said, escorting her to the stairs. "I've heard the stories a thousand times, and the only thing I know about them now is how much work it is to dust them all."

Meredith laughed and went up to the room Charlotte had prepared for her to change in. Her dry clothes were laid carefully on the bed, arranged in an orderly fashion. For a moment, Meredith allowed herself to ponder what it might have been like to have Charlotte for a mother. She couldn't help but wonder how different her life might have been had her mother lived. Meredith quickly dismissed the thought. It was pointless to dwell on the past. There was no changing her circumstances. Meredith swiftly stripped off the wet clothes and cast them aside.

When Meredith came downstairs with her wet clothes bundled together, Charlotte hurried toward her and took them. "Let me hang these on the line to dry," she offered, heading toward the kitchen and the back of the house. "Henry can show you around while I do that."

Meredith wandered hesitantly toward what she thought was the parlor and found Henry sitting in a comfortable chair, reading the paper.

He lowered his reading and smiled affectionately at her. "Well, are you ready for the grand tour, then?"

She nodded and smiled, her curiosity aching to be quenched. Henry got to his feet and placed his arm around her shoulder as he guided her toward the east wall of the parlor. He spoke with great knowledge about every culture he'd encountered, how the people lived, what they thought, what gods they worshiped, what they wore, even what they ate. Listening to him was like opening a door to an unfamiliar world and stepping through to live in it firsthand. She was fascinated by Henry's tales of how he'd come to possess each item from the strange and foreign lands he'd seen.

He had completed the tour of the parlor and the study when Charlotte appeared, pausing in the doorway while Henry continued undaunted. "Has he told you about the great elephant tusk hangin' on the wall there yet?" she asked with a sense of teasing in her voice.

Meredith spun toward Charlotte and shook her head. "Well, don't believe what he tells you. He bought it."

Henry gave his wife a chiding look. "Now Charlotte, I wasn't goin' to tell her I'd hunted down the great beast . . ."

"Hmm," she smirked, knowing Henry to stretch a bit of the truth now and then when it came to his adventures and collections. "Come into the kitchen. I've made us somethin' to eat while we wait for President Simmons."

Meredith followed the old couple. She felt comfortable in their presence, as though she somehow belonged. It was an odd and foreign feeling. Generally people were merely inconveniences to her; she had no use for them or for relationships of any kind, unless it was financially beneficial to her. As soon as they were seated in the kitchen, Charlotte smiled and asked Henry to pray.

"Our Father in Heaven," he began softly, "how grateful we are to be gathered at this table as members of thy true Church. We are so thankful for Meredith's decision to be baptized today and pray she will grow in thy Gospel to become a faithful member. Help us to be obedient to thy commandments for we know that true joy comes from livin' them in our hearts, in our minds, and in our souls. We so pray in the name of thy precious Son, Jesus Christ. Amen."

Meredith was reluctant to raise her eyes to meet the Bryants face-to-face. Henry's prayer had caused her another pang of conscience and she was becoming uncomfortable with these new feelings of guilt. She wanted no part of them and tried to push them from her mind. She was only doing what she'd been paid to do and that was all, she told herself. There was no room for developing scruples this late in the game.

⚜

Amelia Kenyon sat dutifully at the dinner table while her parents bickered incessantly. She tried to shut out the vicious sounding voices by scraping her fork forcefully across the plate.

"Amelia!" Abigail shrieked. "A proper young lady does not use her fork in such a way as to make that horrible noise! Stop it at once."

Amelia felt a seething hatred for her mother burning deep within her. Day after day, month after month, the constant criticism and denigration doled out by her mother had built up a volatile pressure inside her, consuming her every waking moment with resentment and rage. She gritted her teeth. Her nostrils flared as she breathed heavily against the impending explosion of emotion.

"No, *you* stop it!" Amelia shouted, pounding her fist on the cloth-covered dining table. She bolted to her feet, her eyes ablaze. "Stop your fighting and bickering! Does it never end with you two?" Amelia stormed from the dining room, leaving her parents stunned by her surprising outburst.

Abigail stood up, throwing her napkin to the table. "Amelia Kenyon, you come back here this instant!" she commanded.

"Oh, leave her alone," Robert grumbled, pushing away from the table. "She's right, and I'm sick of arguing too."

Abigail was indignant by her husband's lack of support. "How dare you take her side," she sneered.

"For once," he said pausing at the dining room entrance, "would you just shut up?"

Abigail gasped and stared at her husband. She made no rebuttal and stormed off after her daughter.

Amelia ran to her room, knowing there was little point in locking the door. She had tried that before, and it only added to her mother's fury. She braced herself for the ugly onslaught she was about to reap for her impetuous outburst. How she wished she could call back her remarks and spare herself the punishment, but that wasn't possible. Fourteen years of obedience and silence had finally given way to an unstoppable compulsion to rid herself of all her pent-up feelings.

Abigail reached for Amelia's door, expecting to find it locked. She was surprised when the knob turned freely in her hand. She flung open the door and stood in the doorway, her skirts filling the opening with dark green taffeta. Her eyes were molten with anger, her nostrils flared. She charged forward, her hand raised to strike, but seeing the look of defiance on Amelia's face caused her to pause. Then, as if to deny her daughter the satisfaction of intimidation, Abigail let loose with a sharp blow to Amelia's cheek, the palm of her own hand stinging with the power of her rage. "What an ungrateful brat you are!" she screamed. "Have you forgotten the most important of God's commandments? 'Thou shalt honor thy father and thy mother.' Until you have repented of this grievous sin and sufficiently begged my forgiveness, you will remain locked in this room!"

Amelia glared at her mother, willing her tears to remain unshed. As Abigail slammed the door shut and turned the key with a loud click, Amelia burrowed her face into her pillow to silence her anguished cries. She felt as if she were suffocating in her mother's presence. How she wished her parents were like her Aunt Leah and Uncle Richard. They were so kind and loving to each another. Amelia imagined life in their household to be peaceful and calm, a place where words were never spoken in harshness or anger.

Her thoughts narrowed to a single vein: she did not want to live in this house another day. As the minutes passed, Amelia realized she needed to extricate herself from her family. She gave no contemplation to how she would care for herself or what tomorrow would bring. Her goal was to get out of this house and run as far and as fast as she could. Without great deliberation, she retrieved a small satchel from beneath her bed. Amelia grabbed her well-loved doll from childhood, a brush and comb, a pair of stockings, a nightgown, and a gingham dress.

She opened the window and peered at the ground from her second story bedroom. It seemed a far distance down, but Amelia was undaunted. Just as she was about to drop the satchel to the ground, she remembered a few shillings she kept knotted in a handkerchief in the back of her dresser. Amelia retrieved the precious coins, tucked them inside the satchel, and then dropped it to the grassy earth below.

She drew in a deep breath of courage and positioned herself on the window ledge as her feet dangled beneath her skirts. She scanned the area surrounding the house to be sure no one was about and then catapulted from the window and landed sharply on the ground below.

For a moment, she was surprised at her success. Her feet stung from the jump, but she had landed without injury. Amelia caught up her satchel and skulked away from the house without a backward glance. She felt the oppression of her life lifting from her body and the misery trickling away until she was almost giddy in her escape.

Amelia ran until she had no more breath. Leaning against the corner of a tailor's shop, she paused long enough to catch her wind then continued to make her way through the gas-lit streets of Cardiff. She clutched her satchel closely as if it provided some sort of protection. Her walk through town was nerve wracking. She prayed no one would recognize her and stop her for questioning. It was only after she reached Cardiff Bridge that she began to loosen her white-knuckled grip on the satchel.

A new apprehension gripped Amelia as she walked beyond the edge of town and along the darkened road that stretched before her. Only a sliver of moon shone in the night sky, filling her journey with uncertain steps and stumbles. The oppressive darkness carried its own foreboding, igniting her fears of uncertainty with doubt and regret.

Amelia came to a stop at the edge of the road and peered behind her. Tears filled her eyes as she contemplated what she had done. She thought for a moment of returning home to its relative safety and her comfortable bed. But going home meant facing her mother's wrath for having run away, and that prospect seemed even more terrifying than the darkened road that lay before her.

Taking a deep breath into her lungs, Amelia exhaled slowly and then swallowed hard. She had made her decision, and whatever fate had in store for her, Amelia was determined to see it through. She stepped forward with hesitance. Darkness surrounded her with a thick, palpable intensity as she urged herself forward, encouraging her efforts again and again.

Progress was slow as she faltered along the road's edge, her eyes constantly darting to and fro. She was assaulted with a symphony of unfamiliar night noises, sounds she had never heard from the security of her home. With a racing heart, Amelia drew courage from the thought of increasing her freedom by placing more and more distance between herself and her mother.

It seemed she had been walking for hours, yet she was unable to ascertain any progress. She was growing quite weary, and the night air had taken on a chill. Amelia left the side of the road and walked toward an open area beneath a tree. Using her satchel as a pillow, she lay under the tree, pulling her knees up tight to her chest to fend off the chilly air. She closed her eyes and fell asleep more easily than she had anticipated.

She woke often through the night, the unfamiliar sounds and chilliness preventing any deep sleep. It was uncomfortable beneath the tree with twigs poking her flesh and the Welsh earth damp and cool under her slender body. As dawn crept slowly over the horizon, Amelia awoke to the sound of rolling wagon wheels and horses' hooves pounding the dirt road beside her. Her eyes flew open as she stared between the weedy green stems of undergrowth surrounding her. New apprehensions arose as she thought of her parents travelling the road in search for her. She wondered if they were clever enough to determine which direction she had taken when any number of options was a possibility.

Waiting until the wagon had passed, Amelia crept out toward the road's edge and peered up and down the span of dirt. She saw nothing in either direction and got to her feet, satchel in hand, and veered into the lush green that paralleled the road. Amelia determined she could follow alongside the road from a safe distance, keeping herself concealed from the daily traffic as much as possible.

❧

The morning was quickly slipping away as Leah worked feverishly to complete the wash. She stoked the fire beneath the large cauldron of water suspended within a tripod of slender logs and chains. Taking up a wooden paddle she agitated the clothes and pulled one out from the cauldron to scrub it against the washboard. Her hands were bright red as she wrung the shirt of its heated water again and again and then hung it on the line to dry.

Robert came bolting toward her out of nowhere, his face drawn into a menacing scowl. "Where is she?" he barked.

Leah turned from her wash, startled by his sudden appearance and growling voice. "Robert," she gasped in surprise. "What is it?"

"Is she here?" he charged. "And don't lie to me or so help me—"

Leah wiped her raw hands on her apron and stepped closer to him. "Robert, you're not makin' any sense. Calm down and tell me what's the matter."

Robert ran his fingers through his dark hair, his face turning to one of concern. "It's Amelia . . . she's run away."

"Run away!" Leah cried. "What happened?"

He grew defensive. "Never mind what happened. Have you seen her? I thought maybe she would come to you."

Leah grew instantly worried. She couldn't imagine how Amelia had garnered the strength to do such a thing. "No, she hasn't come here. When did she run away?"

Robert scrubbed his face with annoyance. "Some time last night."

Leah reached out to touch Robert's arm, but he pulled back from her consoling gesture. "What can I do to help?" she asked. "Amelia could be in danger."

"Don't you think I know that?" he spat. "She's only fourteen years old—" A crack in Robert's rigid exterior caused a release of his pent-up emotion. His face clouded with the worry he tried so hard to suppress, and his eyes betrayed the depth of his despair.

Leah's heart went out to her brother-in-law but even more so for her young niece. So many dangers awaited such an innocent and naïve girl. "Let me help you look for her," she said with assurance. "I can call together many of the Saints, and we can canvass the city—"

Robert's look of anguish turned to a darkened anger. "I want no help from any of you *Mormons!*"

"Be reasonable, Robert!" she pleaded. "Amelia's life could be at stake!"

Robert snarled and spun on his heel, swiping his hand against the air in disgust. Leah wasted no time and raced toward Claire's, where Richard had gone earlier to help Samuel load his wagon. She arrived breathless as she charged into the cooperage. "Richard—" she panted. "It's Amelia—"

Richard left his work and hurried toward her, alarmed by her agitated state. "What about Amelia?" he asked, taking hold of her by the shoulders.

Leah tried to catch her breath, her eyes filled with trepidation. "Amelia's run away."

"What?" he countered with astonishment. "Where would she go?"

Leah shook her head. "I have no idea. Robert came lookin' for her at our house. He thought she might have come to us."

Samuel hurried toward them. "We has to find her!"

Richard took on a look of control. "Leah, go back to the house in case she shows up there. Samuel and I will start out right now."

SIX

———— ❧ ————

AMELIA WAS CONFIDENT she was headed back to the road after circling about a growth of trees on the outskirts of a large lush clearing. Just a few more yards and the road would be in front of her again. She was thirsty and hungry from her long journey and hoped she would find a nearby village soon.

Amelia found a slightly smug smile crossing her lips as she thought of how clever she had been to hide herself from the view of the road. No one would spot her, most especially her family—that is, if they were even looking for her. Maybe they wouldn't care that she was gone. Perhaps they were glad to be rid of her. In any event, she was glad to be rid of them.

The sun grew hotter as she made her way closer to the road. She tried not to think about how thirsty she was and kept walking through the trees and thick grasses. Amelia expected the road to appear at any moment. She licked her parched lips and walked further, a feeling of uncertainty creeping into her thoughts. Where was the road? She should have come to it by now.

Coming to a stop, Amelia spun in a slow circle, surveying the landscape before her. Trees seemed to surround her on all sides, and uncertainty suddenly plunged her into despair. The cleverness she had assigned to herself disappeared as well; she was lost and had no idea which way to go. The satchel slipped from her grasp, and tears welled in her eyes as she dropped to the ground in hopelessness.

Amelia cried until there were no tears left to shed. She rubbed her red, swollen eyes and sniffed loudly. *Sitting in the grass like a quivering mass is not going to help*, she thought. She drew in a deep breath and got to her feet. Perhaps if she traced her steps back the way she had come, she would find the point at which she last left the road. With a newfound resolution, Amelia picked up her satchel and began retracing her path.

For several minutes, her newfound confidence led her along with good progress. She was certain it would not be long before she found the clearing where she left the edge of the road in the first place. Nothing looked especially familiar; her surroundings were all just green and encompassing on all sides.

She felt impressed to bear to the left, contrary to her initial inclination to continue to the right. The feeling grew stronger as she continued on, and Amelia accepted the prodding to travel in the new direction. After several yards, she saw the outline of what looked like a farmhouse. She gasped with surprise at the sight of the building. Surely there would be a road leading from the farmhouse and someone to tell her which way to go. Amelia sprinted ahead, smiling with excitement as she came closer and closer to the house.

"Hello!" she called, "Is anyone home?"

The front door was broken and hanging from the top hinge. The slate roof was in severe disrepair, and it was obvious that no one was living in the hovel. Amelia's smile dissolved as she realized there would be no one to give her directions, a drink of water, or a morsel of food.

She sighed deeply in her disappointment and scanned the area for any sign of a path that might indicate a direction for her to go. She spied the makings of a well some yards away and broke into a run, anxious to partake of its cool contents.

Amelia peered over the edge of the shallow stone wall that circled the rim of the well. The dry stacked stones were loose, and many had already fallen into the depths of the well or tumbled onto the ground in disheveled piles, leaving a ragged and uneven formation. A discarded wooden bucket lay on the ground, a long piece of frayed rope still attached to its handle. Amelia anxiously picked up the bucket and prepared to drop it into the depths of the well. She prayed there was water below as she licked her dry lips with anticipation.

Slowly leaning over the well's tenuous edge, Amelia fingered the tattered rope in her hands and bent forward, peering down the dark hole. As she lowered the bucket, her foot slipped on a small mound of loosened rubble, forcing her off balance. She scrambled to keep her equilibrium against the shifting rocks, her arms flailed wildly in the effort, and the bucket flung from her hand to land several feet behind her. She lurched forward and caught herself on the lip of the well, but the stones gave way, dropping from her hands as she was left grasping at thin air. Amelia landed sharply, teetering between the black hole in front of her and the unstable debris beneath her feet. Her body was suddenly propelled backward, away from the well, as if an unseen hand had snatched her from the brink of destruction. She landed on her backside with a firm thud amid the stone rubble.

Amelia's mouth gaped open in disbelief as she tried to grasp what had just happened. Amelia could not comprehend how she could have been thrown backward when surely gravity and momentum should have caused her to careen into the well. Before long, the terrorizing moment took its toll on her emotions. Hot tears came to her eyes, burning as they ran down her cheeks. The stinging scrapes and cuts on her hands started throbbing as she sat helpless and weeping, fully astounded by her perplexing rescue from harm.

Another stone fell freely into the well, clanking and bouncing down the sides and landing with a dull thump below. There was no water in the well. Amelia failed to find the irony amusing. She had never felt more alone in her entire life as her tears continued unabated.

❧

Richard decided to head west, crossing Cardiff Bridge. He wasn't certain why he felt impressed to do so, but he wasn't about to question his inspiration. His heart was pounding as he thought of the poor girl whose life was made so miserable she had felt compelled to run away. It was so painful to watch her suffer such mistreatment and feel helpless to do anything about it. All he ever wanted for her was to be happy and content, neither of which she experienced in the home of his brother. He found himself becoming angry with Robert for his weakness and lack of command in his own home. Richard knew that his brother could help Amelia's self-respect with a bit of love and encouragement. He should have been countermanding his wife's wicked treatment of his daughter, but instead he withdrew and allowed Amelia to suffer.

Richard's swift pace carried him along the dirt road for several minutes before his mind cleared of the anger he felt toward his brother. He hadn't even been truly searching for Amelia, only walking as he thought. Taking himself to the task at hand, Richard stepped from the roadside into a small grove of trees and knelt down in the soft meadow grass. He entreated his Father in Heaven for help and inspiration, that his steps might be guided to the discovery of Amelia's location, and that she would be found safe and well. He prayed for her comfort, that she need not fear nor be distraught, and that all would be well. And then he prayed for the Lord's merciful forgiveness for his anger toward Robert.

As Richard closed his prayer, he felt the warmth of the Holy Ghost encircle him, as if he were being lifted with hope and renewed courage. Getting to his feet, he started for the thicket just beyond where he had stopped to pray, his steps now guided with inspiration.

He was unfamiliar with the terrain, relying only on the strong promptings of the Spirit that accompanied him as he moved forward. He pushed his way through wooded glades and open fields of the Vale of Glamorgan, crossed streams and forged ahead along the countryside with the confidence that he was being guided. As he approached a small abandoned farmhouse, his ears were pricked by the faint sound of crying. Richard darted forward, no longer choosing his steps with care. He ran toward the sobbing cries, the volume increasing as he did. "Amelia!" he cried loudly. "Amelia, is that you?"

Amelia was stunned into silence as she heard her name called from the distance. She groped her way through the rubble and scrambled to her feet, her eyes darting toward the sound of the voice. "I'm here!" she shouted gleefully, searching for the owner of the voice. "Over here!"

Richard ran past the farmhouse and saw his niece waving beside the well. "Amelia!" he called with excitement, racing toward her.

Amelia's heart pumped wildly as she ran toward him. "Uncle Richard!"

He swept her up and kissed her tear-stained cheek. "Thank God," he whispered against her face. "You're all right."

"Uncle Richard," she sobbed against his shoulder. "You found me . . . ."

"Aye," he whispered, his prayer of gratitude repeated again and again in his mind. *Thank you, Father. Thank you for bringing me to her.*

Richard kissed her again and took up her small satchel. "Let's get you back to Cardiff," he said, taking hold of her hand. They walked down the small pathway leading from the cottage. He imagined it connected to a main road somewhere, and then they could head due east back to the city. His mind wrestled with the many questions he longed to ask her and the scolding he felt she deserved, but he could do neither. He was too grateful for his answered prayer and the testimony he'd received from it to disrupt the peace he'd found.

Amelia walked beside her uncle in silence. She dreaded the inevitable end that awaited her. She knew her life would be made far worse for her impulsive actions. "You're going to make me go back, aren't you?" she asked after some time had passed.

Richard paused before answering. "I'll do what I can to change that," he said softly, pausing in his stride. He lifted her chin and peered into saddened eyes. "I can't promise you anything, *cariad*, but I will do everything I can to get you out of that house."

Amelia grabbed him with both arms and clung desperately to him. Her moist tears bled onto his coat with hope and gratitude. She prayed her uncle could somehow perform the miracle that would spare her of continued agony. Oh, how she prayed.

※

Amelia rushed into the cottage, her hands outstretched. She clung to Aunt Leah with hungry arms. "I'm so sorry I made you worry," she began to cry. "I just had to leave. . . ."

Leah found warm tears of relief well in her eyes as she returned the girl's eager embrace. "Amelia," she whispered against the girl's ear. "*Cariad* . . . ." Leah took the girl's hands in hers, scrutinizing the scrapes and cuts. "Oh, Amelia . . . ."

Leah ushered her niece to the kitchen table and took down a

large bowl. She filled it with water, gathered some salve and clean cloths, and began washing and dressing her niece's injured hands.

"Let's get you something to eat," Richard suggested as he gathered some bread and cheese, a mug of milk, and the last of the homemade shortbread. Once Leah had finished cleaning the wounds, Richard placed the food before Amelia and urged her to eat.

Amelia took up the bread and tore off a corner, eating it quickly, her hunger causing her to leave her normal table manners behind as she chewed the welcome food. As she ate, she slowly revealed to her aunt and uncle what had caused her to run away. Richard and Leah listened without comment as their niece told them that it was not the single incident of the night before that had driven her from home but the cumulative and mounting mistreatment she could no longer abide. Tears fringed her dark lashes as she looked at her aunt and uncle. "I've always felt such affection from you both," she said, her chin quivering in an attempt to control her emotions. "I just wanted to get out of that house—to get away from them . . . ."

Leah's heart broke as she leaned forward across the table, wiping Amelia's tears away. "Oh, Amelia," she replied softly.

Amelia's face was a mix of emotions. Her eyes darted between the pair. "Please, don't make me go back," she implored. "I'd rather die than go back."

Leah gave Richard a pleading glance before standing and taking Amelia by the arm. "No more tears, now," she said. "Come *cariad*, I want you to lie down for awhile."

When Leah returned from the bedroom, she found Richard still at the kitchen table, his head in his hands. "What is it, Richard? What are you thinkin'?"

He stood up, his brow furrowed as he studied Leah's kind face. "I don't want to send her back—"

Leah gasped. "And you can't! I won't let you!"

Richard took hold of her shoulders. "Hear me out," he said firmly. "I'm going to try to reason with Robert to let her live with us, or if he won't agree to that, then perhaps he'll send her away to school. But first, we must return her to her parents. We haven't the right to do otherwise."

For a moment Leah rebelled against the idea, her desire to

protect Amelia from further pain overshadowing her reason. Leah lowered her gaze. She drew in a deep breath and released it slowly as she pressed her face against Richard's chest. He was right, and she knew it. "I pray Robert will place Amelia's happiness above all else, just this once."

Richard was doubtful that his brother cared anything about his own daughter's happiness, but he was bound by every fiber in his being to help Amelia find it somehow.

❧

Amelia clung to her uncle as they approached her father's house. She was terrified despite Richard's calm, soothing voice assuring her to be fearless. Lucy answered their knock at the door, and her eyes popped open at seeing Amelia there. "Miss Amelia!" she gasped. "You're all right!"

Richard ushered Amelia inside, his protective arm surrounding her shoulders like a fortress. "Lucy, will you please tell Mr. and Mrs. Kenyon we are here?"

The servant nodded obediently but dreaded having to be the one to approach them with the news. She had been on the receiving end of Abigail's wrath before and, due to her mistress's unpredictable nature, was never quite sure just what would happen. She scurried away, and within moments Robert came charging into the foyer, his footsteps heavy and threatening. His stern manifestation caused Amelia to slip behind her uncle, using him as a shield from the impending confrontation.

Momentarily Robert's face softened at the sight of his daughter but quickly returned to a steeled countenance. "I might have known she'd go to you," he growled at his brother.

"But she didn't," Richard defended. "She was headed west on the road to Swansea when I found her."

"When you found her," he scoffed. "That's a likely story. You expect me to believe you just happened to be on the road to Swansea yourself?"

Richard kept his grip on Amelia. "It was nothing like that at all," he tried to explain. "But I wouldn't expect you to understand the workings of the Spirit of God. I was led to her."

Robert's face reddened in reaction to Richard's religious explanation. He didn't believe it or him. He reached for Amelia's arm, but she ducked further behind Richard. "Don't you shirk from me," he snarled.

Abigail came charging down the stairs, her layers of dressing gown and petticoats gathered in her hands. "Amelia!" she screeched. "You come here this instant!"

Richard stood in front of his niece, sheltering her from the ascending shrew. "Now, just a minute, Abigail," he said boldly. "Before you lash out, I beg you to consider Amelia's future. It's obvious the girl is unhappy. Please, let her come and live with us."

Abigail cackled, finding the proposition more amusing than serious. "Don't be preposterous! She'll live nowhere but here! She is *my* child, not yours!"

Robert narrowed his eyes and glared at Richard. "How dare you ask such a thing! This is Amelia's home. She belongs here."

"Then send her to finishing school, in London perhaps," he pleaded, knowing he was waging a losing battle. "She would do well to learn of the finer things in life."

Abigail leered malevolently at Richard, her temper flaring. "You have no right to Amelia. You're nothing but a beggar in a cleric's frock. How dare you even presume to know what's best for my daughter?"

Robert reached toward Amelia, but Richard shadowed his movement, preventing him from taking hold of her. Robert glowered menacingly at his brother. "Don't toy with me, Richard," he threatened. "Let Amelia go and leave."

"Not until I have an answer," he pressed. "Let her live with us. She'll be well cared for—"

Robert leaned forward, meeting his brother face-to-face. "I should have thought the answer was abundantly clear," he seethed. "Besides, I wouldn't have her destroyed by your loathsome religion!"

Richard bristled, his eyes piercing Robert's. "But you would have her destroyed by your own wife?"

"Get out!" he yelled, pointing sharply at the door. "Get out before I call the constable!"

Abigail maneuvered around the two men and seized hold of

Amelia's arm. "You are coming with me!" she hissed.

Amelia screamed as her mother dragged her toward the stairway. "Uncle Richard!" she pleaded tearfully. "Don't let her—"

A sharp backhand to the mouth silenced Amelia instantly as her mother forced her upstairs. Richard started forward in defense of his niece, but Robert barred his way. "Don't do it, Richard," he warned thickly. "Leave now, or you'll regret it!"

Richard stepped back, his teeth gritted in an effort to constrain his temper. "You will answer to God for this, Robert. You and Abigail both!"

Robert snagged the lapels of Richard's coat and pushed him back toward the door. Richard was caught off guard as his brother threw open the door and thrust him outside with a forceful shove. "You can answer to God if you like, but I answer to no one!" he shouted. "And don't come back here, Richard. I mean it!" Robert slammed the door violently, shaking the very entrance of the house.

Richard stood gaping at the closed door, and his heart sank into the pit of his stomach. He'd failed Amelia miserably, and the thought of her being left in the hands of her immoral parents sickened him. He straightened up and tugged on his coat. Turning from the house, he prayed for his niece's safety and for her parents' hearts to be softened.

President Simmons looked around the small gathering of Saints as he prepared to address them. He was pleased to see Brother Yates present, undeterred by the beating he'd received. His heart was touched by the dedication of the man who'd suffered at the hands of his vile oppressors and yet found the courage to continue his association with the Saints of God.

"The legions of Satan have made another attempt to thwart the progress of the restored gospel of Jesus Christ," President Simmons stated boldly, his voice rising above the congregation of Saints with clear, ringing tones. "Our own Brother Yates was attacked and beaten for his faith. But I testify to you that Satan shall not win this battle for he wages it in vain! The Saints of God are the elect whom He has chosen to bring forth His message to every man, woman, and child upon the face of the earth! God is with us as we go forward in righteousness, preachin' the gospel to all who will listen, gatherin' His sheep to the fold once more. Will we face hardships? We will, brothers and sisters. Of course we will. We are not immune to the actions of the wicked. But will we be blessed for our efforts? I testify without hesitation, absolutely yes!

"We have nothin' to fear so long as our hearts and minds are right with God. Even should we perish at the hands of evil men, just as the prophet Joseph Smith, yet will we be saved through the Atonement of our Savior, Jesus Christ.

"As we labor to build the kingdom of God, take courage, brothers and sisters, for we are engaged in the most important work of our lives. Because of that, we will be tested, we will be persecuted, we will be spat upon, and we will be scourged by those who hate and revile us. Nevertheless, the Lord will bless us with strength sufficient to face our enemies with bravery beyond our comprehension."

Meredith squirmed in her seat as she listened to President Simmons. It was obvious that these Mormons were a tough breed. She could not bring herself to look at the battered face of Brother Yates. It was too painful a reminder that she'd had a hand in the beating—not by her own fists, of course, but by her association with John Morgan. She tried not to think about it and turned her thoughts to the sermon.

"But we must act with compassion toward our adversaries," President Simmons was saying. "We must forgive those who would harm us. We must love our enemies even as our exemplar, Jesus Christ, did. We must stand as witnesses of God, renewed in our faith of that which has been restored to us and be not ashamed of the testimony we bare.

"As Moses counseled Joshua and all Israel, 'Be strong and of a good courage, fear not, nor be afraid of them; for the Lord thy God, he it is that doth go with thee; he will not fail thee, nor forsake thee.' I add my testimony of that wise counsel, brothers and sisters, and do so in the name of our beloved Savior, Jesus Christ. Amen."

Ben Lachlan was uncharacteristically sequestered in the back of the room, withdrawn and sullen looking. After the meeting, Richard and Leah approached him with concern. Ben gradually drew his gaze upward toward the couple, his usual affable demeanor awash in a sea of sadness.

Leah knelt down beside the somber man. "Ben, what is it? What's the matter?"

Ben's eyes filled with tears as he looked into Leah's worried face. He slowly reached into his waistcoat and took out a crumpled letter, handing it to her then casting his absent gaze to a corner of the room.

Her fingers trembled as she unfolded the letter and held it open for her and Richard to read. It was dated March 14, 1847 from Winter Quarters. Leah quickly surveyed the scrawl of handwriting, her heart beating abruptly as she came to the devastating passage. " 'Your boys were playing beside the icy river when the bank gave out. They were swept away instantly. Despite being restrained by some of the other sisters, your wife jumped in to save the boys. The combination of the frigid temperature and the powerful current were too much for them. I am sorry to tell you they all drowned. Their bodies were recovered about a half-mile down river and have been buried.' "

Leah's heart broke as she stood before Ben, not knowing what to say or do. The letter drifted from her hand and fell to the floor. Ben came suddenly to his feet and grabbed Leah and Richard into his arms, shaking as he sobbed against their shoulders. His world was collapsing from within as he released the devastating sadness he'd tried to restrain. Ben withdrew momentarily, struggling to collect his emotions again. He smudged his tears away with annoyance and tried to face his friends with renewed courage.

Richard placed his hand on Ben's shoulder. "Ben, I . . . I'm so sorry for your loss. . . ." His words fell short of expressing the full measure of his sorrow for his dear friend.

Leah managed to quell her own tears. She found solace in Ben's quiet strength. "Oh, Ben," she muttered softly, "I don't know what to say . . . I'm so very sorry."

Richard picked up the crumpled letter from the floor and carefully handed it back to Ben, who tucked it away in the pocket next to his heart. He attempted to smile, but it was fleeting. "I take comfort knowing they died in the fullness of the gospel and that I will see them again. . . ."

Richard peered sadly at Ben. "I suppose you'll be returning to America then?"

Ben looked at him pensively, struggling to keep his tears at bay. "What would I return to?" He absently ran his hand through his hair and then looked down at the floor. "No, I'll stay and continue in the Lord's work. In time, I'll be better prepared to return home."

Richard admired Ben's resolve in the face of so much pain. He was convinced it was the strength found only through the gospel of Jesus Christ that sustained his friend. "Perhaps that is wise," he offered with a deep feeling of ineptitude.

Ben straightened his shoulders and forced a strained smile to his lips. "I'm going to be traveling for the next several days," he said. "I'm heading to Llandaf, Rhymney, Pontypridd, and finally Merthyr Tydfil, where a conference of the Saints will be held at the end of the month. I'm sure I'll see you at the conference."

Richard appeared a bit puzzled. "What conference is this?"

Ben explained how all the Saints in a specific region gathered together to share in the messages from church authorities, some local and some visiting from America. Captain Dan Jones presided over the Merthyr Tydfil Conference as well as the entire Welsh nation. President Jones was a native of Wales but had joined the Church while in America. Ben was certain President Jones would preside over the conference. Richard nodded and looked at Leah. "We'll be there, Ben. You can count on that."

Ben shook Richard's hand, gave Leah a brief embrace, and then left the building. He stepped into the street and began walking, his mind consumed with grief. *I just want to work, Father,* he prayed desperately. *I don't want to think anymore, just work. I don't want to see the visions in my mind of my wife and sons drowned. . . . I just want to work.*

Richard kissed Leah good-bye and stepped outside. His meeting with President Simmons had come as an unexpected request after yesterday's meetings. He had no idea what the president wanted.

President Simmons smiled pleasantly as he answered the door and invited Richard inside. "Thank you for comin', Richard. Please, take a seat," he said, indicating the chair opposite his own.

"Where's Sister Simmons?" he asked as he glanced around the otherwise empty parlor.

"She's with the Barlow family," he replied. "Sister Barlow has become ill and has no one to tend her little ones. Sarah loves children, so she was anxious to step in and help."

"Bless her," Richard said with an affectionate smile.

President Simmons' face grew more somber. "Before I tell you why I asked you here tonight, did you hear about Brother Everest?"

Richard shook his head, reluctant to hear what had happened.

"Another beating, I'm afraid," President Simmons said, his voice a mixture of anger and disgust. "He was not seriously hurt. Fortunately his assistant was in the back of his store and heard the scuffle. When he showed himself, the attackers ran off."

Richard shook his head. The news was shocking but not unexpected. It seemed the harassment was growing in its intensity. "Did he recognize any of them?"

The president shook his head. "No, they were wearing hoods. No one knows who they are."

"Cowards!" Richard shot beneath his breath. "How long will this continue?" he asked, knowing there was no answer. President Simmons sighed and looked into the fireplace for a moment. "You can be sure this is just the beginnin'."

"So who's to be next?" Richard asked rhetorically.

"It could be any one of us, I suppose," he said wearily. "I pray day and night for the protection of the Saints."

"And what of you, President Simmons? Do you fear an attack?"

He half-laughed with his answer. "What is there to fear? If my heart is right with the Lord, then I fear nothin' man can perpetrate upon me."

"And Sister Simmons?"

His features grew sober. "She feels the same as I, but I couldn't bear to see anything happen to her."

"Has anyone reported these attacks to the authorities?" Richard asked leaning back in the wingback chair.

President Simmons snorted. "Aye, they were reported and they were politely told nothin' could be done. Unless the attackers are caught in the act and their identities revealed, the authorities refuse to do anything about it."

"So what are we to do?"

He smiled with confidence. "We will do just as we've always done—preach the gospel to those who will listen, remain strong in the faith, and pray for the Lord's intervention in the matter."

"From some of the stories I've heard Ben tell of his life in America, I guess we can't expect much different treatment. The adversary will do all he can to destroy the Church."

Repositioning himself in his chair, President Simmons looked earnestly at Richard. "Now, let's get on to why I called you here this evenin'. But before we do, let us kneel as elders in Israel and ask the Lord's blessings upon the branch."

Just as the men moved to kneel, a flare of orange light flashed through the windows, followed by a second, and then a third, each in ominous procession. Fiery torches surrounded the house, held by dark-hooded figures. "Get down!" Richard shouted, grabbing President Simmons by the arm.

A torch smashed through the window, setting the curtains aflame as it landed on the floor near the men. Richard seized the torch and wrestled it into the fireplace, but it was followed by another and another, until the furnishings caught fire. The room filled quickly with thick smoke as the flames lapped hungrily at all that would burn.

"Out the back!" cried the president, shielding his face with his arm.

They ran from the parlor, assaulted by the raging fire that seemed to overwhelm the entire house. The kitchen was already engulfed in flames, making their exit to the back door hazardous and terrifying. As Richard struggled to find his way toward the back door, his lungs filled with smoke, and his eyes stung with copious tears. He coughed into his arm and tried to shield his face from the heat and smoke. Another kitchen window shattered as a blazing torch crashed through the window and landed on the floor in front of the men.

Flames surrounded them as the sounds of raucous laughter and gleeful cries from their wicked assailants permeated the night air.

"Burn in the hell you deserve!"

"Death to the Mormons!"

President Simmons collapsed to his knees, his lungs overcome with the heavy, thick smoke. The burden proved too much for his heart. Richard could scarcely see as he reached out for the older man, finding his body sprawled limply across the kitchen floor. He latched onto the president's forearm and pulled him toward the door. Richard struggled for breath, finding himself near collapse. He fell to the floor but would not relinquish his hold of President Simmons.

With the painstaking effort of battling to stay conscious, Richard dragged himself and the president to the door of the kitchen. Richard held his breath as long as he could and dared only breathe when it became impossible to keep his lungs from bursting. Blinded by the smoke and flames, he inched his way closer to the door, reaching upward to locate the latch that would set them free.

Richard's head reeled with dizziness as his body and mind threatened to succumb to the masterful smoking fire. With his last ounce of effort, Richard found the latch and opened the door. He crawled laboriously past the threshold, towing the unconscious man's heavy weight behind him. There was the slightest layer of relatively fresh air hovering at ground level, and Richard coughed and spat as he tried to breathe it in, the oxygen purging the smoke and soot from his lungs.

He gasped over and over, renewing his lungs with fresh air. Richard grew more clear-headed and was able to continue his arduous extrication from the house. Crawling on his hands and knees as he dragged President Simmons behind him, Richard made it several feet from the burning structure before collapsing.

Townspeople had gathered, the flames a horrifying signal of destruction. Firefighters had been summoned though the house burned rapidly. A hand reached down and pulled Richard yet further toward safety, leaving his still and unmoving companion behind. "Is there anyone else in the house?" a voice shouted.

"No," Richard coughed. "We were . . . the only . . . two . . ."

The proximity of the burning house posed no threat to neighboring buildings; the perimeter of land surrounding the house provided a generous barrier from the danger. The bright orange flames leapt into the night sky, and the pungent smell of smoke was sufficient to draw frightened neighbors and curious bystanders.

Richard craned his head around until he could see President Simmons. His friend remained too motionless for Richard's comfort, and he crawled to the president's side and shook him roughly. "President Simmons, can you hear me?" By the red-orange light of the burning fire, Richard peered into the president's face. "President!" he implored, shaking him again.

Someone reached down and took hold of Richard's shoulder. "It's no use," the stranger pronounced grimly. "Your friend is dead."

Richard shrugged the man's hand away. He refused to accept such a sentence. He shook President Simmons forcefully, calling his name with his hoarse, smoky voice. The old man's eyes opened gradually, but he could see nothing in the darkness that surrounded him. "Richard?" he managed to rasp.

"I'm here," Richard said pulling him into his arms, cradling him against his chest.

President Simmons' grasp on life was tenuous and fading. He struggled to remain focused as the flames of his burning home danced behind him. "The Lord . . . needs you," he muttered. "Stay strong . . ."

Tears of sorrow moistened Richard's soot-covered face, streaking the dark stains on his skin. "I will, President . . . ," He tried to raise his fingers toward Richard's shoulder, but his hand fell back against the grassy earth. His lungs exhaled a final breath with the faintest whisper of his wife's name on his lips. President Simmons lay still and lifeless in Richard's arms.

SEVEN

———— ❧ ————

J OHN MORGAN CIRCLED TO THE BACK of the three story building, making certain he was not seen. He entered the back door
and climbed the stairs to the third floor. He knocked on the door of
a small room off of the poorly lit hallway.

"Aye?"

"It's John, let me in," he replied.

Meredith opened the door slowly to reveal a half-hearted attempt
at keeping her robe closed. "Hello, love," she said, smiling.

John encircled her waist with his sinewy arms and kicked the
door closed with his foot. He kissed her passionately, backing her
against the bureau. She laughed and pushed him away playfully. "It
hasn't been that long," she teased.

"Long enough," he whispered, nestling his stubble-covered face
into her neck.

She tangled her fingers in his hair and pulled him closer. Her lips
burned with the want of him. "Why don't you take off your coat?"
she coaxed.

He reached for the buttons and smiled slyly at her. "Tonight was
a great success," he mused, sliding the coat from his shoulders.

"Tonight?" she asked moving toward the bed. "What happened
tonight?"

"Simmons house was burned to the ground," he said with a tri-
umphant grin.

The announcement left her stunned. She never suspected John

would go so far as to destroy President Simmons' house. She worried that her concern for President Simmons would show on her face, so she turned away from him. "That seems a bit much, doesn't it?" she asked trying to sound casual. John came up behind her and pulled her against his chest. "Not for any Mormon," he murmured against her ear.

"I suppose not," she replied, trying to conceal her apprehension. "Maybe 'twill put some of them off a bit."

John laughed throatily, his chest rumbling against her back. "Oh, it will do more than that," he purred, nibbling her earlobe. "The old man is dead."

Meredith felt the color drain from her face as her heart ceased its beating. How could this have happened? It wasn't possible—President Simmons couldn't be dead. She was suddenly repulsed by John's touch and wanted to bolt from his embrace, but she feared the consequences of such a reaction. Instead she struggled to remain calm so he wouldn't suspect how sickened she'd become in his presence. "Died in the fire, did he?" she asked quietly, afraid her voice would betray her.

"No, but he's dead just the same," he laughed turning her around to face him. "Let's see how many will remain faithful with that fate awaiting them."

Meredith closed her eyes quickly as her stomach churned. She couldn't bear to look at him, nor could she allow her face to reveal her revulsion. John kissed her again and pulled her hard against him. "You are magnificent," he murmured.

The long ride to the conference in Merthyr Tydfil gave Richard much time to think. His thoughts rambled as he rode silently in the rented wagon. He couldn't erase the memory of the look on Sarah Simmons' face as they lowered her husband's coffin into the ground. It haunted his dreams, her expression one of utter despair and heartbreaking bereavement. In an attempt to empathize with Sister Simmons, he tried to imagine what it would feel like if he lost Leah. Even entertaining the idea brought him overwhelming grief, and he quickly dismissed the horrible thought.

And then he reflected on Ben, having lost his wife and sons to such a horrible death, separated by thousands of miles and apart for so long and now for all earthly time. His heart ached for Ben too, living with his grief and sorrow yet facing it stoically as he pressed on with his missionary work. Richard looked forward to seeing him at the conference and hoped to see for himself how Ben was doing.

He glanced at his wife, who sat beside him, and reached for her hand. The sun played brilliantly against her auburn hair, which sent him back in time to the day of their meeting. It was that magnificent hair that had first drawn his attention.

Leah had been a member of a choir singing in the annual Festival of Eisteddfod. Eisteddfod was rife with a rich Celtic heritage, revived and sanctioned during the reign of Queen Elizabeth I. The tradition focused on the poetry, storytelling, and choral music of Wales, brought together in a grand competition to vie for the honors as Wales' best.

Richard had been there with his own men's choir as part of the competition. He remembered standing below the platform, scanning the faces of the performing singers, and was quickly drawn to a woman with lush, auburn hair that called to him even beneath her straw hat. Richard hadn't been able to take his eyes from her. She was lovely, taller than average. But her hair—it was as if it sang to him with a siren's song. He had watched, mesmerized by her, as the choir performed. He'd been able to distinguish her voice above the others too—a melodic alto, soothing yet strong. Her voice was second in beauty only to her hair and her dazzling green eyes. In a manner most unlike him, Richard had rushed onto the platform the moment the choir finished to introduce himself.

Their courtship had been brief, just long enough for him to carve a wooden love spoon for Leah. The love spoon was an ancient tradition whereby a young man could show his affection and intentions toward his sweetheart. Richard fashioned his spoon from a single piece of sycamore about twelve inches in length. He carved two intertwined ribbons threaded through two hearts to form the handle, symbolizing true love. At the base of the spoon, he carved their initials into the petals of two flowers, which symbolized affection. He remembered the day she accepted his offering as an approval of his love and proposal. They were married just one week later.

He smiled and raised Leah's hand to kiss it. She looked warmly at him and caressed the side of his face. "What was that for?" she asked.

"For being my wife," he replied with a tender smile.

Leah peered into her husband's handsome face and saw the pensive look in his eyes. She read his thoughts and clung to his arm. "I'm not leavin', Richard. Ever."

He smiled gently and touched her cheek with the back of his fingers. The wagon hit a large pothole in the road and jarred them wildly in their seats. They laughed, and Samuel looked over his shoulder from the driver's seat. "Hold on to your hats, ladies and gents," he joked.

Claire held Caleb and Isaac firmly by their hands as they sat in the seat across from Leah and Richard. The boys squealed with delight at the bouncing ride and begged their father to find another hole. "Don't you dare," Claire called up front. "I nearly lost my stomach in the last one."

Young Jonah Reese sat beside Samuel. The invitation to attend the conference was one he'd been eager to accept. He was anxious to listen and learn away from Cardiff, where he experienced untold harassment from his fellow dock workers. The simple fact that he was even thinking of joining the Latter-day Saints kept him the focus of their constant teasing. He wished that he'd never mentioned his interest in the Church so he could have avoided the ribbing and abuse. There were times when he wasn't sure being among the membership was worth the sacrifice required to endure such treatment. These times of uncertainty were what had delayed his baptism. He was convinced of the truth the very day Reverend Kenyon had spoken it at the pulpit, but every time he tried to learn more, the other dock workers seemed to know, and he suffered for it the next day.

Richard touched his coat pocket. The letter from President Jones was still there. The president had written Richard specifically, asking him to attend the conference and to meet with him following the first assembly on Saturday. He was simultaneously intrigued and apprehensive but was anxious to know the legendary man.

Ben Lachlan stood ready to greet the members as they filed into the White Lion Inn. He smiled and extended his hand to many, recognizing some familiar faces in the crowd. The growth of the Church was astounding, especially in Merthyr Tydfil these past months. The whole of the Glamorgan Conference numbered nearly one thousand, and Ben felt a sense of awe as he surveyed the vast audience of Saints.

As he scanned the gathering crowd, he saw Richard and Leah making their way toward him. He raised his arm and waved with excitement until they looked his way with recognition.

"It's Ben!" Leah exclaimed. "How good he looks!"

Richard waved back as they pushed their way forward. "Come on," he called behind him to Samuel and Claire. "Ben's over there, by the entrance to the inn."

The little group shuffled their way through the crowd. Ben shook Richard's hand with zeal. "How wonderful it is to see you." He beamed, but then his face sobered quickly as his joyous reunion took second place to the heartbreaking truth of President Simmons' death. "How is Sister Simmons? Did she come with you?"

Leah shook her head sadly. "No, she went to Swansea to be with her sister. I can't say that I blame her."

Ben nodded with understanding. He surveyed the crowd once again. "You'd best take your seats, or you might be left standing."

"Come sit with us," said Leah. "We'll save you a seat."

Ben nodded as he continued to greet other Saints to the conference. The air was filled with anticipation; the people buzzed with excitement at the prospect of hearing President Jones address them.

Along the perimeter of the gathering, a group of strangers assembled, watching and waiting. Ben observed them for a few moments. It was not yet clear if they were merely curious on-lookers or if they meant to inflict some sort of harassment to the Saints. There had been much persecution of the Merthyr Tydfil Saints, even death threats to President Jones. Ben was reluctant to leave his appointed duties, but when he saw a constable toward the end of the street, he snaked his way through the crowd and approached him.

"Constable," he blurted breathlessly.

The man arched an eyebrow and rocked back on his heels. "What is it?"

"Constable, I suspect there may be some trouble brewing."

The man frowned and surveyed the crowd. "What sort of trouble?"

Ben jerked his head in the direction of some older boys, their hands stuffed into their pockets, their faces wrinkled with anger. "I believe there may be some intent to disrupt our meeting."

The constable eyed Ben with contempt. "What of it? I should think you Mormons would be used to it by now."

Ben eyed the man sternly. "Constable, your personal opinion of the Latter-day Saints should have no bearing on whether or not you enforce the law. We have a permit to meet in this building, and we have obliged every legal requirement to gather in peace. You, a constable of the law, have a duty to prevent us from potential harm."

The constable narrowed his eyes and clasped his hands behind his back. "Potential harm?" he repeated. "If I had my way, the lot of you would be thrown into a coal pit and buried alive!"

Ben gritted his teeth, fighting the desire to counter the man's remarks. He spun on his heel and returned to the conference, pushing the anger from his mind as he attempted to garner the Spirit once again.

The number of saints continued to swell into the building, filling every seat until there was only standing room in the back, the rest spilling outside near the doorway. On a raised platform sat President Jones and the presidents of each branch in the Glamorgan Conference, their counselors in the rows behind. The president of the Penydarren Branch came to the front, and the crowd hushed their whisperings. He smiled pleasantly, indicating the conference was about to commence. He called upon the Saints to open with song and prayer, and then a vote was offered up to sustain President Jones as the leader of the Church in the Welsh nation. The vote was unanimous in the affirmative.

Each president in turn stood and reported on the activity in his branch: the number of baptisms that had occurred since the last conference was held, the total number of Saints in his branch, and the number of elders, priests, teachers, and deacons. A general summary of each branch's missionary efforts was also detailed as well as a report of how many missionaries were assigned to the branch.

Richard basked in the affirmation of the growing population of the church. He found joy in the numbers and faithfulness of those who accepted the gospel of Christ surrounding him with like dedication. The president of the Penydarren Branch then announced that President Jones would now address the conference, and Richard honed his attention keenly as President Jones stood up and walked to the pulpit.

A small man with coal black hair stood before them. He had a rounded face with a long straight nose and a protruding brow that shaded his piercing dark eyes. Dan Jones was a Welshman through and through and had now returned to his homeland to serve his fellow Saints.

Though short in stature, President Jones appeared as a spiritual giant, his confidence and command compelling the audience's attention. His full bottom lip shadowed the cleft in his chin as he spoke. "My dear Saints," he began with a smile, "I welcome you to this great conference of the Lord's chosen and greet you with joy at your presence. I wish to address you on the Restoration of the true and everlasting gospel of Jesus Christ. But first, I would like to share my thoughts regarding the tragic loss of one of our dearest brethren, President David Simmons."

He grasped hold of the podium and spoke in solemnity, extolling the virtues of President Simmons and explaining that his great sacrifice was not in vain but would propel the Saints forward in the eyes of God. President Jones had a manner of speaking quickly and with passion. His great charisma was palpable, and the Saints were already charmed and drawn into his message with awe. The solid character of his being was evident in the way he spoke and the conviction of his words.

As he continued into his prepared remarks, the congregation of Saints was renewed and uplifted. The passing of two hours slipped away so quickly it was hardly noticed, so enthralled were his listeners. When the conference drew to a close, the Cardiff Saints were captivated. Their testimonies were strengthened as never before, and it seemed as though they had been lifted to unknown heights of understanding.

The president from the Penydarren Branch once again appeared before the Saints. "We will close this session now and reconvene here at half past two this afternoon to partake of the Lord's Supper and receive further words of instruction. The ladies of the Church have prepared a wonderful feast in the building next door for your refreshment."

Richard and Leah excused themselves from the others and sought out President Jones as Richard had been instructed in his letter. Richard approached the corner of the inn where President Jones had gone and showed his letter to one of the men who stood as some sort of watchman. The man showed Leah to a seat and ushered Richard to where President Jones and his two counselors were seated. The man introduced Richard to the president and then left.

Dan Jones extended his hand and offered an easy smile to Richard. "I've heard some remarkable things about you, Brother Kenyon," he said, motioning to the empty chair across from him. "I am very pleased to meet you."

Richard felt himself blush as he sat down. "Thank you, President Jones, but I am only trying to do my part in helping to build the kingdom," he replied with genuine humility.

President Jones looked earnestly at him, studying his face before he spoke. "Brother Kenyon," he began, leaning forward in his chair, "the Lord has great need of your services." He paused dramatically and peered directly into Richard's eyes. "Brother Kenyon, the Lord wishes you to serve as president of the Cardiff Branch."

Richard gulped and felt the color drain from his face. "Surely one of President Simmons' counselors would be more fitting for this calling."

President Jones smiled. "Perhaps in some ways that might be true. But the Lord did not reveal their names to be His chosen representative at this time. He chose you."

The bluntness of the president's statement left Richard both simultaneously thrilled and horrified by the prospect. He felt unworthy of such an office, yet he knew that if the Lord required it of him, he would discover a way to accomplish it. Finding his voice, he finally managed a reply. "I am humbled, president, and feel unworthy of this great call. But, I'll do my utmost to fill the vacancy left by President Simmons."

Dan Jones smiled warmly and shook Richard's hand with enthusiasm as he stood up. "Well done," he said with a satisfied grin. "The angels of heaven rejoice at your acceptance of this momentous task. We shall take care of the ordination at the two-thirty session this afternoon."

Richard felt as though he had slipped into a fog between reality and dreaming. He was overcome with emotion but elated at the same time. "Thank you, President Jones," he said with a still-befuddled mind.

"This calling will require much of your time, but you will be provided a small sum from the Saint's offerings to help support you and your wife." President Jones came to his feet and shook Richard's hand again. "Know this, Brother Kenyon; the Lord will sustain you in every way. Go forth in this calling without fear. Provide Him with your devotion and serve the Cardiff Saints with all your heart."

"I'll do my best," Richard replied solemnly.

As he walked toward the spot where Leah was waiting, Richard was struck by the gravity of his new calling and the overwhelming gratitude he felt for the opportunity. He vowed to do his best to serve the Lord wholeheartedly. Whatever lay in store for him as the branch president, Richard was accepting of it all, even to shouldering the persecution and hatred surrounding the Saints in his care.

Leah could see by the seriousness of her husband's expression that he had received extraordinary news. She hurriedly got to her feet and took hold of his arm. "What is it, Richard? What did he say?"

Richard tried to corral his thoughts so that his words would make sense as he spoke. He looked into Leah's face, wondering how she would take what he was about to say. "The Lord has called me to be president of the Cardiff Branch."

Leah stared at him, momentarily shocked by the announcement. She was tempted to voice her concerns for his safety and for taking on such a grave responsibility, but then a warm feeling of confirmation came into her heart. She knew he had been chosen of the Lord. She kissed his cheek and gave him a hug. "Oh, Richard," she whispered, "this is wonderful news."

Richard sighed with relief, grateful for her understanding. "You're accepting of it then?" he asked, taking hold of her hands.

Leah nodded reassuringly. "Positively."

He took her in his arms and held her for a moment, drawing strength from her reassuring support. "Let's find the others," he said with a joyful smile.

❦

Richard awoke from a vivid dream. He looked around the familiar setting of the bedroom to somehow reassure himself he was in his own home. The dream had seemed so real, as if he had almost lived the circumstances he dreamt. There was no question in his mind that he must get up and dress and put the dream to the test.

He quietly slipped out of bed, trying not to disturb Leah as he quickly dressed. He carried his shoes with him to the door and didn't put them on until after he'd slipped silently outside. Richard walked with purpose toward the burned-out shell of President Simmons' home. There was no questioning the prompting to act upon his dream as he stepped into the ruins. He chose his steps carefully as he made his way through the rubble. Approaching a point near to where the center of the house once stood, Richard reached down into the charred remains and began rooting around. He threw aside partially burned chunks of wood and misshapen pieces of metal—the remnants of a clock, he thought, digging and searching for the item in his dream.

He finally found it—a small cloth bag, blackened with soot and smoke but otherwise in perfect condition. He took it into his dirtied hands and carefully untied the leather string pouring its contents into his palm. There it was; the tithes and offerings of the Saints, unharmed and in perfect order. Richard smiled with heartfelt gratitude for the instruction he had received in his dream. The Lord had been truly merciful, sparing the Cardiff Saints the loss of their meager but honest contributions. Now he could forward this money to President Jones for the benefit of the Glamorgan Conference.

Richard shoved the cloth bag into his pocket and wiped his hands on his thighs. He couldn't seem to erase the smile from his face as he started for home.

❦

John Morgan walked briskly down the street. He didn't break his stride until he turned toward Robert Kenyon's home and bounded up the stairs to the front door. He reached out his fist and knocked on the door in rapid succession. The Kenyons' maid put down her polish and hurried to the door. "Good mornin', sir," she greeted.

"I'd like to see Mr. Kenyon," he announced, pushing Lucy aside as he entered the house.

Lucy looked askance at him. "One moment, sir, I'll sees if Mr. Kenyon's available."

"Tell him it's John Morgan. He'll see me."

Lucy nodded and left the visitor standing in the entryway. John waited with a bit of impatience until Robert appeared, unshaven, hair disheveled, and wearing his dressing gown.

"Good morning, Robert," he greeted optimistically.

Robert's once handsome face was in a constant scowl. "What's good about it?" he snarled. "What reason do you have for disturbing me at home?"

John rocked back on his heels and clasped his hands behind his back. "A very good reason, I'd say, and one you'll be most surprised to hear."

Robert scuffled his way into the parlor, John close behind. "Get on with it, Morgan," he barked. "I'm in no mood for games."

John's demeanor changed to one of soberness as he regarded Robert. "Doubtless you've heard your brother is now leader of the Cardiff Mormons?"

Robert's brow arched curiously. "What do you mean?" he asked, reaching for the decanter of sherry and pouring some into a glass.

"He's replaced Simmons," John said. "Your brother is now the branch president."

Robert's eyes glazed over as the news sunk in. His brother's commitment to these Mormons was even more dogged than he'd bargained for. He leered at Morgan and took up the decanter again. "It changes nothing."

Morgan nodded slowly, taking in Robert's comment. "Perhaps not to you," he replied slowly. "But to me it will make his demise all the more enjoyable."

"His demise?" Robert questioned carefully. "How have you planned that?"

John thrust his hands into his pockets. "I don't know just yet, but trust me, I'll think of something."

Robert downed the second glass of sherry. "Just remember, Morgan: Richard and I share the same last name. Just be sure you don't sully mine in the bargain."

"To be sure," John smirked. "Well, I'll leave you to your morning. Have another glass of sherry, Robert, won't you?"

Robert glowered at him. "Get out of my house," he sneered.

John let himself out, and Robert circled the parlor aimlessly before settling into a chair near the fireplace. He swept the thick dark hair from off his forehead, raking it back with his fingers. His depression seemed darker and more consuming than usual as he contemplated Richard's new position of authority. Robert wasn't sure just how that would play into things, but he remained undeterred in his commitment to drive the Mormons out of Cardiff or destroy them trying.

Abigail came into the parlor, her dark plum colored dress rustling as she walked. "Why aren't you dressed yet?" she demanded sharply.

Robert barely raised his eyes. "What do you care?"

She pursed her lips as she noticed the empty glass in his hand. "You're drink—" The menacing glare she received from her husband stopped her in mid-sentence. "Who was just here? I heard you talking to someone."

Robert stood up and went to the decanter. "No one you know," he replied. "He just stopped by to tell me Richard has become the head of the Mormons."

Abigail blanched. "What are we to do? This could ruin the Kenyon name!"

"I am well aware of that," he said, filling his glass again.

Abigail puffed up in indignation. "Well, what are you going to do about it?" she asked pointedly.

Robert stared at her and then tipped back his head and drained the glass of sherry. "You don't need to know the details, just know that it will be taken care of." Abigail reached out and snatched the glass from Robert's hand and flung it into the fireplace. "I want to know!" She narrowed her eyes and leaned menacingly toward him.

"Richard's involvement with the Mormons affects me too!"

Robert's temper snapped, and he shoved Abigail back with such force that she toppled onto the settee with a thud. He loomed over her with heated vengeance and struck her repeatedly across the face with his open hand. Abigail cried out with each blow, attempting to protect herself with her raised forearms.

Lucy loomed in the shadows of the kitchen, listening, but too fearful to intervene. She did not want Mr. Kenyon's rage turned on her, nor did she feel any real sympathy for Mrs. Kenyon that would cause her to risk her own fate.

With his anger spent, Robert withdrew and stood over his sobbing wife, feeling numb. There was no remorse in his actions, nor sorrow or pity for her. He was an empty vessel, one void of compassion and tender feeling. His heavy footsteps took him upstairs, leaving his hysterical wife to find her own consolation.

From Amelia's locked room, she could hear the argument and her mother's bitter sobs. She held her pillow over her ears, but it did little to drown out the hateful words and the sharp ring of her father's blows. She looked at the window of her room, nailed shut now to keep her prisoner. For a moment she contemplated smashing the glass and jumping to the ground, but she would not risk her parent's further retribution.

It was more than she could bear, being locked in her room day after day, trapped and sentenced to a life of solitary confinement. Her mother brought her meals, carrying the only key to the room. Even Lucy was forbidden to enter except once a week when Abigail allowed for a cleaning of the room and the emptying of the chamber pots. At those times, Amelia was locked in her wardrobe with no escape as Abigail oversaw Lucy's every movement.

Amelia had sunk into a world of despondency and utter despair, drawing her mind inward to shelter her from the horrible existence she endured. Her daydreams consisted of imagining a life with her Uncle Richard and Aunt Leah, where she was loved and wanted. There she lived a happy life, free of her hateful parents. But then reality disrupted her fantasy world with the ugly sounds of arguing and angry cries. Amelia prayed for the only deliverance she believed would free her; she prayed to die. Death seemed a far greater alternative to the hell she endured on a daily basis. *If this was all my is holds for me,* she thought, *then perhaps death would be welcomed relief.*

❧

The sky was gray and filled with rain-laden clouds. Ben bent down and whisked his hand through the river at its banks. It was cool, but not terribly cold. He stood up and smiled at Richard. "Not so bad," he commented.

Richard and Leah stood waiting for Jonah to arrive. The Bryants were walking along the road in the distance, wanting to be a part of the boy's baptism. Leah waved eagerly to them.

Richard smiled as the elderly couple drew nearer. "Thank you for coming," he called, reaching for Leah's hand. "I know Jonah will be pleased to see you here."

Henry Bryant shook Richard's hand and smiled. "We wouldn't miss it for anything. It seemed only natural since we all share a common beginnin' in the gospel." Charlotte Bryant extracted her gnarled hand from beneath the blanket draped over her arm and touched Leah's shoulder. "I brought a blanket, just in case," she said. "It's warm enough on dry ground, but the river will be cold."

Richard spotted Jonah running hard up the road, glancing over this shoulder as he did so. He arrived breathless and panting as he came to a stop before the gathering. "What is it, Jonah?" he asked with alarm.

"I was . . . followed . . ." he said, trying to catch his wind. "I thinks . . . I lost 'em . . ."

A momentary shiver ran through Leah's insides. "Lost who?" she asked, not certain she really wanted to hear the answer.

"Take your time," Richard encouraged. "Catch your breath and tell me what happened."

Jonah was young and recovered from his run quickly. His panting steadied, and he wiped the sweat from his brow with the back of his arm. "It's two of the boys I works with," he began, "They threatened me when they found out I was bein' baptized. They chased me for a time, but I led 'em in circles before comin' here."

The Bryants looked with concern on the boy. "Threatened you how?" asked Henry.

"They said if I joins with the Latter-day Saints, they would beat me within an inch of my life," he explained. "But I told them they couldn't make me change my mind for any beatin' they could give me."

Leah was touched by the lad's conviction. "You're very brave to stand against them."

"I'm not afraid of them or anyone," Jonah said firmly. "They can't take away my testimony no matter how they tries."

Ben glanced down the road, satisfied that Jonah's pursuers had lost the trail. "Let's get started."

Three passers-by had stopped to watch the proceedings. They stood at a curious distance but made no motion to leave. Within a few moments, others traveling the road and seeing the unusual gathering stopped to inquire what was happening. Ben entered the water, and Jonah followed. Once again, the simple ordinance was performed. Jonah rose from the water with elation and shook Ben's hand vigorously. "Thank you, Elder Lachlan! Thank you!"

Jonah made his way to dry ground, where Charlotte was waiting with her blanket. "Am I really a member now?" he asked her with excitement.

Charlotte smiled. "Most certainly, Jonah, you are a member."

The gathering of onlookers murmured as they observed the proceedings, asking each other questions and making comments on what they saw. Someone recognized the missionary and began making disparaging remarks about the Mormons. Soon the murmurs became more audible, fueled by the inflammatory comments.

Richard encircled Leah's shoulders with his arm and looked at the crowd with concern. He gave the Bryant's a nod as if to motion them on toward the house.

"There he is!" shouted one of Jonah's coworkers, running toward them.

Suddenly the two young men burst through the crowd, pushing people aside as they honed in on Jonah. Richard held up his hands in an attempt to halt the imminent attack, but the boys came at them with fists flying. Jonah shrugged off his blanket and swung hard at the first boy, hitting him squarely in the jaw. Richard stepped in front of the second boy, fending off blows with his forearms. Ben ran toward the fray and helped restrain the first boy before he could fully recover from Jonah's blow. Richard took the second in a bear hug, locking the boy's arms at his sides.

Leah instinctively placed herself in front of the Bryants as the onlookers encouraged the two boys with shouts of support. Some even came forward with threats of participation. Leah had scarcely begun to pray for the Lord's help when the constable shoved his way through the crowd to confront the assailants.

"Everyone back!" the man shouted. "Be on your way," he ordered to the crowd. "This has nothin' to do with you."

The constable glowered at the lads held in restraint. "What's the meanin' of this?"

Richard released the boy from his grasp and faced the officer. "These two boys attacked us without cause," he explained.

The officer eyed the boys. "Is that true?"

The first boy wriggled free from Ben's loosened grip and stood before the officer with clenched fists. "Aye, we attacked 'em," he admitted. "But we was right to do so." The boy turned toward Jonah and spat willfully in his face.

"That's right," shouted the second boy. "Don't you know these people are Mormons?"

"Right!" cried the second. "Mormons! We only wants to stop our friend from makin' a damnin' mistake!"

"That's not true!" Jonah barked vehemently. "They threatened to beat me if I joined the Mormons!"

The constable grabbed hold of the two boys by the back of their necks. "You're comin' with me," he commanded. "We'll let the magistrate sort this out." He looked at Richard and Jonah. "You two as well."

Leah looked fearful as Richard turned briefly back to the others. "Don't worry," he said with reassuring calm. "Go on home and wait for us there."

"Take the blanket, Jonah," Charlotte called. "You'll catch your death."

Jonah declined her offer with a wave and then looked at Richard. "I'm not a bit cold," he said with a beaming smile. "The gospel's warmed me from the inside out."

The constable took his charges through town and stopped as they approached the governor's residence. Beside the house were three detached wings that held, among other things, the magistrate's office. They entered the appropriate building, walked down a lengthy hall, and the constable opened a door without knocking and pushed the two young men in front of him.

The magistrate looked up from his desk and scowled. "What's this?"

The officer took a step forward. "These two ruffians admitted to threatenin' these Mormons," he said, stabbing his thumb over his shoulder. "They was caught in the act of a public disturbance. If someone hadn't come to complain about 'em holdin' their baptisms, there's no tellin' what might've happened."

The magistrate eyed the two boys over the top of his glasses. "And you admit to this charge?"

The boys stood tall and unrepentant, glaring at the magistrate. "Aye, we threatened him," said the first, "and we would've thrashed him good if it hadn't been for his Mormon friends."

The magistrate removed his glasses and placed them carefully on his desk. He peered at Richard and Jonah and motioned them forward. "Are you two Mormons?"

"Yes," Richard replied without hesitation.

"I see," the magistrate replied. He picked up his glasses and set them back on his nose as he addressed the two boys. "Inasmuch as you have admitted your intent, I charge you guilty of attempt to commit bodily harm and causing a public disturbance. This sentence carries with it a fine of ten pounds, or three days jail time."

Jonah couldn't help a smile from creeping to his lips. He felt some vindication and relief that his would-be assailants would pay for their crimes.

"Sir," the second boy cried, "we has no money—"

The magistrate held up his hand to silence the protest and turned his attention to the constable. "Release these two boys. They are free to go."

The boys looked incredulously at one another and darted out the door as the echo of their racing footsteps resounded down the hall.

"Excuse me, sir," Richard interjected. "I don't understand. You just pronounced them as guilty, yet they are to be released and without paying the fine?"

The magistrate glared at Richard. "Yes, the boys are free to go, and *you* are to pay the fine."

"What?" Richard exclaimed incredulously. "Why should I pay the fine? We've done nothing wrong."

The magistrate narrowed his eyes. "Pay the fine or go to jail," he ordered.

Richard clamped his hands on the edge of the desk. "This is an outrage! We are not the guilty parties—"

"Silence!" barked the magistrate. "I will mete out the law as I see fit. Maybe you Mormons will learn your lesson once and for all."

Jonah shot forward. "But sir, we was the victims—"

The magistrate slammed his fist on the desk with force. "Do you want to double that fine?"

Richard braced his arm across Jonah's chest to restrain him from further angering the magistrate. "I haven't that sort of money, sir. I will take the three days in jail."

"Very well," the magistrate said with satisfaction. "Perhaps while you're sitting in jail, you will rethink your foolish choice of religion."

The constable took hold of Richard's arm. "Come with me," he said.

Richard glanced at Jonah. "Go to the house and tell Sister Kenyon what has happened. I know she'll be worried." Jonah nodded obediently as the constable escorted Richard from the room. He followed behind them down the hall and out to the street. The constable took Richard to the jail near the governor's house, and Jonah left to inform Leah and the others.

As Jonah ran from the building he unexpectedly met Ben coming up the street just in front of him. Jonah ran toward him. "They's taken President Kenyon to jail!"

"What?" Ben exclaimed. "Why?"

As Jonah related the story, Ben felt his blood boil. The indignation of suffering such treatment at the hands of the law was more than malevolence, it was evil. "I should have known," Ben said with disgust. "I've encountered the magistrate before. He has no sympathy for the Latter-day Saints."

Jonah followed as Ben headed to a sizeable stone building surrounded by a towering wall with a massive gateway entrance, over which stood the gallows where criminals were hanged. Ben approached the gate. "A man named Richard Kenyon was just brought here. We wish to see him."

The guard peered through the bars of the gate. "Wait here." He disappeared from sight and then returned momentarily. He opened the gate and motioned for them to enter. "In the day room. Follow him," he said, indicating a waiting jailer.

The jailer led them to an expansive room, the windows secured with bars and the perimeter fitted with sparse furnishings. Only a few wooden chairs and a table were available for the twenty to thirty men inside. Most of the men sat on the floor. Ben scanned the group for Richard and called to him when he spied him leaning against the opposite wall. Richard pushed himself away from the wall and met his two visitors.

Ben's face was stern as he spoke. "Jonah told me everything. I'll find the ten pounds and have you free as soon as I can."

Richard shook his head. "No, Ben, it's far too much money to spend in such a way. I'll serve the three days and be done."

"Don't be ridiculous," Ben countered. "You can't let the magistrate win."

"And where do you suppose the ten pounds will end up?"

"In the magistrate's pocket," Jonah answered with disgust.

"Exactly," said Richard. "Three days' time is a small price to pay. I'll be home in no time, and we can forget this ever happened."

Ben shook his head slowly and placed his hand on Richard's shoulder. "I won't argue with you," he conceded.

Richard's eyes filled with apprehension. "Watch after Leah for me. . . . She'll only worry."

"That she will, but I'll do my best."

Jonah looked at Richard with admiration. He believed him to be a brave man for taking such an unjust punishment so well. Jonah wondered if he possessed the same courage as Richard and vowed that he would try to be like him when it came his time to be tested. Ben and Jonah bid Richard good-bye and left him in the dismal depths of the prison's day room.

EIGHT

CHARLOTTE BRYANT WAVED with a beckoning hand toward Meredith as she entered the Tredegar Arms for church services. Her smile was warm and genuine, her fondness for the girl obvious in her expression. "Come sit with us," she urged.

Meredith moved across the room toward the Bryants and took a seat beside the old woman. "Good mornin'," she smiled.

Henry stood until Meredith was seated and then sat beside his wife. " 'Tis so good to see you, Meredith," he greeted.

Meredith nodded and looked around the room for moment. "Someone new, is it?" she asked, pointing to Jonah Reese.

"He's our latest convert," said Charlotte. "His name is Jonah Reese. He used to attend President Kenyon's church . . . well, I mean his old church . . . the Methodist one."

"Oh," Meredith replied, eyeing the young man. "Very tanned, isn't he?"

"Aye," Henry commented. "He works on the docks."

Charlotte placed her hand on Meredith's forearm. "Before I forget, my dear, I want to invite you to have dinner with us on Thursday evenin'. Are you free?"

Meredith felt a bit uncertain about accepting. It was hard to pretend in front of the Bryants; they were so likeable. "Well—"

"Charlotte's famous for her *whipod*," he grinned. *Whipod* was a favorite of Henry's. He loved the spicy rice pudding, still warm from the fire.

"Oh, say you'll come," Charlotte insisted gently. "We would so love your company."

With some reluctance, Meredith acquiesced and promised them she would come to dinner. She was tiring of living the lie that at first seemed to enthrall and challenge her. The more she associated with these Mormons, the more she came to know them and to learn of their good hearts.

After the sacrament was passed to the congregation, Richard went to the podium and scanned the eager looking faces before him. They were anxious to hear what he had to say.

"No doubt you have heard of the unscrupulous act which sent me to jail this week," he began. "Falsely accused and sentenced without cause, I, by any right, should be an angry man." He paused for effect. "But I am not an angry man, and I seek for no vengeance, for anger is Satan's tool. Should we harbor anger as offenses come to us, we are damaging only ourselves by allowing that anger to corrode our testimonies and drive the Spirit's influence from us. I, for one, choose to forgive my enemies."

At the conclusion of his remarks he took a seat, and the meeting was opened to testimonies. He listened intently to those who spoke, pledging their own resolve to offer forgiveness and love toward their enemies. The spirit of the Holy Ghost permeated the meeting, and as it came to a close, the congregation of Saints was edified, strengthened, and confident in their new branch leadership.

Meredith sat motionless at the meeting's conclusion. The words that President Kenyon had spoken struck a blow to her conscience. She got to her feet and hurried from the room without saying goodbye to anyone. It was too uncomfortable to remain in their presence with such feelings of guilt.

Jonah approached Richard after the meeting and extended his hand. "Thank you, President Kenyon, for your fine words. I was strugglin' with some hard feelings toward those boys and the magistrate, but now I knows 'tis wrong to do so."

Richard smiled. "Good," he said, patting the lad's shoulder with affection. "And speaking of the boys, how are things now between you?"

Jonah shrugged. "I don't works on the wharf no more," he said.

"They made such trouble for me that I was sacked."

Richard scowled with disapproval, but the young man grinned, and his voice filled with excitement. "But not to worry, President Kenyon," he replied. "I went straightway to the woolen mill and got work there. I even makes a bit more money. So, I sees the Lord's hand in it all along."

Richard chuckled, pleased by the pleasant outcome. His attention was suddenly drawn to the sound of heated voices outside the building. Richard put his arm around Leah and went to see about the commotion. He stepped onto the street to find Reverend Trahern and some of his followers shoving pamphlets into the hands of the Saints as they exited the building. "Read this and be saved from the devil's church!" he shouted vehemently.

The members either refused to receive the papers or crumpled the pamphlets in their hands and threw them onto the street in disgust. Trahern continued, impervious to the rejection. "Come into the full knowledge of the evil you now embrace!"

Richard and Leah were some of the last to leave the building, and once he spotted them, Trahern bolted toward them. "Repent!" he yelled into Richard's face. "Repent of your sinful and false beliefs!"

Richard was unshaken and held the reverend's gaze. "Isn't that a bit like the pot calling the kettle black?" he replied with a thin smile.

Trahern reared back in offense to Richard's comment. His expression changed to one of indignation. "How dare you speak to a man of God like that!" Trahern spat, his eyes glowing with noxious loathing as he pushed a pamphlet into Richard's hand.

Richard took the pamphlet and tucked it inside his coat. "Thank you for the literature, Reverend Trahern. Good day."

Leah resisted the urge to laugh out loud. What a sight the puffed up, red-faced reverend presented, and how aptly her husband handled him. She linked her arm through Richard's, and they began their walk back home.

Richard retrieved the pamphlet from his pocket and glanced at the title. *Satanists Revealed: The Mormons Are Devils*, it read. He scanned down a few lines and read some of it aloud. "Joe Smith claims to be Christ. . . . Mr. Smith states the Bible is false and has replaced it with a new Golden Bible. . . . He believes God speaks to man—such blasphemy prevails . . ." Richard crumpled the pamphlet in his hand and threw it to the ground. "If Trahern could turn his zealous hatred of us toward a righteous cause, imagine the good he could do."

Leah nodded and held tight to his strong arm. "Aye, but would it pay him well enough?" she laughed.

❧

Meredith waited in the small apartment John rented for her. She had promised him more information to use against the Saints, and he was expecting her to deliver. As she stared out the window of the room and onto the street below, she found a lump in her throat that wouldn't go away. Her hands were bloodied with guilt. Everything had changed now. What began as providing a charming man with seemingly harmless information had turned into something ugly.

She jumped with surprise at the sound of John's unannounced entrance. Meredith turned to face him but found she was lacking in her usual amorous feelings for him. He approached her with hungry eyes and snagged her by the waist, smothering her mouth with his.

Meredith gently pushed him away. He scowled and pulled her hard against him. "What's the matter? Not in the mood?" he teased with a taste of vindictiveness to his words.

She moved toward the window and kept her back to him. "I am not feelin' so well," she said, "that's all."

John came up from behind and slid his arms around her waist. "Let Doctor John make it better," he rasped against her ear.

Meredith tried to pull away from him, but he held her fast. "No, really, John," she insisted. "I'm not feelin' well."

He spun her around and slapped her forcefully across the face. "I don't care one way or the other how you feel," he snarled. "I pay you to feel how I want you to!"

Meredith placed her fingers over the throbbing red mark on her cheek. She sidled around him and stood in front of the bed. "Aye, of course, John."

He smiled smugly and shoved his hands into his pockets. "That's much better," he said with satisfaction. "Now, let's get on with business before we move on to pleasure."

Meredith shifted her weight from one foot to the other and kept her back to him to avoid his leering glare. "Tain't much new to report," she said.

John reached out and pushed her face first onto the bed and pinned her in the back with one knee. "Liar!" he shouted. "You forget I have eyes and ears all over this city. I know for a fact there was a baptism just last week." He grabbed her by the hair and pulled back her head. She winced in pain as he twisted her head to face him. "Now, do you have something to say?"

Meredith was sick inside, but her fear of John compelled her to answer him. "Aye," she said timidly.

John released her hair and withdrew his knee from her back. "I find your reluctance to provide me with the information I seek somewhat concerning, Meredith. If you're growing sympathetic to these people, you will no longer be of any use to me." His voice was thick and threatening.

Meredith rolled over on the bed and sat up. "No, 'tis not that," she tried to explain.

John's arm reared back menacingly, held at the ready to strike. "But?" he coaxed narrowing his eyes.

"There is a new convert," she said.

"Better," John said, lowering his arm. "And?"

Meredith swallowed hard, the lump in her throat even larger than before. "Jonah Reese, he's called. He's livin' in a boardin' house on Lisvane Road."

John peered down at her. "That's it?" he growled.

"He's workin' in the woolen mill," she replied. Meredith looked up at him imploringly. "He's just a lad, John. What threat could he be?"

John's face filled with contempt. "I don't like this, Meredith. You've changed."

She bolted to her feet and threw her arms around his neck. "No! No, I haven't," she cried. "I told you all I know. I'll find out more, I promise."

John worked the muscles in his jaw as he pried her arms from his neck. He wanted to believe her. He'd developed feelings for her, more so than with any other woman he'd ever known. "Don't fail me, Meredith," he warned, his eyes searing through to her soul. "I promise you'll regret it if you do."

Henry pointed to the painting on the wall using his pipe as an indicator. "That's the Indigo Star," he said with pride. "I served aboard that ship for near ten years. Oh, the crossin's I sailed on her bonnie decks," he sighed.

"You must have had some excitin' adventures," Meredith said, enthralled with the romantic notion of sailing across oceans to other continents.

"Aye," Henry nodded with a wink. "Ports in the raucous Caribbean, the wildest Africa, the exotic Orient, even America," he said with fond reminiscence. "Great adventures, all."

"Don't let him fool you," Charlotte said, coming toward them from the kitchen. "To hear him talk, you'd think he was some sort of privateer instead of a merchant seaman."

Henry appeared wounded by her comment. "A captain, my good woman, not a seaman. And nonetheless, I had many a great adventure."

Meredith chuckled. "I imagine you did, Brother Bryant."

"Come you two, dinner is ready," Charlotte said.

Sailor jumped to his feet and followed the group into the dining room, his tail wagging with excitement. Charlotte smiled at the intelligent and devoted creature with great fondness. She pointed to the corner of the room, and the dog obediently went to his appointed station to wait for the table scraps that would soon be his.

Meredith eyed the beef roast with delight. She had not had such a treat in ages, and the smell of it enticed her quickly to the table. The place settings were neatly arranged with beautiful silver and elegant dishes upon a fine linen tablecloth. "You shouldn't have gone to so much trouble, Sister Bryant," she said, fingering the edge of her china. "I never seen nothin' like this."

"Oh, think nothin' of it," the old woman smiled as Henry helped her to her seat. "I enjoy havin' company, and we don't do it often enough."

Henry stood across the table from his wife. "Meredith, would you be kind enough to offer a prayer upon this fine meal?"

Meredith gulped. She hadn't counted on such a request. She was about to decline the offer when Sailor's ears pricked up and he shot to his feet. He began barking, his demeanor tense with unease. "Sailor," Charlotte chided. "Settle down."

The dog looked at his mistress, bounded toward her, and continued to bark. He was more insistent than usual, and Charlotte frowned as she leaned over to gently reprimand him for his poor behavior. "Listen, you naughty pup, you be quiet."

"Sailor, sit!" Henry commanded, but the dog only veered toward him, barking even more intensely.

"Take him outside," Charlotte told her husband. She looked apologetically at Meredith. "I'm so sorry; he's not usually like this."

The glass from a bay window suddenly shattered, and Sailor ran to investigate. Henry hurried after the dog, finding a large rock in the center of the room as Sailor stood growling in front of the broken glass.

The door flew open abruptly, and four men raced inside, their faces concealed behind hoods and each brandishing a knife. Henry stood before them, his heart pounding as they circled him. "What do you want?" he demanded. Sailor growled menacingly, his teeth bared as his hackles stood on end. Charlotte and Meredith rushed into the room, coming to an immediate stop as the men neared Henry.

"What is the meanin' of this?" Charlotte shouted. "How dare you enter our house!"

One of the men stepped aside, a large sack in his hands. He filled it with items from the room—porcelain figures, silver, anything that appeared to have value. Charlotte's heart sank. These were things Henry had collected for her over the years, irreplaceable things from faraway places that were precious to her. "Stop it!" she cried, confronting the man with the bag. "You can't have them!"

Charlotte reached for the bag before Henry could stop her. The man reared back a clenched fist and hit her in the face, knocking her to the floor. Sailor instantly charged the man, lunging at him with all his strength, his teeth sinking sharply into the man's arm.

"Get him off me!" the man cried in pain, trying to shake the tenacious dog free.

A second man sprinted forward and stuck his knife deep into the dog's belly, but Sailor managed to hold fast. Henry started to advance but was held helpless as the other two men barred his way. Sailor refused to release his hold. The second man began beating the dog on top of the head with the butt of his knife.

"Stop! I beg you!" Charlotte screamed as she watched her beloved pet's struggle with the assailant beginning to fail.

"Take what you want!" shouted Henry. "But don't harm us!"

Meredith seemed frozen, unable to react, and watched in horror as the scene before her unfolded.

Sailor's jaws released, and he dropped to the floor. Staggering, he fell on his side, bleeding and broken. From across the floor, he could see Charlotte, her arms outstretched to him. He made an attempt to lift his head as if he were trying to affirm she was safe, but the effort was too much. Meredith suddenly came to her senses and knelt beside Charlotte to bury the woman's face in her shoulder.

The wounded man handed the bag to his friend but stood attentive, his eyes darting from face to face. "Get the rest of it," he ordered, "and let's go."

"We've done nothin' to you. Why are you doin' this?" Henry asked beseechingly.

"You're Mormons," the man growled with disgust. "That's reason enough!"

Once the sack was filled with valuables, the four men backed their way toward the door, their weapons still at the ready. As they crossed the threshold, they turned and ran into the night, leaving the scene of havoc and carnage they had created.

Henry ran to the door, his eyes straining against the darkness as the figures disappeared from view. "You cowards!" he shouted after them. "You miserable cowards!"

Charlotte crawled toward her beautiful dog. She stroked his head and lifted his paw into her hand. He was still. He had given his life to protect her. Tears came into Henry's eyes at the sight of his wife's devastation as he bent down to comfort her. He peered at Meredith. "If this is the sort of thing we can expect to receive as Mormons, then I want no part of them."

Meredith was in tears, her heart twisted with sorrow for the

Bryants. She had no words of comfort for them, nothing that would take away their pain nor restore their faith. Her contribution to this wicked deed filled her with disgust and self-loathing. The sight of Charlotte stroking Sailor's head again and again caused her to sob openly.

"I think it would be best if you go," Henry said to Meredith as he cradled Charlotte in his arms, her poignant sobs muffled against his chest. "Tell President Kenyon of this," he said with a tone of bitterness in his voice. "And Meredith, get out before 'tis too late."

Robert locked the door to Kenyon & Sons and headed straight to the Lamb and Flag for a drink before going home. He hoped to delay his arrival at home as long as possible. He despised having to exist in the same house as Abigail. He hated her treatment of Amelia and hated himself even more for tolerating it. *My own daughter*, he thought with bitter regret, *how I've failed her*. Robert pushed his thoughts away and concentrated on making his way to the inn.

The night air of late summer was warm and balmy. He passed beneath the gas streetlights along his way and opened the door to the Lamb and Flag, looking for an unoccupied table. Motioning to the barkeep, he ordered a glass and a bottle of port and found a table in the corner of the room where he could begin the process of banishing his thoughts to oblivion.

Robert took the bottle and glass from the barkeep and dismissed him summarily. He drank a glass of port quickly and then refilled it and drank a second. Already the noise in the room began to fade as he felt himself melting into the warmth of the liquid relief. He closed his eyes and let the numbness wash over him.

"May I join you?"

Robert's eyes shot open. He peered up at the familiar face before him. It was Calvan Garrett, a longtime associate whose wife was close to Abigail. "Perhaps another time," he suggested.

Calvan ignored his friend's comment and sat across from Robert. "Haven't seen you in a while," Calvan said, filling his own glass from Robert's bottle.

Robert stared at him. "Look, Calvan, I'm not really in need of company tonight."

Calvan stretched out his legs beneath the table and pulled back the front of his coat to expose the pale gold vest beneath his dark suit. "Now, that's no way to treat an old friend, Robert," he said. "We go back quite a way, don't we?"

Robert sighed heavily and gave him a piercing look. "What do you want?"

Calvan pulled in his legs and leaned over the table. "Well, I just wanted to pass along some rather disturbing rumors your wife is spreading about you."

Robert drained another glass of port and snorted aloud. "Abigail was never one to tell the truth," he said with a cynical smile. "She's happiest when fabricating her lies. What is it this time?"

"I'm aware of Abigail's penchant for fibbing," Calvan remarked. "My wife, for some reason unknown to me, tells me everything Abigail tells her. I usually dismiss it as the drivel it is." He paused for a moment and tried to decide how he should formulate his next words.

"Go on," Robert encouraged, his curiosity getting the better of him.

"When Tressa asked Abigail why she hadn't seen Amelia lately, well—" Calvin paused a moment to gauge Robert's expression. "Well, her answer was rather shocking."

Robert narrowed his gaze. "Go on."

Calvan licked his lips and swallowed. "Abigail said she had taken to locking Amelia in her room for her protection," he said gingerly, as if revealing only a layer of the situation. He paused again. "To protect her from you."

Robert reared back in his chair. "Protect her from me?" he exclaimed. "From what? I've never laid a finger on that child."

Calvan held up his hands defensively. "Believe me, Robert. I've never questioned your behavior toward Amelia in the least. But your wife has implied that your daughter needed protection from your . . . amorous and intimate designs."

Robert exploded from his chair, causing it to topple over behind him. The blood in his veins boiled with heated rage as he pivoted toward the door. Calvan was left with his mouth agape as Robert stormed from the inn without another word.

Robert's fists clenched and unclenched as he pounded the streets with his heavy, angered steps. He felt a burning wrath grip his soul, seizing his will with purpose. Bounding up the front steps of his home, Robert threw open the door and stormed through it, yelling Abigail's name.

Abigail was already dressed for bed and reclining on the chaise in her room. She paused in her needlework as her husband's voice reverberated throughout the house. Leaving the sewing behind, Abigail came to her feet and padded to her bedroom door. His bellowing annoyed her as she opened the door and came into the wide hallway. "Robert!" she called stridently. "What do you want? And why are you yelling?"

Locked in her room, Amelia heard her mother's piercing voice and grabbed her pillows to the sides of her head. She couldn't bear another argument, another violent episode from her parents. She prayed for silence—for relief—anything that would bring her peace.

Robert vaulted up the stairs, taking them two at a time until he reached the landing and turned down the hall toward Abigail's room. His nostrils flared as she came into sight. His steps made a heavy thudding sound through the carpet as he charged toward her. Confused but frightened by his obvious anger, Abigail spun around and tried to close the door behind her, but she was too late, and Robert pushed his way in and bore down upon her.

"Robert," she cried, her voice trembling. "What are you doing?"

Robert's heaving chest blasted his hot, moist breath into her face, and Abigail cringed beneath his towering frame. She stiffened her arms in an attempt to push him away, but Robert had no difficulty in overpowering her weak challenge. His hands seized her slender neck and tightened around her throat as he squeezed and crushed the life from her body. Abigail's eyes bulged in terror as she pawed and slapped at his strong hands. His powerful grasp continued to constrict her breathing. He shook her like a mad dog until her struggling stopped.

Amelia heard none of the usual yelling and shouting between her parents. She climbed off her bed and went to the door, pressing her ear against it. There was nothing—no sound, no arguing, just the silence for which she had prayed. She returned to her bed and stared out the sealed window at the large full moon and counted herself fortunate.

Abigail went limp in Robert's hands as he let her fall to the floor in a lifeless heap. He peered down at her. The rage and hatred were gone, sated by his violent act. He felt liberated and even started laughing quietly with the recompense of his freedom. He was oddly relieved of the years of pent-up abhorrence, feeling no remorse in the violent explosion of his actions. Slowly, the realization of what he had done replaced his sense of release with the acceptance of his vile deed—his crime. He welcomed it.

Robert left her where she lay and turned to go downstairs. His footsteps were slow and plodding as he made his way to the parlor. The room was dark but he knew his way around and easily found the decanter of whiskey. He removed the crystal stopper and sat heavily in the wingback chair. Robert drained the decanter until it was as empty as he felt inside. He let it slip from his fingers to the floor beside him and stared at the full moon through the window. When Lucy arrived in the morning he would send her for the constable.

❦

Meredith continued along Duke Street until she came to the house with bay windows, one of which was covered with boards. She hesitated before approaching the handsome building, still questioning her motive for the visit. Taking courage in the moment, she knocked on the door and waited.

Several seconds went by without response, and she thought perhaps the Bryants weren't home. Then gradually the door parted and a single eye peered from behind it. "What do you want?"

Meredith smiled. "Sister Bryant?" she asked. "Can I come in?"

Charlotte revealed more of her face as she pulled back the door. There was a nasty bruise to her cheek, the result of the fisted blow. "Please, go away," she said weakly. "We don't want any more to do with the Mormons."

Meredith was persistent and smiled. "Aye, but I has somethin' for you."

Charlotte pursed her lips as she weighed the offer. Her fondness for Meredith caused her to open the door. "Come in," she said finally.

Meredith tried not to look at the woman's damaged face. It was too painful to know she had caused the injury. She held a small, lidded basket in her hands. She stepped just inside the door. "I wants you to know how very sorry I am about the other night," she began, extending the basket toward Charlotte. "I hopes this'll ease your pain."

Charlotte eyed her curiously. "What is it?"

"Open it and see," Meredith encouraged.

Charlotte's gnarled fingers took hold of the lid and lifted it from the basket. As she peered inside, she saw a tiny puppy, a black and tan fluff of fur. She looked up at Meredith. "Oh, I can't," she said quietly, tears welling in her eyes. "There'll never be another dog like Sailor."

The puppy whimpered and stood on his hind legs in an attempt to escape the basket. Charlotte instinctively picked up the little creature and held it to her face. "Don't you cry now, little one," she whispered. The puppy licked her with an eager greeting, and Charlotte felt him making inroads to her broken heart.

Meredith placed the basket on the floor. "He likes sleepin' in it," she said, turning to leave.

Charlotte touched her sleeve. "God bless you, Meredith," she said, nestling the pup beneath her chin.

Meredith blushed and smiled softly at the old woman. "No," she replied, "God bless *you*." She left the house with a sense of accomplishment. It was the first good thing she had done in a long time, and it was a welcome feeling. She tried to keep her focus on the warmth of the moment instead of the horrible guilt she felt in exposing the Bryants to harm. As she began her journey home, she vowed there would be no more incidents like this as a result of her betrayal of the Saints.

Her fear of John Morgan was very real, but Meredith's determination to refuse him access to the Saints was also very real. She realized there would be danger in refusing him, but she would no longer play a willing part to the endless persecution. She realized it most likely meant she would have to leave Cardiff and start a new life somewhere else.

Meredith climbed the three flights of stairs to her flat. As she approached her room, she saw that the door was ajar. She frowned, remembering distinctly that she had closed the door behind her on her way to visit Sister Bryant. A chill ran through her as she pushed the door open.

"Well," John said from the wooden chair in the corner of the room. He leaned against the wall, the chair balanced on two legs. "I see you're finally home."

Meredith tried not to show her alarm at John's presence. She took off her hat and placed it on the bed. "Waitin' long?" she asked casually.

John shifted his weight, and the chair rocked forward onto its front legs. "No, not really. Where have you been?"

"Just runnin' errands," she said, opening the wardrobe to return the hat to its rightful place. She hoped she sounded convincing enough to satisfy his curiosity.

"I just stopped by to inform you of your next assignment," he said, glancing absently out the window.

" 'Assignment?' " she questioned as her heart raced wildly in her chest.

John turned his gaze on her. "Yes. I've been thinking about Richard Kenyon," he said, rising from the chair. "Since he's the new Mormon leader, I believe he needs to be made an example of."

Meredith looked at him in disbelief. "An example?"

"An example of the treatment the Mormons can expect if they continue to follow him." John took a few steps forward until he was standing in front of Meredith.

Meredith turned back to the wardrobe, trying to appear cool and unaffected by his plans. John smiled and grazed the back of her neck with his lips. "You are going to seduce him," he murmured, "and then expose him to the others as a fallen prophet."

Meredith couldn't help but laugh. John scowled with disapproval. "You don't know Richard Kenyon," she said. "If you could see the way he looks at his wife—"

"It doesn't matter whether you succeed or not," he argued. "You need only give the appearance that you did. It'll be your word against his. That will be enough to discredit him before the eyes of his followers. And then he will unexpectedly commit suicide, his shame too horrible to bear."

Meredith shook her head and moved away from him. "It won't work, John. Everyone'll see through it. They won't believe me, and they won't believe he committed suicide."

John snagged her by the crook of the arm and spun her about. "They will believe you. You'll make them believe you."

Meredith stared at him, strengthened by her resolution. "Let me help you understand somethin', John," she began, the commanding tone of her voice a surprise to her. "These people don't follow Richard Kenyon. He's not their prophet. Their prophet's in America. Doin' harm to Kenyon won't sway 'em. Don't it seem obvious by now?" She continued, gaining more confidence as he remained silent. "These folks is committed to their faith in a way we can never hope to understand. You're never goin' to change 'em, John, not in a thousand years. And murderin' an innocent man won't help your cause. So why don't you just give up and save yourself the trouble?"

Suddenly Meredith's blood ran cold. She knew she had said too much. John glared at her, his lip curled in disgust. He struck her suddenly with a knotted fist, and she collapsed to the floor. "How dare you presume to tell me what I should do?" he seethed.

Meredith tasted blood in her mouth as she stared up at him. "I'm not tryin' to tell you what to do," she cried, "I'm only tryin' to make you see that you can't win—"

John reached down and grabbed her arm with his left hand while swinging sharply with his right. The blow split her lip and caused blood to trickle from her nose. He struck her again as she raised her arm to fend off his blows. Dropping to his knees beside her, he held her by the wrists and shook her. "If you ever betray me, I'll kill you!"

Meredith could scarcely see as her eyes swelled shut from John's crazed blows. Her ears rang, and his words sounded muffled as she fought to remain conscious. He released his hold with a forceful last shove and stood up. Meredith curled into a ball as the pain of his beating ripped through her head. She stifled her moaning for fear it would elicit him to further anger. As she heard the door slam shut, Meredith started sobbing in open release of her pain.

She hated John Morgan and cursed him for what he had done

to her. *There is no place for me in Cardiff now,* she thought. Meredith crawled toward her bed and pulled herself to her feet. She was afraid to look in the mirror as she poured water into a basin and rinsed her face. As she raised her eyes and peered through the swollen lids, she scarcely recognized her own image. Meredith gingerly wiped the blood away and attempted to soothe her wounds with the cool water.

As she changed her clothes, Meredith knew she had to warn President Kenyon. He had a right to know who was behind so much of the persecution of the Saints and the devious plan John had to destroy Richard, with or without her help. But even beyond that immediate threat, she needed to confess her part in the horrible events of recent weeks.

It seemed an irrational thing to do. Her instincts urged her to run, and to run now, but her conscience pled with her to mend the wrongs she had committed and to beg for forgiveness before leaving Cardiff. She took a satchel from the wardrobe, determined to set things right.

※

Leah and Claire worked together in Claire's kitchen, making one of Richard's favorites—currant cake. He loved the heavy, bread-like treat made with currants, raisins, dried peel, and pungent spices. Leah loved making it for him too, and with Claire's help, she could make a double batch for everyone to enjoy.

"Richard's settlin' into his presidency, is he?" Claire asked as she measured out some flour.

"He seems to be adjustin'," Leah replied, dusting her hands free of dried peel. "I suppose after years as a minister, this callin' is a natural fit for him."

Claire glanced askew at her sister. "And what about you? How are you adjustin' to his callin'?"

Leah looked at her. She knew Claire would be able to read her face if she tried to conceal her true feelings. "I'm worried," she said honestly, "all the time. But I know without a doubt that this is what Richard should be doin'. I would never dare let him know how much I fear for his safety every time he steps foot outside or visits one of the branch members, or even just sittin' home readin' . . . "

"Aye," Claire said, echoing her sister's concerns. "It seems as though the Saints are nothin' more than targets, waitin' to be picked off one by one."

"My heart just aches for the Bryants," she sighed. "I've tried to visit them twice, but I've been turned away both times. They refuse to have any more to do with the Church."

" 'Tis a pity they've turned away," Claire lamented. "Still, it makes me wonder who'll be next. Which one of us will it be? I don't mind tellin' you, thinkin' of it puts me in a fearful state."

Leah measured out some cinnamon and sprinkled it on top of the mound of flour in the large mixing bowl. "On the night of the fire, Richard asked President Simmons if he was fearful of an attack, and he told him he had no reason to fear so long as his heart was right with the Lord. That thought keeps runnin' through my mind over and over. Somehow it helps me accept the risks we must take to continue on if we're goin' to endure Satan's thrashin'."

Claire nodded in agreement and checked the fire. Caleb raced into the kitchen with a wooden horse in his hands, pretending to gallop it through the air as he ran. Isaac did his best to keep up with his older brother, trailing behind with his shorter legs. "Whoa-a-a-a," Caleb exclaimed as he stopped in front of his mother and placed the wooden horse on the table.

Claire looked adoringly at her boys and slipped her fingers through Caleb's dark hair. "Are you playin' nice with your brother?"

Caleb stared up at his mother with a scowl. "You don't hear him cryin', do you?"

Claire tried not to laugh at the boy's declaration of innocence. Just then, the kitchen door flew open, and Richard filled the door frame with his presence. "Robert's been arrested," he announced abruptly. "I must go to him."

Leah's eyes widened as they registered her disbelief. "Robert? Why would he be arrested?"

Richard struggled to keep his emotions from showing. "He's confessed to the murder of Abigail," he stated bluntly.

The sisters gasped in shock as they looked at each other with looks of horror.

"Where's Amelia?" Leah cried in panic. "Is she all right? Was she—?"

"No, she's unharmed," Richard said, alleviating Leah's fears. "Take her home and do what you can for her. Lucy said Amelia's been locked in her room now for weeks and wasn't aware of what had happened last night."

"Locked in her room?" she repeated aghast. "What have they done to her?"

"Just go get her," he ordered as he charged out the door, "and hurry."

"Aye," she said, wiping her hands on her apron. "I'll fetch her directly." She looked at Claire momentarily as if to share in her agonizing over Amelia. "My poor little lamb," she lamented mournfully as she stripped the apron ties loose from her waist.

"Let us know what we can do," Claire said as Leah rushed from the kitchen.

"I will," she answered over her shoulder.

Leah's only thought now was to get Amelia out of her parent's house and home to a safe and loving environment. She thought of the horrible tragedy Amelia now faced, and it broke her heart in two. How many times had she prayed Amelia would be spared cruel treatment and daily ridicule? Perhaps the cruelty and ridicule were now ended . . . but at what cost?

When Leah arrived at the Kenyon family home, the constable was just preparing to leave. He was making some notations in a book as he stepped away from the house. Lucy stood on the front portico, her apron crushed in her hands. She saw Leah and ran toward her. "Oh, Mrs. Kenyon," she sobbed, " 'tis just awful. I knew your husband would want to know. I hopes I did the right thing."

Leah touched the servant gently on the shoulder. "You did the right thing, Lucy. Where's Amelia?"

"I let her out of the room after her mother's body was removed and they took her father away. I didn't want her to see that," she said. "The poor thing's already been through enough . . ."

"I'm glad she didn't witness any of it," Leah said with gratitude. "Thank you for sparin' her that memory." Leah lifted her skirts and dashed up the front stairs and into the foyer. She quickly looked about, calling Amelia's name. She raced through each of the downstairs rooms and could not find the girl, so she hurried upstairs. "Amelia? Where are you? It's Aunt Leah." She looked in the first bedroom at the head of the stairs, Abigail's room, and saw Amelia standing near the chaise, staring at the floor, motionless and silent. Leah cautiously approached, her arm extended toward her niece. "Amelia?" she called softly.

Amelia continued to stare at the floor and said without emotion, "This is where Lucy said they found her." She pointed at the carpet.

Leah took hold of her niece by the shoulders and gently turned her about. "Amelia, don't torture yourself," she said with desperation. "Come with me now."

Amelia looked her aunt square in the eyes. "This is not torture, Aunt Leah. This is liberation."

Leah pulled Amelia into her arms and held her. The tearless, unemotional girl seemed empty inside as her aunt held her close. There was nothing Leah could say to counter Amelia's claim because it was true. For the first time in her young life, she was free. "Come home with me," Leah urged, drawing the girl from the room. "Everything is goin' to be all right."

⁂

Richard was numb as he ran toward the jail. His heart was heavy with despair, his soul wracked with anguish. He struggled to comprehend and accept what his brother had done. He came to the gate and faced the guard with urgency. "They just brought my brother here," he blurted. "Robert Kenyon. May I see him?"

The guard shook his head. "No, sir. He's bein' questioned. Come back tomorrow."

"Questioned? But why? I was told he confessed," Richard argued.

"He might have confessed, sir, but there's lots of people who confesses to crimes they didn't commit."

"Please, let me see him," Richard pleaded. "I just need to speak to him."

"Sorry, sir," the guard replied. "I has my orders."

He grasped the bars in frustration. "I beg of you—"

The guard raised his weapon, and Richard let go of the bars. He backed up and turned away from the gates, disappointed by his failure. He couldn't imagine the torment Robert must be suffering. Though he was repulsed by his brother's crime, Richard loved Robert and wanted him to know that. Richard pondered with eternal perspective the outcome of Robert's actions and found himself weighed down by sorrow.

As Richard left the prison, he realized the news of the murder would circulate throughout the city within hours, not to mention a write-up in the newspaper. He decided to visit the store and break the news to Niall before an endless flow of people assaulted him with their questions and curiosity.

Niall had barely arrived at the shop when Richard opened the door. "Niall," he called without stopping. He went toward the back of the store to find the man hanging up his coat.

"Why, Reverend Kenyon," he greeted jovially. "What brings you here so early this mornin'?" The look on Richard's face caught him off guard. "What is it, sir?" he asked with concern.

The words seemed stuck in Richard's throat, but there was no way to communicate the horrible deed other than to force the words out in the open. "Niall, something terrible has happened. I want you to lock the store and go home for the day. I'll see to it you won't lose any wages."

Niall still held his coat in his hands. His face drained of color. "Please, sir, what's happened?"

Richard swallowed again. "My brother has confessed to the murder of his wife." There, he'd said it aloud, but it made it no more acceptable.

Niall gasped. "Oh, no . . . this is heartbreakin' news." Niall looked at Richard with sympathy. "What happened? Your brother was still here when I left last night."

"I don't know," he said sadly, "but it appears as though Abigail . . . was strangled."

Niall slowly shook his head. "Poor Mr. Kenyon," he sighed. "A terrible burden he's carried these last months."

"What burden, Niall?"

"Well, he never really spoke of it, but I knows the business was not fairin' so well, and he seemed a different man . . . unhappy and moody, he was."

"I didn't know about the business," Richard said, as though trying to piece together the circumstances that drove his brother to such extremes.

Niall looked at Richard with deep sympathy. "I'm so sorry, Reverend."

Richard was touched by his old friend's tenderness. "I fear there will be nothing but curious on-lookers and strangers seeking morbid details from you all day, Niall. That's why I believe it best to keep the store closed."

Niall hung his coat on the hook in spite of Richard's suggestion. "And what would keep 'em from comin' tomorrow, or the next day, sir?" he asked with determination. "I'm not afraid of 'em. Let 'em come and see what they get for their trouble."

A small smile crept to Richard's lips. "Very well, Niall. Do your best then."

"That I will, sir."

NINE

ICHARD WALKED HOME SLOWLY, his grief-stricken heart weighing heavily in his chest. He contemplated the fate appointed to his brother and then thought of Amelia. What a wretched future awaited his niece with her mother murdered and her father to hang for the crime. He couldn't help but feel as though he had failed his family, but guilt would do little to remedy things now. He knew his focus must now be on Amelia. Perhaps it was not too late to turn her life around with the love and affection he and Leah so desperately wanted to share with her.

When he walked into the house, it was eerily quiet. He expected sobbing and wailing, but there was no sound. Leah appeared from the kitchen, her face as sullen as the mood in the house. She opened her arms and went to him, finding solace in his embrace. "Oh, Richard." Her tears flowed in sympathy for the girl and the tragedy they'd experienced.

Richard held his wife tightly, forcing back his own tears. He knew he must remain strong for her and for Amelia. "Hush now," he said, stroking her rich, auburn hair. "We'll get through this, *cariad.* I promise you that."

Leah had faith in the Lord and faith in her husband. She knew that somehow they would survive, but she was not so certain about Amelia. The girl had said little in the time since Leah had brought her home, and Leah hoped that Richard could draw her out of her silence. "Speak with her," she prodded. "Maybe she'll respond to you."

Richard released Leah from his embrace and kissed her. "Where is she?"

"She's outside, sittin' under the oak tree."

Richard took Leah by the hand and led her through the house. "I wasn't able to see Robert," he said quietly. "Perhaps tomorrow."

They walked slowly toward the oak tree where Amelia sat, her face lifted to the sun, her eyes closed. It had been weeks since she'd felt fresh air on her skin or smelled the air rising from Cardiff Bay. She seemed to relish the delight of her freedom. Amelia opened her eyes and looked up at her aunt and uncle as they came toward her and sat on the grassy earth beside her. Richard leaned forward and took Amelia's hand. She did not grasp it in return; her fingers remained limp and unresponsive to his touch. "Amelia," he began softly, "we want you to know how much we love you and how sorry we are this has happened."

Amelia withdrew her hand from his, and her jaw clenched as though she were fighting to maintain her composure. Within moments, the floodgates of her emotions opened, and tears welled in her eyes. "She made him do it!" she accused hotly, the tears streaming down her cheeks. "She never loved my father! It was her fault. She drove him to it!"

Richard reached for his niece, but she shrank from his attempt. "Please, *cariad*, you mustn't—"

"It's true," she spat. "I know it is!"

"Amelia," Richard said in a low, controlled voice, "we don't know what was in your father's mind. He was under many pressures and—"

"Uncle Richard," she blurted, stopping him from completing his thought, "every day my mother needled him. She destroyed everything good in him. She was wicked to the core!"

How could Richard counter her claims? He knew they were true. But he also knew his brother's weakness was a great contributing factor to the situation. "None of us is perfect, Amelia. We all have our weaknesses."

She snorted and pulled some blades of grass into her fingers. "Believe me, I know that all too well." Amelia peered into their faces, her eyes edged in hardness. "I had a lot of time to think while I was locked in my room with all the windows sealed shut and no way to escape."

Leah's heart melted, and tears pooled in her eyes as she looked at her niece. "My Amelia," she wept softly. "How you must have suffered . . ."

Amelia lowered her gaze and concentrated on the blades of grass between her fingers. "I prayed to die, Uncle Richard," she said quietly, without shame. "I wanted to die. I thought at least then I would be free."

Richard and Leah looked upon their niece with great tenderness but remained silent. They felt only sorrow for her and heartache for the pain she had endured. Richard stroked the back of Amelia's hand. "Things will be different now, *cariad*. All of that is behind you now."

Amelia knew he was right, but the prospect of a brighter future did not erase the years of neglect and haunting memories. Another wave of sorrow rose as a tide of despair and dashed itself upon her broken soul. "What will happen to my father?" she whispered between quiet sobs.

Richard shook his head. "I can't say for certain," he hedged, knowing his brother's prospects were grim. Robert had confessed, so there would be no trial. The penalty for murder was death. Richard couldn't bring himself to inflict even more pain on the girl. She would learn of her father's fate in due time.

Leah moved closer to Amelia and took her in her arms. She softly stroked her hair and hummed quietly against her ear. Such a genuine outpouring of love overwhelmed Amelia with emotion. She had never felt such tenderness before, and with that realization, a rush of remorse claimed the void in her soul. Now she knew what she had been denied, what had been withheld all of her life. Something so simple as to be held and loved filled Amelia with a saddened regret for all the empty days spent in her parents' house.

Richard stood up and motioned for Leah to stay with Amelia a few minutes more. He felt he could endure little else as the weight of the day's events smothered him from all sides. He absently walked around to the front of the house, his mind numb and unfocused, hoping in vain that a new landscape would bring clarity of a new perspective.

A woman with a veiled face approached him with hurried steps, a small satchel clutched in her hand. She was petite and seemed familiar, but the veil concealed her full identity. A man trailed her in the distance, his stride turning to a jog as she neared the cottage. Richard strained to see beyond the covering and thought he recognized her. "Sister Cullen?" he asked, unsure of his guess as the woman stopped in front of him.

"President Kenyon," she said breathlessly, "I has somethin' important to tell you."

Richard's face darkened with concern as he made out the bruising on Meredith's face, her split lip, and her swollen eyes. "Meredith? What's happened to you?"

"Never mind that," she said urgently, dismissing his question.

The man who had been following Meredith bolted forward and caught her by the crook of the arm. "There you are, Miss Cullen. For a minute I thought I'd lost you." The sound of John Morgan's voice iced the blood in Meredith's veins. Her eyes widened in shock as she swiveled her head toward him, his smug smile a symbol of his victory. John looked at Richard. "I apologize for the intrusion," he said with a slight bow. "I'm John Morgan."

Richard glared suspiciously at the two of them. "What's going on here?" he demanded. "Do you know this man?" he barked with authority.

Meredith dared not open her mouth but managed to nod. She waited for John, knowing he held her captive with his presence. He looked disapprovingly at Meredith. "Miss Cullen, you really should have stayed and given a statement to the constable." He turned his eyes to Richard. "I was just leaving the Blue Anchor when Miss Cullen was attacked," he explained. "I managed to control the assailant and held him down until the constable arrived, but she would not press charges."

Richard stared at Meredith with astonishment. "Is that true?"

She gave a slight nod of her head. Why hadn't she run from Cardiff when she'd had the chance? Now she was trapped, and all because she'd wanted to warn President Kenyon. "I thought . . . it would only make m-m-more trouble," she stammered.

John puffed out his chest and spoke before Richard could object to the pretended reasoning. "I was detained by the constable just a few moments longer than Miss Cullen. I wanted to escort her safely home and have been trying to catch up to her ever since," he said with a gallant note in his voice.

"As you can see, Mr. Morgan, I'm fine now," she said, trying to disguise the panic in her voice. "I was only comin' to tell my friend good-bye when you come along."

Morgan arched his brow and looked at the satchel in her hand. "Are you leaving Cardiff?"

Richard's brow furled in confusion. He could tell by the look on Meredith's face that something was wrong. He glanced at Morgan, trying to read the man's placid and unyielding expression. "I don't understand," Richard charged, his over-burdened emotions causing his temper to flare. "Why are you leaving, Sister Cullen? Is there something I can do to help?"

Meredith waved her hand. "Oh, no, I'm goin' to visit . . . some family," she offered lamely. "I-I won't be back for awhile."

Richard knew she was lying. Even behind the veil, the frightened look in her eyes spoke otherwise. "Come into the house," he urged. "I think we should talk about this."

Meredith tried not to look at John. Her voice was quivering as she spoke. "No, 'tis all right. I has train tickets," she lied. "I needs to go, or I'll miss my train."

"Now that I see you are faring well enough, Miss Cullen, please allow me to escort you to the train depot," John said nobly, though his grip on her arm only tightened.

" 'Tis not necessary, Mr. Morgan," she said with greater control of the quaver in her voice than she expected. "There's no need for your trouble."

"It's no trouble at all," John assured her. "It's on my way."

Meredith's eyes darted between Richard and John as she struggled to control the alarm rising in her throat. Richard could see the terror in her eyes as she glanced at John Morgan. His suspicions were aroused even further, and he felt uneasy about Meredith's sudden departure and her flimsy excuse to do so. "Good-bye, President Kenyon," Meredith said weakly. "I'll see you soon."

"Perhaps I should see Meredith to the station," Richard stated as he tried to press his way between the two.

John tightened his grip on Meredith's arm. "No, no. It's no trouble, I assure you."

He steered Meredith from the cottage and onto the street. Richard couldn't ignore the nagging need to follow the pair. Leah walked up from the back of the house. She had heard the last vestige of the conversation and came to Richard's side. "What was that about?" she asked skeptically. "And did I hear you say Meredith's name? Who's that with her?"

Richard's jaw was set, his gazed fixed on the disappearing couple. "Something's not right," he said. "I think I'd better follow her."

He tried to press his way between the two.

Meredith's heart pounded as John dug his fingers tightly into her arm. She knew of his intentions even though she had not revealed the truth surrounding her beating nor had she betrayed Morgan. She had meant to though, and she was well aware John knew it.

John maneuvered her through the busy streets away from the Kenyons. "You're not the clever girl you thought yourself to be, are you?" he hissed between his teeth.

Meredith tried to pull free, but his hand was on her like a steel vise. "I hates you!" she seethed.

"Shut up!" he ordered under his breath.

His eyes darted about until he saw a narrow alley between two buildings. He pushed her in front of him and drove her into the shadows. John grabbed her wrists and pinned them beside her head against the brick wall. "We were doing so well together," he breathed. "It's a shame you had to spoil things."

Meredith struggled beneath his painful hold. "Let me go," she begged. "I didn't betray you, and I won't. I'm leavin' Cardiff, and I'm never comin' back."

John smiled cynically. "Wouldn't that be convenient for you?" He pressed his body against hers as he transferred her wrists into one hand. Reaching behind his coat, John extracted a knife and flashed the pointed blade in front of her face. Meredith tried to scream, fighting against him, but John forced his forearm against her mouth, the knife gripped in his fist. "Shut up!"

She frantically scanned the alley for something, anything she could use to defend herself. As she looked down the darkened alley toward the busy street, she could see people passing by, oblivious to her plight. She had to make them hear her, make them see what was happening only yards away.

John's breath seared its way through her veil, his maniacal expression terrifying and horrible. "I'm sorry it has to end this way," he whispered.

Meredith sunk her teeth into the flesh of his forearm while at the same time pounding the heel of her shoe onto his instep with all her might. He yelped in pain and in reflex, he pulled away just far enough for Meredith to escape his grasp. She ran screaming toward the opening of the alley, praying she would reach the sunlit street and get the attention of someone passing by.

John chased after her, the knife still in his hand. He was larger and much stronger than Meredith and gained ground quickly against her. His outstretched hand reached toward her as she neared the opening to the alley. She screamed sharply as he touched the back of her bonnet, knocking it from her head.

Blinded with fear, Meredith broke into the street directly in the path of an oncoming wagon, John inches behind her. Her frantic screams startled the team of horses. They reared up, each of them feeding on the panic of the other as the shocked driver tried to manage the terrified animals. A hand reached out and pulled Meredith from in front of the flashing hooves.

"Look out!" someone yelled as the hysterical horses stamped and pounded their powerful hooves against the ground.

It was over in a split second. John lay motionless on the street as two men grabbed the horses' reins, and another threw a large cloth over the heads of the frightened animals. People shouted orders, working the horses away from the body, as others surrounded the trampled form.

Meredith stared at John. Her senses returned as the reality of the scene sunk into her mind. The hand that had pulled her free from disaster was still clutched about her arm. "It's all right now, Meredith. You're safe."

Meredith spun around and looked into Richard's reassuring

face. She broke into tears and buried her face against his chest, sobbing and trembling with relief. She had survived what she thought was her certain death. As Richard quickly ushered her away from the crowd, she knew John Morgan could never hurt her again.

Richard continued against the flow of onlookers. He turned the nearest corner and wound his way back home, Meredith leaning weakly against him. When he opened the door to the house, Meredith collapsed before him. He scooped her into his arms and carried her to the sofa as Leah ran toward them.

"Richard!" Leah cried. "What happened?"

He placed Meredith carefully on the sofa and then turned to his wife and pulled her close. "I was able to keep up for awhile and then lost sight of her. I had stopped on the side of the street when I heard a scream and saw Meredith run out from an alley. Her screams frightened a team of horses, and they reared. I grabbed her just before that Morgan fellow was trampled—it just happened so fast . . . "

She clung to her husband in desperation. Leah kissed him, grateful he had been spared any harm. "Then he's . . . dead?"

Richard nodded and looked into her eyes with intensity. "Leah, he had a knife in his hands."

Leah blanched to a pale white. "Oh, Richard." She looked down at Meredith, her unveiled face now in full view, showing the brutal beating she'd sustained. "What happened? Who did this to her?" she gasped.

"I'm guessing it was Morgan," Richard said with an undertone of anger.

"Who is Morgan?" she wondered. "I don't understand."

Meredith moaned softly, and Leah placed a pillow beneath her head for support. "It's all right," Leah said soothingly. "You're with the Kenyons."

Meredith's eyes opened against her painfully swollen lids. She peered up at Leah and grabbed for her hand. "Thank you . . ." she whispered.

Richard knelt beside Meredith, his face worn with worry. "You're safe now," he said reassuringly. "You just lie here and rest."

Amelia heard the commotion and crept toward the parlor to listen. She could just make out her aunt bent over a woman lying on the sofa. She felt the tension of the atmosphere and kept herself hidden from view as she observed the scene. Keeping below notice was a priceless skill, one she had used many times to spy on her parents when they argued.

Meredith drew in a deep breath and closed her eyes. She couldn't rest. Her soul was still tortured by a shadow of misdeeds. She sat up despite Leah's attempt to keep her unmoved. Meredith peered at the pair and then steadied her gaze on Richard. "President Kenyon, I needs to tell you some things."

"Whatever it is, it can wait. You should rest now."

Leah moved to leave. "I'll fetch some cool cloths for your face—"

"No, Sister Kenyon," she said, reaching for Leah's hand. "I wants you to hear this too. And what I has to say needs to be said now. It can't wait. It's why I come earlier."

Leah sat on the sofa beside Meredith and studied the poor woman's worried face. "Go on. We're listenin'."

Meredith lowered her gaze and wrung her hands as she formulated her thoughts. She couldn't bear to look up as she unraveled the sordid details of her involvement with John Morgan. She explained how he had convinced her to join the Church so that she would be above suspicion as she fed John with information about the Saints. Tears pooled in her eyes as she told them how she listened and laughed as John would tell her about his exploits and what great fun they seemed to be.

Leah and Richard were stunned as Meredith continued. She finally drew the courage to face them and raised her eyes. "But that was before," she said softly. "Little by little, it wasn't funny anymore. And every time I was with the Saints, I come to know you more, even when I was pretendin' to be one of you. Everyone was so kind to me and lovin', and as I hears more and more of what you believe, it began changin' me . . . inside."

"And that's what Morgan suspected—that you were changin'," Leah said, finally understanding.

Meredith nodded. "After the Bryants was attacked, I knew I couldn't go on bein' a part of his plans. I tried to make John see that what he was doin' was a waste, that he could never stop the Church from growin'."

"And the beating you received was to help you see differently." Richard surmised.

"That's when I knew I had to leave Cardiff." Meredith confirmed. "He'd never let me live knowin' what I knows about him, about what he planned next. That's why I come to see you. I didn't know John was followin' me."

Leah touched the woman's hand with sympathy.

"I come to warn President Kenyon," she blurted, her emotions taking control. "He was goin' to kill you . . . I couldn't . . ." Meredith covered her face with her trembling hands. "I knew he'd kill me if I betrayed him . . ."

An icy shiver ran through Leah's spine. She trembled inside at the thought of John Morgan's evil intent. Leah looked at Richard with fearful eyes. He met her gaze with a calm resolution that quickly melted her apprehension.

Meredith sobbed into her hands as tears of shame and sorrow drenched her cheeks. "I didn't know 'twas goin' to come to this . . . I would never have been a part . . ." she sobbed.

"Hush now," urged Richard. "Morgan has no power over anyone now."

Meredith swallowed against the final detail she had yet to share with him. She worried most of all about this revelation. "There's one thing more, President," she started cautiously. "Your brother was payin' John and his men," she said as if the words were stinging her tongue.

Richard felt as though he'd been slapped in the face. It was an incredible thing to contemplate, that his own brother had been a part of the horrendous treatment of the Saints in Cardiff. Had Robert hated the Church so much that he would even destroy his own flesh and blood? Richard was numb. Gradually, the depths into which his brother had sunk registered in his mind, and an overwhelming sadness and sense of betrayal enveloped him.

"I'm so sorry," Meredith wept. "So sorry . . . for everything . . . please, forgive me."

Leah's heart ached as she witnessed the true pain of remorse and regret Meredith now suffered. Instinctively, Leah took the broken woman into her comforting embrace and rocked her slowly back and forth. Her love for the repentant woman penetrated deep into Meredith's soul until she felt forgiveness in Leah's arms.

Amelia felt faint as she absorbed the news of her father's involvement in the Saints' persecution. A whirlwind of conflict swept through her. She crept to the door dizzily and went outside. Hot tears streamed down her cheeks as she slumped beneath the arching branches of the old oak tree. She had tried to convince herself that somehow her father was justified in what he had done to her mother, as if there could be some rightness to it. How else could she keep from hating him? But now hate was all she felt—hate and contempt. She saw her father now for the malevolent and immoral man he was. Amelia grew sick inside, repulsed to be a part of him. Again, her yearning for relief overtook her thoughts. She prayed for death to take her, for God to be merciful and remove her from this suffering. She wanted only to be void of all feeling. Amelia cried until she had no more tears to shed. She curled up on her side and fell asleep beneath the sheltering branches of the forgiving tree.

✻

Richard quietly left the house without waking Leah or Amelia. He wanted to see his brother alone. The walk to the jail seemed long and tedious, his emotions slowing the passage of time with their relentless assault. He had slept poorly, tossing and turning in frustration of needful rest, but it only caused him to believe Robert was suffering in far worse ways. The jail was bleak and unwelcoming as he asked the guard about Robert. The man opened the heavy gate and allowed Richard entrance. The guard gave him a cursory patting down for hidden weapons and found only an orange stuffed into Richard's coat pocket. The guard inspected the orange by rotating it in his thick fingers and handed it back to him. Soon, the jailer arrived and motioned for Richard to follow him.

He was taken through a very different part of the jail than he had previously experienced. They walked down a long, darkened corridor with small cells on either side, isolated from the less dangerous criminals. The jailer inserted the key and swung open the cell door. Robert sat on the edge of a flimsy cot, his arms draped over his knees, his head bowed. He looked up without expression as the guard stepped aside to allow Richard access. "You have fifteen minutes," the jailer said, locking the cell door with the brothers inside.

Robert's eyes were sunken within dark circles. Pale and unshaven, his face mirrored the emptiness he felt inside. He displayed little emotion as Richard sat beside him on the cot. "They wouldn't let me see you yesterday," Richard began, shocked by his brother's hollow appearance.

"They insisted on questioning me even though I told them there was no reason for it." Robert's voice was barely above that of a whisper. It conveyed the mechanics of speech but lacked any feeling. "I explained everything that had happened and that I was the one responsible for Abigail's death." He was quiet for a moment and then looked at his brother for the first time. "Does Amelia know . . . about what happened that night?"

Richard peered at his brother. He seemed a stranger to him, void of life and emotion. He was an empty vessel, a shell of what he once was. "Not until afterward. Lucy kept her locked in her room until you were both taken away," he explained.

Robert nodded slowly. "Good . . . good . . . at least she won't have that to relive . . ."

Richard reached into his pocket, retrieved the orange, and gave it to his brother. "Leah asked me to give this to you," he said lamely. "She was worried you'd get scurvy in a dark place like this."

The corners of his mouth slightly responded with a brief smile. "I won't live long enough for that to be a worry. But tell her thank you anyway."

Richard swallowed hard in an effort to keep his emotions in check. "Robert," he said with an ache in his voice, "what happened to you? How did you—"

"You want to know how I could have killed Abigail?" his brother finished for him. A sardonic grin touched his lips and then disappeared. "I wouldn't expect you to understand, Richard. But that's because you don't understand the ugliness of what she did to people, the manipulation, the deceit . . ." His eyes clouded for a moment, and then he steeled himself against the rising tide of emotion. "She lied to people . . . about me . . . that I made improper advances toward my own daughter . . ."

Richard's blood seized in his veins. It was beyond his comprehension to understand how Abigail could do such a thing. What had she expected to gain? The answers lay on a dead woman's lips, and there would never be understanding of it in this life. For the briefest of moments, though, Richard grasped what might have driven his brother to such tragic action, the culmination to a bitter marriage rife with hatred and contempt.

His brother's despair was palpable, and Richard's heart sorrowed for him in a way that tore at his insides. Richard placed his hand on his brother's arm, but Robert slowly withdrew from Richard's touch and stared at the filthy, straw-covered slate floor.

"I feel pity rising in you, Richard," Robert said in a rasping voice. "Don't waste it on me. The truth is that I'm glad I did it." He raised his face to meet Richard's, almost daring him to be anything but shocked. "I'm glad she's dead, Richard. I'm glad she can no longer harm Amelia . . . and I'm glad even to have an end to my life—to finally be free of my misery." He let his heavy lids close.

The anguish of the situation choked off any words Richard wanted to speak, the events too weighted with sorrow. He finally placed his hand on Robert's shoulder, and his brother let it rest there, to Richard's relief.

"How is Amelia?" Robert asked, scrubbing his eyes in annoyance as tears threatened to spill onto his cheeks. "She must hate me or wish me dead—which will come to pass soon enough."

"Robert—"

He shook his head. "I wouldn't blame her . . ."

"It will take time," Richard explained. "She's very confused, but she'll come through it, I promise you."

Robert peered deeply into the mirror reflection of his brother's eyes. "Take care of her, Richard. Help her to be happy."

"I'll do my best."

"Good." Robert licked his dry lips. "Good . . . I know you will."

The jailer's key slid into the lock, and the men came to their feet. Richard embraced his brother and could no longer restrain his tears. A wave of sorrow overtook him. "I love you, Robert," he whispered raggedly. "I always have."

Slowly, Robert allowed his arms to encircle Richard's shoulders.

"I . . . ." But his voice fell silent as the jail door swung open.

In his heart, Richard knew what his brother was unable to say, and it was all right. He knew Robert loved him.

⁂

Amelia chose not to attend her father's sentencing. She wanted no part of it. She was already saturated with an overabundance of conflicting emotions. She couldn't bear to see her father's face again or hear the judge impose the sentence: to be hung by the neck until dead. Amelia stared up into the cloudless sky as her gaze traced the flight of a pair of swallows. She watched, mesmerized, as they circled and swooped through the sky, paired in a flawless aerial ballet. Swallows mated for life, she had learned. What an amazing thing, she considered, that even birds shared something she would never know. She mourned the idea that there would be no mate for her. No one would wish to be saddled with damaged goods. When the birds disappeared beyond the treetops, she turned her eyes to the road ahead. She expected her aunt and uncle but instead saw a young man coming up the road, and she hoped he would hurry by. She lowered her gaze and stared at her shoes tucked beneath the hem of her skirt.

Jonah Reese walked with purpose, his stride long and sure. He saw Amelia sitting in front of the house and recognized her as President Kenyon's niece. He knew of her father's sentencing today, as did all of Cardiff. He couldn't help but feel a twinge of pity for the poor girl. As he drew nearer, he smiled, but she didn't look up.

"Is President Kenyon home?" he asked, coming to a stop.

Amelia's face drained of color, unnerved that the young man had spoken to her. She shook her head without looking up.

"I'm Jonah Reese," he said, bending somewhat forward in an effort to get the girl to look at him.

Amelia glanced up at him quickly and then lowered her face again. She was struck by how handsome he was and even more embarrassed at having thought so. Jonah squatted down beside her and met her gaze with his, enticing her to look at him. "Your name's Amelia, right?" She darted her eyes in his direction. "Yes," she replied quietly. "I'm Richard and Leah's niece."

Jonah smiled. "I thought so," he said with a light tone. "Why hasn't I seen you at church?"

Amelia felt uneasy talking to the young man. She felt sullied by the deeds of her father; she certainly wasn't worthy of anyone's company. She wished he would go away. "I am not a member of your church," she finally said.

Jonah scratched his head and screwed up his tanned face. "No? Well you should be," he said without apology. "Why don't you come Sunday next?"

Amelia flushed and bolted abruptly to her feet, turning away from him. She was too embarrassed to be seen in public, let alone in a church. The thought of facing people who knew about her parents was more than she could bear. Her utter disgrace made it impossible to interact with others, so she sought anonymity instead and wanted only to fade into the background, where no one would take notice of her.

Jonah stood up, confused by the girl's reaction. "I'm sorry," he said, sensing her great discomfort. "I meant no harm. I'll come back when President Kenyon's at home."

He wished he had the courage to say something more to the poor girl, to tell her he was sorry about her mother and father. But he felt he should leave well enough alone. As he turned to leave, he glanced back over his shoulder. He thought she was pretty in spite of her forlorn expression. As Jonah walked along the road, he whistled a pleasant tune, and the lilting notes floated onto the warm summer breeze and back to Amelia.

TEN

———— ❧ ————

IT HAD BEEN NEARLY THREE WEEKS since his brother's execution. Richard reflected on the incident, ruminating on the tragic events that led to his brother's death. He couldn't help thinking of his brother's unmarked grave. The city's clergy refused burial in any churchyard, stating that such sacred and hallowed ground was forbidden to murderers. He didn't even know the exact whereabouts of Robert's grave. By order of the magistrate, his brother had been taken from the gallows and buried outside of town. It was a hasty and unceremonious procedure, a conclusion to the final detail of the legal obligation following the execution.

Richard stared out the window, lost in his thoughts. It had been drizzling continuously for several days, leaving everything sodden and damp. He watched the rain drip from the tips of the leaves of the oak tree outside the cottage and pool below its trunk in a murky brown puddle. The gloomy weather only added to his somber mood.

Leah tore off another piece of newspaper, crumpled it, and stuffed it into the crack between the kitchen window frame and the wall. It seemed the drafts were endless in the small cottage. She had filled nearly every gap with rags and more paper, but it never seemed to suffice. She pulled her shawl more tightly around her shoulders and glanced into the parlor, where Richard sat hypnotized. The pensive look on his face concerned her. Quietly, she approached her husband and bent down to kiss him on the forehead. "What's got your head in the feathers?" she asked softly.

Richard looked up at her and smiled. "Did I worry you? I'm sorry." He reached out and pulled her onto his lap. He kissed her as she nestled herself into the warmth of his arms. "Just thinking about Robert," he offered. Leah nodded knowingly. She stroked his handsome face with her slender fingers. It pained her to see her husband in such a state of melancholy. "Let me give you somethin' else to think about," she murmured. Leah kissed him ardently as her fingers tangled in his thick, dark hair.

Richard returned her kiss with equal fervor, his thoughts of Robert fading to shadows of the past. "How I do love you," he whispered.

There was a knock at the door. Leah reluctantly left the warmth of Richard's embrace and opened the door. "Ben, come in!" she exclaimed. "You're soaked to the skin."

Ben took off his hat and shook the water from his coat as he entered the cottage. "I feel like a drowned rat," he chuckled.

Richard stood up and shook his friend's moist hand. "Come sit by the fire," he encouraged. "I'm glad you stopped by." He reached for a letter from the table and handed it to Ben. "This came for you yesterday."

Ben looked at the letter curiously as he scrutinized the handwriting. "Hmm, doesn't look familiar," he remarked casually as he slid his finger beneath the flap of the envelope. Ben unfolded the paper and began reading.

Richard observed in silence as he took a seat in the chair next to Ben. He glanced at Leah as she went into the kitchen to prepare some coffee. Richard waited until Ben had finished reading. The disappointed look on Ben's face left him curious about the letter's content. "Anything wrong?"

Ben folded the letter and tucked it inside his coat pocket. "It's from President Jones. He says I'm to be released from my mission next month," he reported with a somber tone. Richard knew what was troubling Ben. Missionary work had become insulation against the aching void left by the tragic drowning deaths of Ben's wife and children. With his mission ending, Ben would return to America to face those grave markers and battle with his memories. "I don't know what we'll do without you," Richard said, hoping to ease the man's discomfort.

Ben smiled absently. "I knew this day would eventually come," he said, "but I'm not going back to America. There's nothing to go back to. It just wouldn't be the same."

"Aye, it'll never be the same. But you can begin again," Richard encouraged.

Ben tried to push from his mind the faces of his wife and children. It was too painful, too heartwrenching to know he would not see them again. "I'm not sure about that," he replied with a half smile. "I might just stay here in Cardiff."

"There's a lot of momentum building for the Saints here to emigrate. President Jones spoke of it in the last conference." Richard wished he'd kept quiet about that news. It was Ben's decision whether he returned to his homeland.

"Yes, I remember . . . to the valley of the Great Salt Lake." Ben grew quiet as his thoughts retreated to another time. "Sometimes I can't help myself from thinking, what if I'd never left on this mission . . . what if I'd stayed with my family . . . ."

Richard reached across to his friend and touched him on the shoulder. "And what if you'd never come here?" Richard pressed firmly. "How many people would never have heard you preach the gospel? How many would not be baptized because you weren't here to convert them?"

Ben smiled. He appreciated his friend. "Thank you, Richard, for reminding me."

Leah came in from the kitchen with a tray. She'd heard the conversation between the men as she prepared the refreshments. Placing the tray on the side table, Leah poured some coffee into her Blue Willow china and handed a cup to each of them. "Ben, I would be very happy if you'd stay in Cardiff," she said, taking hold of her own cup, the warmth of the liquid welcome to her cold fingers. "Your missionary efforts don't have to stop just because you're no longer a missionary."

"That's true, Ben," Richard agreed. "There is still a lot of work to do in Wales."

"Speaking of work to do," Ben said, reaching into his pocket. "I almost forgot why I stopped by." He handed Richard a newspaper clipping. "Look at this. The good Reverend Trahern is still at it. Now he is publishing articles in the paper."

Richard took the clipping and focused his eyes on the print. " '. . . Those who follow the false prophet to America are sold into slavery,' " he read, shaking his head. " '. . . Women are subjected to unspeakable tortures at the hands of the elders, forced against their will . . .' " Richard scrubbed his face in disgust. "How can he publish such tripe?"

"Does the man have no conscience?" Leah complained. "Sometimes I just get so angry!" She snatched the clipping from Richard's hand and crumpled it in her fist. She went to the window and shoved the paper into a crack in the sill. "There!" she said with satisfaction. "That's where he belongs."

Richard couldn't help but chuckle to himself, but he knew she spoke for all of them. The seemingly endless persecution took a toll on all of the Saints. Their frustrations mounted daily as the barrage of lies and harassment followed them constantly. He empathized with his wife's irritation.

After finishing his coffee, Ben got to his feet. "Well, I'd best be off," he said, secretly reluctant to leave the warming fire.

"As should I," Richard replied. "I promised Niall I'd be in today."

Leah sidled up next to Ben and placed her arm around his shoulder. "You are always welcome here, Ben. Richard and I think of you as family."

He offered her a sheepish grin and blushed. "Thank you, Leah. I feel like a part of the family."

Meredith finished dressing and glanced out of the window of her tiny room. The bleak rainy day seemed to mirror her feelings this morning. She dreaded the thought of another afternoon serving hungry and thirsty patrons at the Blue Anchor. The noise, the lewd comments she endured, the long hours, the men's groping hands— they were at times too much to bear. It made her feel unworthy of the gospel she had grown to love. But what could she do? She knew nothing else. Thoughts of spending her life working in such a way left her feeling hopeless and disparate.

She sighed deeply and turned away from the window. Perhaps

a visit to the Bryants would help lift her burden. They had a way of making her feel special even if that feeling faded the moment she left their presence. Meredith visited them every so often, but she had never revealed to them her part in the vicious attack that had cost them so dearly. There were times when she had wanted to tell them, to confess her hand in the tragedy, but when she looked into their sweet, aged faces, it became impossible to disillusion them with her true self.

It pained her even more that the Bryants had rejected their membership in the Church as a result of the persecution they'd received. Meredith felt largely responsible for that too. Though it was John Morgan's despicable acts that had rendered the evil, it was Meredith's betrayal of their trust that had set the wheels in motion. She had begged the Lord's forgiveness for the part she played in the Bryants' ordeal. But no peace would come to her, and she knew it wouldn't until she had the courage to confess to the Bryants and beg their forgiveness.

She prayed for the strength she needed to declare her wrongdoing to the couple, even if it meant the loss of their friendship. Meredith realized that was the reason she had so hesitated to tell them the awful truth. Steeling herself against the consequences of her impending actions, she slipped into her inadequate coat and out into the rain.

Walking briskly toward the Bryants' home, partly due to the dampness urging her on and partly to at last face them with the truth, Meredith felt sick to her stomach as she knocked on the Bryants' door.

The boisterous yapping from her puppy alerted Charlotte to a visitor even before she heard the knock. The elderly woman got up from her comfortable chair and followed the dog.

"My goodness, Captain," she mildly complained of the dog's barking. "You'll likely scare them away with that noise."

Charlotte opened the door, and an immediate smile illuminated her face. "Meredith!" she exclaimed. "Come in, come in. How wonderful to see you!"

Meredith attempted a smile, but the heaviness of the task before her left her bereft of the joy she found in her usual visits. "Is Henry home as well?" she asked.

"Oh, yes," she replied. "We were just sittin' quietly by the fire to chase away the chill." The old woman draped her arm around Meredith's shoulder. "Come in where it's warm. I'm so happy to see you, but my goodness! You shouldn't have braved such a dreadful day to visit us." Captain danced in front of Meredith's feet, his tail wagging an eager greeting. She reached down and patted him on the head. He had grown so much since the day she had brought the tiny puppy to the Bryants. She was glad the pup had brought some comfort to Charlotte after the tragic loss of her beloved dog, Sailor.

"Henry," Charlotte called as they approached the parlor. "Look who's come to visit!"

The old man craned his stiff neck around and broke into a smile. "Meredith!" he beamed, coming to his feet. He took hold of her cold hands and frowned. "You poor girl, you've nearly frozen." He looked at his wife. "Charlotte, get Meredith some coffee to warm her up."

"No," Meredith said quickly, withdrawing her hands from his. "I needs to talk to both of you. Please, sit down."

Charlotte noticed Meredith's somber mood. She was instantly concerned as the young woman took a seat before the couple. "Meredith, what is it, child?"

Her voice was filled with tenderness, making it all the more difficult for Meredith to speak. "There's somethin' I've kept from you for some time," she began slowly, wringing her fingers nervously. "Somethin' I has needed to tell you . . . wanted to tell you, but I has been too afraid."

Henry offered her a consoling smile. "My dear," he replied warmly, "you needn't be afraid to tell us anything. We're here for you," he said, reaching for Meredith's hand. "Aren't we, Charlotte?"

"Please," Meredith implored, pulling her hand away from Henry's once again. "Don't make this harder for me."

Henry and Charlotte looked at each other with apprehension and turned their gazes to Meredith. The young woman swallowed hard against the lump in her throat. She pressed her fingers against her mouth in an effort to keep from crying. Meredith averted her eyes from the Bryants' worried faces and began unraveling the fabric of shame she wore.

"The night you was attacked and Sailor was killed," she wept, her heart aching with emotion, "I was so ashamed that I'd played a part in bringin' such pain to people I cares about . . ." Meredith smudged the endless tears from her cheeks. " 'Twas me that told John about you, where you lives, how easy it would be for him to. . . . 'Twas me who led him to you." She covered her face with her hands, too mortified to look at them. "I tried to tell you so many times . . . so many times . . . " Meredith sobbed into the palms of her hands as the Bryants looked on in stunned silence.

Charlotte looked at her husband, the sounds of Meredith's mournful cries tearing at their hearts. It seemed impossible to believe she was not the girl they thought they knew. They had only known a kind, sweet, young woman who brightened their lives with her mere presence. Her affections were genuine; they felt them; they believed them. She was not the terrible woman she made herself out to be. Before them sat a repentant, sorrowful child, and they loved her.

Charlotte opened her arms and beckoned Meredith to her. The young woman rushed to her and fell at her knees, sobbing against the folds of her dress. Charlotte stroked Meredith's dark hair and then lifted her tear-stained face with her gnarled fingers. "My dearest," she wept, "your burden is no more." Charlotte gently wiped Meredith's tears with the corner of her apron. "We forgive you . . . and now you must forgive yourself."

Henry sniffed against his own tears, his emotions unsuitable for a hearty sea captain. But he couldn't help them. He was fond of Meredith and looked upon her as a daughter. He reached for her hand and patted it softly. "There, there, no more tears now," he said soothingly. "I can tell this has taken a great toll on you, my dear. Rest assured, all is forgiven."

Meredith hugged each of them tightly, her conscience now liberated from guilt and remorse. She felt renewed and miraculously healed of her pain. The Atonement of Jesus Christ had washed her clean of sin. His merciful love made this moment possible. Meredith smiled lovingly at the old couple and offered a silent prayer of gratitude.

Richard walked the short distance to Kenyon & Sons and opened the door, triggering the welcoming sound of the door's tinkling bell.

Niall rushed from the back of the storeroom and appeared within seconds. "Ah, Reverend Kenyon," he greeted with a smile. "I'm glad you've come."

Richard removed his hat and shook the man's hand. "I should have been here sooner, I know."

" 'Tis no problem, Reverend," he replied, resting his hands on either side of his small protruding belly. " 'Tis a slow mornin' anyway."

"Aye," Richard smiled as he shrugged off his coat. "Come and sit down," he said to Niall, leading the way to the storeroom. "I want to talk to you."

They sat before a small stove, and Richard gave his old friend a look of guilty concern. "I'm afraid I've not been very attentive to your needs, Niall," he said, stabbing a poker into the coal fire. "I've expected an awful lot from you these last few weeks and given little thought to the burden you've shouldered in Robert's absence."

Niall sat on a wooden chair across from Richard. "I understands, sir," he replied quietly. "You've had much to overcome. I've been happy to look after things here."

Richard reached over and patted the man's knee. "You're a good man, Niall, and I thank you for all you've done."

"I had great respect for your father and your brother," he said, rubbing his hands before the warm stove. "I done it for them, and I done it for you with pleasure."

Richard had been thinking of how often he was called away from the shop in performance of his duties as branch president and how Niall was often left alone. He felt guilty leaving the man to take care of the business without help and believed he had come up with a plan. Richard leaned back on his wobbly old chair and allowed his thoughts to find voice. "I have an idea, Niall."

Niall's eyes grew wide with interest. "Yes, sir?"

"I would like to bring in a young man to help you in the shop," he began. " You can teach him all you know and allow him to relieve you of as many of your mundane duties as possible. That way you'll be able to fully manage the business when I can't be here, and in return, you'll have an increase of salary and a portion of the profits."

Niall's mouth fell open, his eyes fluttering in surprise. "I couldn't . . . that's far too generous, sir . . . I . . ."

"Now I've given this some thought, Niall, and I trust you completely to run this business with all competence. I've made commitments to my church, as you are aware, and I don't always have the time to devote my full attention to operating the business. I believe this solution will help us both."

"Well, sir, I doesn't know what to say," he said with a look of bewilderment. "You're certain you want me to run your business? I has never taken to such a task before . . ."

"But you already have," Richard exclaimed. "I'm convinced you can do it, Niall. Are you willing?"

Despite some misgivings, Niall considered the increase in salary and what it would mean to his family. "I am, sir, most willin'."

Richard thrust his hand out to seal the bargain, and Niall shook it enthusiastically. "Good!" Richard stood up and smiled. "Now, I need to speak to the young man I have in mind for the position. He has no formal business experience, but he's polite and intelligent, and I believe he will catch on quickly."

Niall smiled, got to his feet, and clasped his hands behind his back. "If you believe in the lad, then I does too."

"Good. Then it's settled." Richard turned to leave the storeroom as the bell at the front door sounded.

Niall excused his way past Richard and hurried to the front of the store. Richard put on his hat and quietly slipped from the storeroom and into the shop. He gave Niall a nod of encouragement and left Kenyon & Sons, pleased with his new plans.

Outside, Richard retrieved his pocket watch and glanced at the time. He had plenty of time before his council meeting at six. He put the watch away and buttoned his coat against the damp air rising off the bay and turned in the direction of the woolen mill to find Jonah Reese.

ELEVEN

———— ❧ ————

S UNDAY FOUND THE SAINTS among friends. Milder weather
had given way to sunshine as they gathered together to partake of
the sacrament. Richard took his place between his two counselors as
the meeting began. As he scanned the growing congregation, there
were still three faces he longed to see, three souls he yearned would
embrace the gospel, Charlotte and Henry Bryant and his own niece,
Amelia.

The Bryants continued to make good on their promise to reject
their membership in the Church, having been driven away by the ugly
handiwork of his brother and John Morgan. Sadly, they had succeeded
in crushing the Bryants' convictions. Amelia, on the other hand, was
curious about the Church and asked question after question, seeming
to agree with the principles presented to her. She was reluctant and
unwilling to attend the various Church meetings, despite her uncle's
urging. She hadn't explained her reluctance, but Richard and Leah
suspected her reasons surrounded her feelings of dishonor and had
nothing to do with her growing testimony of the gospel.

The girl's shame and disgrace filled her with such self-loathing
that she was trapped in a self-imposed prison of humiliation. No
consolation could sway Amelia from her destructive feelings. Richard had often tried to help the girl understand how wrong she was
to feel as she did, but he knew that feelings were powerful masters—
stronger than words, reason, or logic. He had resigned himself to a
sense of helplessness, but he would never stop praying for a miracle.

Richard watched Jonah as he helped pass the sacrament to each of the Saints. It seemed the boy had shot up six inches in the last few weeks. His new suit of clothes, purchased for his position with Kenyon & Sons, testified to the growth spurt. The arms of the coat rose far above his wrists, and the trousers revealed several inches of leg. He chuckled to himself at the sight of the gangly adolescent and promised himself to take the boy to the tailor for some alterations.

As the sacrament services concluded, Meredith appeared at the back of the room, arriving late. She caught Richard's eye with a look of apology and found a seat. Getting time away from the Blue Anchor had been a challenge, and today she had been granted only thirty minutes. She was disappointed that she had missed the sacrament.

Richard motioned for Jonah and whispered something in his ear. The young man smiled and happily took the bread and wine to Meredith. She took the offering with humility and gratitude, believing now she was truly cleansed of her past.

The meeting proceeded to the bearing of testimonies and concluded with the singing of hymns. Afterward, Richard stood at the front and looked upon the gathering of Saints. He smiled benevolently and brought the meeting to a close with solemn prayer. "We will meet again, brothers and sisters, at six o'clock, at which time we will greet any and all people who wish to join us. Elder Lachlan will offer his thoughts on the restoration of the priesthood."

As the Saints filed from the room, they found the door braced shut by a group of troublemakers, mostly young lads looking for a laugh. "It's locked," cried one of the women. "We can't get out!"

Richard wove his way through the gathering to assess the situation. He pounded on the door and could hear the boys' laughter from the other side. "All right," he called through the door. "You've had your fun, now open the door."

The young men laughed again, delighted with their mischief. "Where's the match?" one of the boys shouted with a threatening tone. "Let's burn 'em out!"

The women inside gasped. Richard snagged the doorknob firmly and shook the locked door. "Open this door!" he commanded. "You've gone far enough."

They heard the key turn in the lock, the door flung open, and the boys scampered away, hooting and laughing with excitement. The Saints gave up disgruntled murmurs as they left the meeting, weary of the harassment they received at every turn. Whether harmless or not, it became tiresome at times to face the ceaseless persecution.

Leah found Meredith and smiled as she approached, dismissing the young ruffians' annoying prank from her mind. "I'm so glad you were able to make it," she said, linking her arm through Meredith's.

"It's gettin' harder all the time," Meredith complained. "I has to bargain two extra hours tomorrow in exchange for half an hour today. Mr. Flanagan wasn't keen on lettin' me leave at all, even at that."

Leah sighed and patted Meredith's hand. "Take courage," she replied. "At least you were able to partake of the sacrament, and that's the most important thing."

"Aye," Meredith nodded, " 'Tis the truth." They walked a few steps, and then Meredith stopped. "I visited the Bryants," she said, almost as an afterthought.

Leah was surprised, but pleased. "How are they?" she asked anxiously. "And how is that little pup you gave them?"

Meredith smiled. "They's well, and that little pup isn't so little no more. Captain is growin' like a weed. Charlotte seems to love him so."

"I'm so glad you've been in contact with them," Leah replied with a tone of gratitude. "I've tried to visit them more than once, and they've refused to let me in."

Meredith looked surprised. "They's never mentioned it to me."

Leah sighed. "I suppose they wouldn't. They won't see Richard either."

"Then I'm grateful the Lord's allowed me into their home. I hopes somehow . . . I prays I can bring 'em back. 'Tis my fault—"

Leah gave the petite woman a squeeze. "There now, Meredith. Just keep tryin'. Love is a powerful motivator."

❦

Richard sat at Robert's old desk in the office at the back of the store. He felt increasingly uncomfortable, as if he were somehow intruding on his brother's sanctuary. Richard shuffled through papers on the desk and tried to push his unease to the back of his mind. As he forced himself to review each document, Richard became increasingly aware he was looking at letters requesting past due payment to importers, shipping lines, warehouses, and other business entities. He shook his head as he glanced at the pile of unopened mail and correspondence.

"Niall," he called, walking around the large desk, his hand filled with papers. "Niall, will you come here for a moment?"

The balding man appeared almost immediately, his hands resting characteristically beside his rounded belly. "Yes sir? What is it?"

"Niall, did you know about these past due notices?" he asked without accusation. "There must be dozens of them."

"I'm sorry to say I was aware of some," he explained. "Your brother was, well, he seemed to ignore 'em toward the end."

Richard bit his lower lip. "I see," he said, sorting through the bills. "I should have gone through these before now anyway . . ."

"But, sir, you was mournin', and no one expects you to carry on without proper time—"

Richard held up his hand and smiled disarmingly. "It's all right, Niall. Together I'm sure we can get things in order."

Niall smiled, eager to offer his assistance. "Yes, sir," he said. "What can I do to help?"

Richard grinned and touched the man on the shoulder. "Well, first of all, you can call me Richard," he said.

Niall almost blushed, the response to the unfamiliar relationship foreign to him. "Aye, sir . . . uh, Richard, sir . . . I means, Richard."

The men laughed, and Richard glanced up at the clock. "I'd better get cracking on this mound of paperwork."

Niall nodded and suddenly leaned forward, speaking in a whisper. "Young Jonah is doin' a fine job. He's a tidy lad and sharp as a tack."

"I'm glad to hear it," Richard replied with a pleased look on his face. "And from what I've observed, he's bound to make a good missionary one day."

Niall chuckled. "Well, I don't take no offense in it. 'Tis interestin' what you two believe, and he do like to talk about it."

"Who knows," Richard said, tamping a pile of papers into order. "Maybe one day they'll be more to you than just interesting stories."

❧

Meredith placed a glass of stout in front of the last of the three men at the table. He reached out and grabbed her wrist with force and glared up at her. "I knows you," he slurred. "I seen you before. You used to work the Golden Lion, didn't you?"

Meredith's past returned to haunt her. Yes, she had worked there, and it was a well-known fact that any man could have her company for a fee. Meredith tried to twist free from his grasp, but he dug his fingers into her flesh. "Let me go!" she ordered.

"Now, now," the man persisted, reaching for her other arm in an attempt to pull her onto his lap. "You shouldn't play so 'ard to get."

The other two men laughed as she struggled against the drunkard. "Let me go!" she shouted. "Mr. Flanagan!"

"Mr. Flanagan," he mocked, laughing. "Save me, Mr. Flanagan."

His friends roared with laughter, further provoking the man. Meredith fought to free herself from the man's steely grip, trying to pry his fingers loose with her other hand. As her frustration mounted, she slapped him sharply across the face.

The man's cheek reddened as he bolted to his feet, his hand still clenched about her wrist. "Why you—" He reared back to retaliate as Mr. Flanagan came rushing forward.

"Here now!" Flanagan shouted. "What's goin' on?"

The man released Meredith with a glare of contempt and turned his heated stare to Flanagan. "She hit me!" he hissed through clenched teeth. "Nobody does that and gets away with it!"

Mr. Flanagan looked at Meredith with narrowed eyes. "Is that true? Did you strike him?"

Meredith rubbed her throbbing wrist. "Mr. Flanagan, he grabbed me—"

"I asked if you hit a customer!" he repeated angrily.

"She did," encouraged one of the other men at the table. "We seen it with our own eyes."

"Is this how you treats a payin' customer, Flanagan?" the man charged. "You let a common trollop lay a hand to him?"

Mr. Flanagan balled his fists and turned to Meredith. "You've been a thorn in my side ever since you started here, always askin' for time off when you should be workin'. And I was nice enough to give it to you, and this is how you repay me?"

"Mr. Flanagan, just listen," she argued.

"Get out!" he ordered. "Get out of here and don't come back."

Meredith glared at the drunken man who had riled her temper. Her nostrils flared in anger as she marched to the back of the tavern for her cloak and hat. She went out the back door, not wishing to engage the men or Mr. Flanagan again. As she stalked off, she continued to rage, not so much because she'd lost her job, but because her past followed her relentlessly. Why couldn't anyone see she wasn't the same person? She'd changed! She'd repented.

Gradually her anger gave way to melancholy as she ambled aimlessly through the streets. She got lost in thought and realized she was only fooling herself. How could she hope to attain respect toiling in the same sordid atmosphere, trying to ignore the same crude comments, pushing away the same unwanted advances? It wasn't as if she possessed other employable skills. Serving spirits to lewd men was the only trade she knew.

As she wandered the town, her thoughts turned to prayer. Help me, Father. Help me find a way . . . I'm not who I once was . . . I wants to be a good Latter-day Saint . . . but how can I support myself when all I knows how to do isn't pleasin' to you? Please, Father, have mercy on me and show me what to do. Without realizing it, Meredith found herself near the Bryants' home. She had given no heed to her direction, propelled only by thought and prayer. Glancing toward the large house, she thought about the old couple. Perhaps now more than ever Meredith needed their gentle kindness. As she approached the house, she noticed Charlotte struggling with a large bucket of coal. The old and bent woman stopped every two or three steps to rest, the burden too much for her to carry much farther. Meredith broke into a run and hurried to help her.

"Let me help you," Meredith said, taking hold of the bucket.

"Why, Meredith!" Charlotte gasped with surprise. "Where did you come from?"

Meredith capably handled the generously filled bucket. "I was just walkin'," she said, "and happened to come by."

"Bless your heart," Charlotte said with a smile. "You came just in time. I was havin' a bit of a struggle."

"But where's Henry? Shouldn't he be helpin' you with this?"

Charlotte reached for the kitchen door and held it open for Meredith. "Aye," she said. "But he's not feelin' well today. I put him to bed so he could rest."

Meredith placed the bucket near the stove and dusted her hands together. "Then I'm glad I happened by." Meredith peered beseechingly at Charlotte. "Is there anything I can do for Henry?"

Charlotte offered a tender smile. "He just has a little cold. I gave him a dose of honey and coal oil. He should be right as rain in no time."

"I'm glad 'tis nothin' serious," Meredith said, moving toward the door.

Charlotte motioned for her to come back. "Won't you stay a bit?" she asked hopefully. "Unless you have somewhere else to go, that is."

Meredith laughed to herself. The only place she had to go was her flat. And even then, she only had a few more days' rent saved. "I can stay, if you'd like."

Charlotte smiled and went to the stove. "Oh, I'm so pleased. I was just about to start some tea for Henry."

Meredith untied her cloak and hat. "Let me do that, Charlotte. You sit for a spell."

Charlotte gave in easily. She was more tired than usual, especially having run up and down the stairs to see to Henry's needs. "How sweet you are, Meredith."

"Are you feelin' peckish?" Meredith asked. "I'd be glad to make you somethin' to eat."

"Well, I was goin' to fix a little bite for Henry . . ."

Meredith reached for an apron hanging on a peg beside the kitchen door. She slipped the bib strap over her head and secured the ties in the back. "Sit, sit," she said, waving Charlotte into a kitchen chair. "Just let me take care of everything. Point me to some bread, eggs, and butter, and I'll have you a meal in no time."

Charlotte watched as Meredith took down a heavy skillet and placed it on the coal-fired range. It was refreshing to see someone working with such vitality. Charlotte remembered how she had worked that way once, with quick, sure movements made by toned muscle and a straight back. She had always insisted on keeping her own home and never allowed Henry to hire a servant. Charlotte took pride in servicing the large house, even though its size had outgrown them years ago. Charlotte found she grew weary of the daunting chores. It was difficult for her to admit she no longer possessed the strength and stamina of her youth. The floors were scrubbed less often, the windows hadn't seen a rag in months, the carpets were in need of a good beating, and she barely managed the laundry.

"Where's Captain?" Meredith asked as she stirred the eggs in an earthen bowl.

"He's with Henry," she replied. "He hasn't left his side since he went to bed."

Meredith smiled and took down some plates from the dish rack. "I'm glad Captain's good company for you." As if by some psychic communication, Captain appeared at the entrance of the kitchen, wagging his tail, his nose sniffing the air at the smell of food. Charlotte lowered her hand and snapped her fingers. Captain obediently trotted to her side. "Speak of the devil," she chuckled.

Meredith turned and smiled at the pair. "And there he is," she said to the dog.

Captain went to the door and hopped up on his hind legs while bobbing his forelegs up and down. "Do you want to go outside, Captain?" Charlotte asked.

The dog yapped and turned in an excited circle. Charlotte opened the door, and a blast of cool air swept into the room. It had begun to drizzle. The unwelcome rain sent a shiver through Charlotte as she stood against the open door. "Hurry up," she ordered.

The dog hesitated for a second and then darted outside into the inclement weather. Charlotte closed the door and took her seat at the kitchen table. She continued to watch Meredith work as she plated the food. "You're good company," she said to Meredith.

Meredith smiled and reached for the pot of tea. "And so is you," she said, filling the cups with the hot amber liquid. "You and Henry's very special to me."

"You're like the daughter I never had," Charlotte said with a wistful smile. "The good Lord never saw fit to bless us with children of our own. And now you've come along . . . well, you'll never know how much your visits mean to us."

Meredith lowered her head in humility. "You'll never know what it means to me to have your friendship . . . most people won't . . . well, most people—"

"Most people," Charlotte finished for her, "don't know what a lovin' and carin' girl you are, and if they can't see that, well then shame on them."

Meredith felt warmed inside. It was Charlotte's kindness that did more to heal her wounded heart than anything. Her visit to the Bryants was just the medicine she needed.

Captain yapped and scratched at the door. Meredith opened it, and the dog shook himself vigorously, freeing his fur from the icy rain. "That was mighty quick, Captain," she commented.

The dog ran to Charlotte and put his front paws on her thigh. She went to pet Captain's wet head and instead asked Meredith for a towel. As she wiped the dog down, she looked up at Meredith with a guilty smile. "I know . . . he's just a dog, but he means the world to me."

Meredith couldn't help but smile as Captain stared up at his mistress with trusting brown eyes as he held still for her doting attention. Charlotte had an abundance of love to give, even to a dog. Meredith placed Henry's food on a tray and then set a plate before Charlotte. "I'll take this up to Henry. You go ahead and eat while 'tis still hot."

As Meredith picked up the tray from the table, Charlotte touched her arm. "When you come back, perhaps we could sit in the parlor for awhile. I've been tryin' to read *The Old Curiosity Shop*, but my tired eyes aren't what they used to be. Maybe you could read to me for a few minutes before you go?" she asked hopefully.

Meredith smiled warmly at the elderly woman. "I'd be happy to," she replied while crossing the kitchen. "Though my readin' might not be too good."

"Don't be too long," she urged, "Henry can wait for a long visit another day, but Mr. Dickens and Little Nell cannot."

Meredith laughed and headed upstairs with the tray. While in this house, among people who cared for her, she was able to forget her own concerns. Only here did she feel accepted and valued. She pushed the thought of leaving to the back of her mind and concentrated on the moments she gladly spent in service to the Bryants.

TWELVE

———— ❧ ————

Leah tied a beautiful red ribbon around the towel covering the currant cake she'd baked this morning. She hoped the Bryants would accept her offering. The elderly couple weighed heavily on her mind of late. She couldn't shake the feeling that she needed to pay them a visit, even if they continued to refuse her entrance.

Taking her cloak from the peg beside the door, Leah swirled it about her shoulders and cradled the gifted cake in the crook of her arm. There was a prayer on her lips as she headed for the Bryants', the brisk air embracing her with its cool reminder that autumn was near. When she arrived at her destination, Leah paused a moment to complete her prayer and then knocked lightly on the door.

Captain barked from inside as Charlotte made her way from the warmth of the parlor to the front door. The dog followed her like an inseparable shadow. Charlotte reached for the doorknob and looked down at Captain. "Sit," she said in a low tone. The dog immediately obeyed and sat next to her, panting, his pink tongue pulsing in and out of his mouth. "Good boy," she praised as she pulled open the door.

Leah smiled warmly. "Charlotte, how are you?"

The old woman appeared weary, her husband's increasing illness taking a toll on her own stamina. "I feel as though I've been killin' snakes," she said with a slight smile.

"What's the matter?" Leah asked with concern.

Charlotte let out a sigh, her usual defensiveness lowered for the moment. "I don't want to burden you with it, my dear."

Leah braved a step inside the house, and Charlotte didn't object. " 'Tis no burden. Please, tell me."

Charlotte glanced toward the staircase, where the sound of Henry's coughing resonated from above. She pushed a strand of loose hair back from her forehead, her gnarled hands slightly trembling. "Henry . . . he seems to be gettin' worse. I thought it was just a cold, but now . . ."

Leah untied her cloak and discarded the currant cake on the foyer table. "Have you tried a mustard plaster?" she asked with a tone of knowing authority.

Charlotte shook her head. "I don't know what that is."

" 'Tis a remedy taught to me by my mam." Leah unbuttoned the sleeves of her dress and rolled them to her elbows. "You've dry mustard and flour? And some towels?"

Charlotte again nodded, relieved that someone seemed to know what to do for her husband. "Aye, all. Come to the kitchen."

Leah measured out some of the dry mustard and flour and added water to the mixture until it formed a thick, paste-like substance. She spread it over a towel and covered it with another. Immediately, the mustard gave off heat, and she handed it to Charlotte. "Place this on Henry's bare chest, but mind you don't let it rest too long, just until the skin begins to redden. The heat will penetrate his lungs and should help to clear his cough."

Charlotte took the warming towels and nodded with amazement. "I don't know how to thank you!"

Leah made a shooing motion with her hands. "Go on, get that up to Henry before the heat is gone."

Leah offered a prayer of gratitude for having acted upon the Spirit's prompting. She cleaned up the kitchen and went to the foyer to retrieve the currant cake. She took the opportunity to make some tea and sliced the cake, waiting for Charlotte to return.

After several more minutes, Charlotte came into the kitchen, a smile of relief on her lips. "Henry says he feels much better," she said. "Thank you for your kindness."

Leah lowered her gaze in humility and motioned toward the slices of cake. "I brought you some currant cake and took the liberty of placin' some water on for tea."

Charlotte sunk into a kitchen chair, her eyes wet with tears. "Oh, Leah, I've been such an old fool!"

Leah clasped Charlotte's hand in hers. "Now, don't be silly."

"No, 'tis true. I realize it now," she insisted, raising her lined face to meet Leah's gaze. "Not knowin' what else to do, I've been prayin' for Henry, and here you are, an answer to my prayer. Oh, Leah, I'm so ashamed I turned away from the truth, from my testimony of the gospel."

Leah encircled the sobbing woman in her tender embrace and held her tight until Charlotte's tears subsided. Words were not necessary, the Spirit having touched each of their hearts with comfort and peace.

Leah busied herself with dusting the parlor while Amelia made the beds. Leah was preoccupied with thoughts of her visit to Charlotte's the day before, her dusting a mechanical effort disconnected from her attention. The Lord had made her an instrument in His hands. How humbled she was to have been a part of Charlotte's reawakening. Amelia finished with the beds and came into the parlor to see what her aunt would have her do next. She saw the distracted look on Leah's face and hesitated to speak. After a moment, she cleared her throat. "Is everything well, Aunt Leah?"

Leah spun about, startled back to the present. "Aye, *cariad*. I was just thinkin' we should visit the milliner's shop today. It would be fun to look . . ." She trailed off at the look of horror on her niece's face.

Amelia shook her head adamantly, the wounds of her father's crime and execution still fresh and raw. "Oh, no, Aunt Leah! I couldn't bear to go out. I can't abide the jeers and pointing fingers."

Leah's heart ached for the young woman. She felt powerless to help Amelia move beyond her self-destructive feelings. No amount of conversation or cajoling seemed to have an effect on the girl, and Leah was beside herself with feelings of helplessness. Prayer was her only solace.

A knock sounded at the door, and Leah went to answer it. She was surprised to find Meredith there with dark circles beneath her eyes and a startling paleness to her skin. Leah reached for her, taking the woman's thin, icy fingers. "Meredith, what is it?" she gasped, pulling her into the warmth of the house.

Meredith attempted a smile as she folded her arms tightly across her chest. The thin coat she wore did little to keep out the moist and chilly air. "I'm sorry to bother you, but might I warm myself for a bit?"

Leah frowned as she led her toward the fireplace in the parlor. "Of course, Meredith." She looked to her niece. "Bring a blanket," she said.

"No," Meredith declined. "Don't trouble yourself. I'll be fine by the fire." Leah pulled a chair closer to the hearth and helped Meredith settle into it. She knelt down beside her and rubbed her frozen fingers. "What's goin' on, Meredith?" she asked with concern. "How long have you been outside in this cold?"

Meredith closed her eyes and slowly shook her head. "I didn't want to bother you," she said weakly. "I just didn't know what else to do."

"Please, tell me what's happened." Leah took off her shawl and placed it over Meredith's legs.

Amelia handed her aunt a blanket and stood back to watch, her eyes wide and unblinking.

"I've been lookin' for work," she began, her face pained as she spoke. "I was sacked from the Blue Anchor a week ago and been lookin' ever since. I couldn't pay for my flat no more."

Leah's heart swelled with sympathy for the young woman. Meredith had been through so much and had tried so hard to change her life. "Oh, Meredith," she breathed softly.

"Mr. Flanagan put the word out, so no one'll hire me," she said, tears beginning to stream down her cheeks. " 'Tis all I knows, Leah. 'Tis the only work I've ever known." Her eyes seemed to be searching Leah's for understanding. "I spends last night in a barn and snuck out early this mornin' so I wouldn't get caught."

"Oh, Meredith, you foolish woman," she whispered. "You should have come here. We would have welcomed you with open arms. We do welcome you with open arms," she said sincerely.

Meredith wiped her tears with the sleeve of her coat. "I knows it now," she said. "I just . . . somehow thought I deserved it as some sort of punishment. Or maybe 'twas my pride . . . I don't know."

Leah lifted Meredith's chin with her finger and peered deeply into her eyes. "Listen to me," she began softly. "None of this is your fault. Now, you're goin' to stay with us until we get things figured out. You can room with Amelia."

Meredith looked to Amelia, her eyes circled in worry. "Oh, that wouldn't be fair to Amelia. I can sleep right here."

Amelia felt drawn to Meredith. It was as though they shared kindred feelings of disgrace and humiliation. She stepped forward, her voice filled with understanding. "I would be happy to share my room with you, Meredith, for as long as you need."

"Thank you," she whispered against her fingers. "Thank you."

Leah smiled and touched Meredith's shoulder. "And in the mornin', you and me are goin' to see Charlotte. She needs some help, Meredith. She needs your help."

"Is it Henry?" she asked with alarm.

" 'Tis the both of them," she replied. "And I think you need them as much as they need you."

※

With the family retired for the evening, the house was quiet as Amelia stood in front of the mirror that hung on the wall. She brushed her hair as Meredith put on her borrowed night clothes. Meredith slipped between the covers of the narrow bed and watched Amelia. The flickering candlelight cast dancing shadows on the wall with every stroke of the brush. In the warm glow of the light, she thought she saw a tear on Amelia's cheek in the reflection of the mirror. Meredith could only speculate as to the cause of the girl's unhappiness. It pulled at her heartstrings, though, to see her filled with such sadness. Finally, Amelia placed the brush on the bureau and blew out the candle. She pulled back the covers and climbed in beside Meredith. The bed was cold and unwelcoming as she lay on her back, her eyes open as she stared at the ceiling for several minutes.

"Meredith?" she whispered softly, finally gaining the courage to speak.

"Aye?"

"Do you ever wish you were someone else?" Amelia's voice sounded fragile.

Meredith pondered the question for a time. She wasn't sure what answer Amelia was searching for, and it caused her to pray she might know what to say to the girl. "Well, I guess I am someone else now."

"How do you mean?" asked Amelia, her gaze still fixed to the ceiling.

"I mean, I'm not what I used to be," she explained softly. "The Church changed me. Repentin' changed me, and lettin' the Lord change my heart made me a different person too."

"But that doesn't make you someone else, really."

"Maybe not in the eyes of the world, but it does in the eyes of God. I knows some people still thinks of me as what I was—what I did, but, the difference is I know, and God knows I'm not the same person. If others think bad of me, then they answer to God for that."

Amelia pondered Meredith's words for a moment. "But what if it's not something you did, but something someone else did that makes you look terrible—makes you unworthy?" she questioned.

Meredith prayed she was saying the right things. She knew about the girl's parents and the horrible shame she must feel. It was evident Amelia felt some affinity toward her. Perhaps, in the tender mind of the young girl, she felt they both were shunned by the world. "Not too long ago, I learned somethin', Amelia, that helped me. There's a scripture in the Bible, and I'm sorry I can't say just where 'tis, but 'twas like 'twas written just for me."

"Do you remember it?" Amelia asked, rising up on her elbow.

"Well, the important part, anyway," Meredith replied. She turned on her side and raised herself to one arm. The silvery moonlight shed just enough light to distinguish the features of Amelia's face in the darkened room. "For man looketh on the outward appearance, but the Lord looketh on the heart."

"The Lord looketh on the heart," repeated Amelia, mulling over the words in her mind. "Do you really believe that?"

Meredith found a part of herself feeling maternal and loving toward the girl. She couldn't help reaching out and stroking the girl's hair. "I do. And like the Lord looks on your heart, one day, so will the right young man."

It was as if she could read her thoughts. Amelia threw her arms around Meredith's neck and hugged her tight, sniffing back her tears. She found comfort in Meredith's wisdom. "Thank you, Meredith," she whispered, wiping her tears with the sleeve of her nightdress.

Meredith warmed inside. She marveled at the intricate workings of the Lord's hand in all things, that she would be in this house on this night, available to a young girl yearning to be free of her inner demons. For the first time in her life, Meredith was grateful for her past, for she knew what it was like to feel like an outcast. Through the miracle of repentance, she could see with new insight and offer empathy to the heart of a hurting soul.

THIRTEEN

───────── ✦ ─────────

RICHARD SAT IN THE BACK OFFICE of Kenyon & Sons, poring over the books. Business was down from last year. No matter how he figured the numbers, the outcome was always the same. There was at least a thirty percent loss in sales. He shook his head, bewildered by the downturn. He would have to cut back on his orders and perhaps eliminate some of the more costly teas—at least until things improved.

Niall was out front with Jonah, taking an inventory as requested by Richard. Jonah scratched down the numbers Niall provided from his count. Their inventory became sidetracked with Jonah's continued attempts to educate Niall about the gospel. Niall was intrigued by the stories Jonah had told him, but he couldn't bring himself to be influenced by them. Nevertheless, he held Richard and Jonah in high esteem and regarded them to be honorable men.

A customer opened the door, and Niall hurriedly climbed down his small ladder to greet the man. "Aye, sir?" he smiled affably.

The man had a permanent pinched expression on his face, his nose long and narrow. "I'd like to speak with Mr. Kenyon, please. Tell him it's Charles Ormond."

Jonah nodded and quickly disappeared to the back of the store to notify Richard of his visitor. Richard looked up from the books with slight annoyance at the disturbance. "Charles Ormond?" he repeated. "He was Robert's solicitor. What would he want with me?"

Jonah shrugged. "He didn't say, President."

Richard stood up and smiled at the young man. "Please bring him back."

Charles Ormond made his way to the office, where Richard greeted him with an extended hand. Charles offered his limp hand, and Richard tried to look beyond the weak handshake. "What can I do for you, Mr. Ormond?"

Ormond opened a satchel and withdrew several papers, placing them on Richard's desk. "I'm afraid there are some affairs your brother left unattended prior to his death which now, unfortunately, fall upon you."

Richard glanced at the papers then back to Ormond. "Very well. Please, go on," he said, motioning Ormond to take a seat.

"I received a notice of unpaid taxes on your brother's home and also on the business," he began, his narrow expression giving him the look of a shriveled prune. "As legal recipient of his estate, you must bring the taxes current or face additional fines and, if they remain unpaid, perhaps imprisonment."

Richard held up his hands, startled by the thought of such a punishment. "Mr. Ormond, I assure you the taxes will be paid. I apologize that I was unaware of these outstanding debts. How much is required?"

Ormond thumbed through the papers he'd placed on the desk. "The house amounts to fifty pound ten with penalties, and the business forty pounds and . . . six shillings."

Richard's mouth gaped open. How was he to procure such a sum? The store barely cleared two pounds a month after expenses and wages. "There must be some mistake," he said, flabbergasted by the sum.

Ormond pursed his lips and pushed the papers toward Richard. "See for yourself, Mr. Kenyon. You must have these debts cleared by month-end." He got to his feet and closed his satchel. "I'm sorry to be the bearer of bad news, Mr. Kenyon. I will meet with you again soon."

Richard slumped into his chair as Ormond retreated from the office. He closed his eyes and shook his head slowly from side to side. He could never obtain over ninety pounds by month-end— not by year-end. Sighing heavily, he took the papers into his hands to inspect them more closely until his attention was drawn to loud voices emanating from the front of the store.

"See here!" Niall shouted. "What's this all about?"

Three men, each with a heavy bludgeon in his hand, stood menacingly before Niall and Jonah. They moved forward, their eyes narrowed with malice. "What do you want?" Niall demanded again.

The first man shoved Niall aside as the others began smashing the shelves and canisters of teas, swinging their clubs in all directions, crashing products to the ground. Jonah lunged toward the man closest to him, catching the club as it came down. He wrapped his foot around the man's ankle and pulled, sending the assailant off balance as Jonah jerked the club from his hands.

Richard sprang to his feet at the sound of breaking glass and cracking wood. He ran from the office, past the store room, and into the front of the shop. One of the men targeted Niall with his club and reared back to strike. "Niall! Look out!" he yelled.

Richard ran into the midst of the destruction and pulled the man away from Niall's vicinity. Without warning, another of the men took a swing at Richard from behind and hit him in the head. Richard fell to his knees as Niall swung his fist into the man's stomach. The man groaned and dropped the club beside Richard.

"That's enough!" one of the men ordered. "Let's go!"

"That's what Mormons deserve!" shouted another.

"Filthy Mormons!" yelled another as he ran through the door.

Jonah raised the confiscated club and threatened to race from the store. "Jonah, no!" Richard shouted from the floor, still gasping for breath. "Let them go."

Jonah lowered the bludgeon and went to the spot where Richard sat reeling from the blow. "President! Are you all right?"

Richard felt the pounding knot on the back of his head as a trickle of blood ran down his neck. "I think so," he answered.

"Niall, was you hurt?" Jonah asked as he discarded the club from his hands.

"No, thank goodness," he said, shaken by the assault. He started for the door. "I'm goin' for the constable—"

"Wait," Richard ordered as he reached toward the two men for assistance getting to his feet. "Don't go, Niall. It won't do any good."

"But Richard," he implored. "Look what they've done . . . they've destroyed the store. They might've killed us. You can't let 'em get away with this."

Richard's entire head felt as though it was going to explode. His vision blurred as he tried to focus on Niall. "Who were they, Niall? Did you recognize any of them? Do you know their names?"

"Well, no . . . I thinks one of 'em . . . I don't know . . ."

"It won't be of no use if we can't identify 'em," Jonah said. "We's been on the losin' side of justice before."

"But 'tisn't fair," Niall protested. "No one's the right to destroy a man's business because he disagrees with his religion."

Richard managed a brief smile as he leaned heavily against the counter. "There's nothing fair about persecution, Niall. Not to any right-thinking man, at least."

Jonah took Richard's arm and slung it across his shoulder. "Let me help you home," he said, taking charge. "I'll come back and help Niall clean up this mess."

"I can make it," Richard insisted as he tried to take a step. His knees were like rubber, and he found he could not walk unassisted.

"No you can't," the boy replied with authority. "I'll see you home."

Niall began making a pathway through the rubble. "That's right, Jonah. Take him home," he said in agreement. "Get him a doctor."

"No doctor," Richard scowled as he staggered toward the door with Jonah's help.

Jonah was surprised at how heavily Richard leaned against him for stability. It must have appeared as though he were helping a drunken man home from the pub. He was worried for Richard. A blow to the head was a serious thing. He knew it all too well. His older brother died in a mining accident when a chunk of coal gave way from the ceiling of the mine and crashed onto his brother's head. One moment he was alive and the next he was dead.

Jonah shifted his weight beneath Richard's arm as they approached the house. He reached out for the doorknob and called for Sister Kenyon.

Richard didn't want to frighten his wife and tried to stand on his own to show her he was all right, but his world was swirling before him. His knees buckled with the effort, and he collapsed back against Jonah's capable frame.

Leah hurried toward Jonah's insistent call. She blanched at what she witnessed. "Richard! What happened?" she cried, maneuvering beneath his other arm for additional support.

"I'm all right," Richard slurred, "I'm all right."

"Some men attacked the shop," Jonah replied breathlessly. "He was hit from behind."

"Amelia!" she called frantically. "Amelia, we need your help!"

Leah tried to keep her wits about her as they made their way toward the bedroom. "Richard," she implored, "stay with me, it's just a few more feet."

Amelia came running from outside the kitchen, where she had been feeding the chickens. Her face registered the same panic as Leah's. "Uncle Richard!"

"Turn down the bed," Leah ordered.

Richard was like a rag doll, his head rolling back and his limbs of little use. Leah's heart pounded as they managed to get him to the bed, terrified by his lack of his response.

"I'll send for a doctor," Jonah said as he took off Richard's shoes.

"No . . . no doctor," Richard muttered, unable to help with his undressing.

Amelia looked pensively at her aunt. "I think you should," she said.

Leah looked at her husband, his eyes opening and closing repeatedly in a slow, deliberate effort. He was disoriented and near unconsciousness. What could a doctor do for such injuries? "Go find Samuel," she said decisively to Amelia. "He can administer to Richard."

Leah went to the washstand, pressed a clean towel into a pitcher of water, wrung it out, and returned to the bed. She turned Richard's head and parted his hair to inspect the injury. The split in the scalp had stopped bleeding, and she gently cleaned the cut with the moist towel. The large knot at the base of his skull was already bruised and red.

Jonah felt helpless as he stood behind Leah. He looked down on the man who had become like a father to him and began to pray.

Richard was still and unresponsive as Leah draped the moistened cloth across his forehead. She placed her hand on his chest. He was still breathing, but her stomach wrenched at the sight of his motionless frame. "Richard?" she whispered near to his face. "Can you hear me?"

He made no sound, nor did he open his eyes. Leah's heart fell with his silence. She heard Samuel and Claire racing through the house and pivoted toward them. "Samuel," she entreated, extending her hand to him.

Claire's face shadowed her sister's concern as she approached Leah, reaching out her hands to sustain her. "Don't worry. Everything'll be all right," Claire soothed, embracing Leah with all the supportive courage she could muster as Leah absorbed her sister's strength.

Jonah looked at Samuel and was hesitant to leave, but he knew he would be of no use to the family and had promised to assist Niall with the righting of the shop. "I'll come back," he said quietly as he turned to leave.

Samuel let out a slow, steady breath and prepared his mind and spirit to receive the will of the Lord. He briefly glanced at the two women and then placed his hands atop Richard's head. The blessing was short and to the point. He promised Richard would be healed and made well.

Leah felt herself breathe again at the conclusion of Samuel's blessing. She hugged him tightly and thanked him, confident that Richard would be all right. Claire brought a chair from the kitchen and placed it beside the bed. "Sit here," she instructed.

Leah nodded and adjusted the bed covers over Richard's shoulders. She sat down beside him and caressed his cheek. She continued to beseech the Lord as she watched and waited for her husband to regain consciousness. She stroked his dark hair as she hummed quietly to him. The minutes passed slowly, dragging against the hours.

It was nearing evening when Claire returned from checking on Amelia and the boys. Leah scarcely noticed her sister as she stood behind her and lit a candle. The room was cold and damp with the humidity from the bay. Claire reached for a shawl at the foot of the bed and draped it around her sister's shoulders. Only then did Leah glance up at her. "No change?" Claire asked quietly.

Leah shook her head. "I keep waitin' for him to open his eyes, or make a sound, move a finger—anything—but he doesn't."

Claire placed her hand on Leah's shoulder. "Have faith," she said softly.

"I'm tryin'," she replied with a catch in her voice. "I had hoped Samuel's blessin' would be enough, but I don't know." Her throat tightened as she struggled to keep back a flood of tears. "He said he would be made well . . ."

Claire bent down and pressed her cheek against Leah's. "Be strong, Leah. Perhaps it'll just take time." She kissed her sister and left the room to get Leah something to eat.

Leah held Richard's hand, her fingers pressed against his palm. Why wasn't he made well? Had the blessing gone unfulfilled? Or worse, unanswered? She had witnessed miraculous results at the pronouncement of other blessings. Why not Richard? Why, with the life which mattered most to her, must she wait?

Claire came back to the bedroom. The sight of her sister's worn expression and tear-filled eyes tugged at her heart. How she wished she could ease Leah's worry. She set down a plate of bread and cheese and a cup of tea. "Take a moment and eat somethin'," she encouraged. "It's near eleven."

Leah motioned with a nod, her face drawn and haggard. In the shadowed light of the candle, she looked older and pale. "Maybe later."

"I understand," Claire said softly. "I'll sit here with you then. Amelia has the boys already down for the night and is doin' her best to keep her Uncle Richard in her uppermost thoughts and prayers."

Leah turned her face toward her sister. "You must be tired. Why don't you rest for a spell? I'll be all right."

I should be the last of your worries, Claire thought, *but you've always looked out for me.* "You're sure?"

"I'll call if I need anything."

Claire turned and hesitantly started for the door. "I'll leave it open a bit. I'll hear if you call."

Leah stood from the chair and hugged her sister tightly. She held her for a long time as if she might draw strength and comfort from her body. "Good night," she finally said.

Claire found it difficult to withdraw from their embrace. She kissed her sister's cheek and left the dusky room.

Leah's limbs were stiff from the hours of sitting and watching. She stretched her aching back and then removed her shoes and dress. She pulled back the coverlet and slipped into the bed beside her husband, weary and filled with anxious thoughts.

Leah drew herself near to him and rested her arm across his chest. The rhythmic motion of his breathing was somehow comforting, but she couldn't keep the tears from sliding down the side of her face. She looked up at her love spoon hanging on the wall, the symbol of Richard's love for her, and a bittersweet smile brushed her trembling lips. "Richard," she whispered, "you've got to come back to me. I need you too much . . . I can't do this alone."

She wiped her cheeks with the edge of the sheet and stroked his handsome face. "Remember when we met? Remember?" she breathed above a whisper. "When I first saw you, I knew I loved you. No man had ever touched me that way. I'd waited only for you and no one else."

The candle sputtered as it neared the end of its life. The flame flickered and extinguished in a puddle of melted wax. The room grew dark, and Leah sighed heavily. "I needed you then," she murmured, "but I need you even more now, Richard." Leah pushed back a lock of hair from his forehead. "I'll tell you a secret. . . . I was savin' it for a bit longer, but I think now I'll tell it to you. We're going to have a baban." She waited as if he might respond, but she was answered only by his slow, steady breathing.

Her tears came once again, hot and moist against her cheeks. "Our little one needs you," she wept softly against his chest. "I love you so much, Richard . . . so very much . . . Oh, Lord, please don't take him from me. . . ."

Exhausted and drained, Leah's eyes closed as she listened to the cadenced sound of her husband's breathing. Within moments, she was sleeping and dreaming of the time they first met. The clock chimed three times, and Leah awoke with a start. It was still dark. She felt ashamed she'd fallen asleep for the short time she had. Richard's steady breathing brought her some reassurance that he was still with her.

At once the feeling of dread flooded back, and she felt the sickening knot tighten in her stomach. She lay beside Richard for what seemed an eternity, waiting, praying, driven to madness with worry. How long was he to remain unconscious? She could not contain her tears as she wept bitterly against his chest. "Is this a test?" she whispered aloud. "If 'tis, I fear I'm failin' it. . . . Please, have mercy on my weakness, Lord, and forgive my doubtin' heart."

Richard felt his mind opening, as if he was being pulled through a murky tunnel toward a beam of light. As the darkness abated, he became aware. His eyes opened, and he could make out the slight shadows of his room. He could hear something, faint at first, but growing more prevalent with each passing moment. The sound of a woman crying registered to his senses, heartbreaking in its sorrow. It was Leah, he knew. His mouth opened, but he struggled to find a voice. Then a hoarse whisper came. "Don't cry . . ."

Leah's head bolted up, and she stared at him through the darkness. "Richard?" she gasped, her heart racing in her chest.

"I'm here," he said as he reached for her. His arms felt heavy to him, but he was able to make the moves his mind commanded.

She buried her face against his chest and muttered a prayer of thanks as grateful tears of joy wet her cheeks. "Oh, Richard, I thought you were lost to me."

"Hush," he murmured, stroking her hair. "Everything's all right now."

FOURTEEN

As Richard continued to recuperate the next day, Leah scarcely left his side. She was attentive to his every need, although he felt as though it was he who should be tending her. Leah had lost so many babies that it worried him to a frenzy to see her scrambling about the house in her normal fashion.

He held out his hand to her as she scurried by with a fresh candle for the parlor. "Put the fiddle on the roof for a minute and sit down," he said with a bemused smile. "There's something I need to tell you."

Leah paused and took hold of his hand as he pulled her onto his lap. She laughed with the surprise of it and then tried to pull herself up. "You've not been well—"

"I'm well enough to do this," he smirked as his lips met hers.

She placed her slender fingers against his cheek as a look of pained gratitude clouded her face. "Promise you'll never leave me . . ."

He cupped her face in his hands and kissed her again. "Never, *cariad* . . . never."

They fell silent for a moment as Leah traced the line of his jaw with her finger and then gave him a playful tap on the end of his nose. "Now, what was it you wanted to tell me?"

Richard refocused, and his expression slightly darkened. He told her of Mr. Ormond's visit the day of the attack and of the large debts he now owed. He cast his eyes down and took hold of her hand as a weighty anguish encompassed him.

Leah's heart sank. Ninety pounds was an incredible amount of money. She would never see that much in a lifetime, or even two life-times, much less by month-end. She beseeched her Father in Heaven in silent prayer as she wracked her brain for something, anything, that would help them find the needed funds.

Richard sighed. "I could sell the house or maybe the business, but it would be impossible to do so in such a short amount of time."

"Aye," she agreed glumly, her mind still searching for a plan.

He stared at the floor and worked the muscles in his jaw. "I don't know how I can possibly pay it." The thought of debtor's prison mortified him, especially with a little one on the way.

Leah felt the inkling of an idea begin to grow, sparked by something Richard had said. She lifted his chin until their eyes met. There was something in her gaze, a glint of inspiration in her mossy green eyes. "I do," she said with self-assurance.

"How?" he asked incredulously. "We have nothing—"

" 'Tis true, Richard, but your brother does," she said, grinning. "That big, overstuffed house full of clutter Abigail so selfishly collected can all be auctioned. There should be plenty to pay the taxes from that with more to spare."

It was an excellent idea—an incredible idea. How Richard wished he could realize the solutions to problems as quickly and easily as Leah did. He gave her a squeeze and a kiss. "We'll auction off the bed sheets, if we have to," he laughed. "Let them have it all."

"And good riddance to it!"

Within the week, the auction was arranged and advertisements placed in several publications. Samuel and Richard had handbills printed and passed them out on the city streets of Cardiff and placed them in every business that would allow it. The auction would be held with just two days to spare for the payment of the taxes, but Richard was confident the time frame allotted would prove to be sufficient.

Richard, Leah, and Amelia stood on the front steps of the house in anxious anticipation as the crowds gathered. Richard leaned toward Amelia and took hold of her arm. "I know I've asked this of you before," he said above a whisper, "but are you sure there is nothing in the house you want to keep? Anything at all you would like to have as a memento?"

She shook her head. "I'm certain, Uncle Richard. Nothing in this house would bring me a pleasant memory."

Sadly, he knew she was probably right. He squeezed her arm with affection and let go as the auctioneer approached. The man's bustling team was at the ready to bring each tagged item from the house to the front for bidding. The house had been open for viewing, and the potential bidders had made a cursory tour of the contents inside. The auctioneer raised his arms and called for the crowd's attention.

Leah scanned the audience of strangers, and her eyes settled on a familiar figure. It was Reverend Trahern, surrounded by several of his followers. She glared at him suspiciously and tugged on Richard's coat sleeve. "Look over there," she rasped. "It's Trahern."

He focused on the crowd until he found the place where Trahern stood, a smug look on his face as he stared back at Richard. He saw Trahern nod as if giving a signal, and the auctioneer called for the first item. Richard's neck swiveled toward the auctioneer and then back to Trahern. The reverend touched the brim of his tall hat and flicked his hand forward in Richard's direction.

A marble bust of Caesar was brought to the auctioneer's table, and the bidding began.

"The opening bid is a thruppence," the auctioneer shouted.

"A thruppence?" Richard charged beneath his breath as he confronted the auctioneer. "Why are you starting so low? It's worth at least five pound."

The auctioneer glowered at Richard and fingered the wooden gavel in his hand. "Patience, Mr. Kenyon. We must start low and increase the amount with each bid," he answered with annoyance.

"A thruppence!" came a bid from the crowd.

The auctioneer looked in the direction of the bidder. "We have a thruppence," he repeated. "Do I hear a penny?"

Reverend Trahern raised his gloved hand. "A penny here!"

The auctioneer slammed the gavel down on the table. "Sold to the gentleman in the back for one penny."

"This is outrageous!" Richard charged, his fists knotted at his side. "I demand you let the bidding continue until a fair price is reached."

The auctioneer seemed to bristle and then turned to the crowd. "Is there anyone willing to pay more than a penny for this marble bust?" he called.

A round of murmuring circulated through the crowd. No one came forward with a higher bid. Richard felt as though he had been slugged in the stomach. The auctioneer faced Richard again. "There, you see? 'Tis what the market will bear, Mr. Kenyon."

"I see," he conceded bitterly. "I see all too well."

Leah took hold of her husband's hand and clung tightly to it. "Have faith," she said into his ear. "The Lord is mindful of us."

The auction continued, each item bringing far less than its value. Richard wasn't quite sure how Trahern had managed it—what he had done to influence the crowd or what he held over the auctioneer—but only a few times did any item rise beyond one or two bids before the gavel crashed to the table and a boisterous *Sold!* ejected from the auctioneer's mouth.

Richard could scarcely contain his temper, the ire rising in him until it nearly choked the breath from him. But he would not concede to Reverend Trahern's despicable behavior and instead prayed for his temper to subside and for peace to come to his heart.

At the auction's conclusion, the clerk finished tallying the count and subtracted the auction house fees. He gathered up the remaining money and slipped it into a large cloth bag. He went to Richard and handed him a notebook. "I've made an accountin' of your proceeds, sir, and the total comes to ninety-seven pound, five shillin's, and four pence. If you'll sign this receipt, I'll be done."

Richard looked at Leah with a surprised and pleased expression on his face. He took the man's pencil and signed the book and then hefted the bag of money between his hands. It was enough to pay the debt, and that was all that mattered. Despite Trahern's effort to thwart a fair bidding, his brother's debt would be paid.

❧

Leah sat in her mother's kitchen, tracing her finger about the rim of her teacup. The relationship with her mother had been somewhat strained since her baptism, but Leah was hopeful with the baby coming it would help mend the relationship again. "Richard is hopin' for a boy," she said absently. "He won't admit it, of course, but I can tell."

"Well, what man doesn't yearn for a son to carry on his name?" Gwendolyn replied, pouring more tea into their cups.

"What does he do when he has two daughters then?" she asked, indicating her own father.

Gwendolyn smiled. "He loves 'em just the same." She placed the teapot on the table and settled back in her chair. "You girls have always been the candle of my eye, just as you was to your tad."

Leah got a faraway look in her eyes. Only fleeting memories of her father floated through her mind now as wisps of fading reminiscence. She wondered what it was like for her widowed mother, alone all these years.

Gwendolyn picked up the lull in the conversation. "You've been feelin' well?" she asked with concern. She suddenly sprang to her feet and went to the larder. "I wants you to take this."

Leah watched as her mother took a handful of leeks from the larder and placed them on the kitchen table. "Now put these 'neath your pillow at night to keep away the evil spirits."

Leah gave her mother a sideways glance. She didn't hold to the old ways as her mother did and wasn't about to sleep with the strong smelling roots under her pillow.

"Don't you look at me like that," Gwendolyn warned. "I knows you think I'm just a foolish old woman, but heed what I tells you to do!"

Leah nodded and promised she would take the leeks home with her, though she didn't promise to place them under her pillow.

Gwendolyn took her seat at the table once again and placed her teacup to her withered lips. "I hear one of your church people's prize ewe was found dead the other day."

Leah absently fingered the edge of one of the leek's thick green leaves. "Aye, 'twas a horrible thing," she said, taking a sip of her tea. "Someone slit the poor thing's throat and left her there to die. She was found the next mornin'."

Gwendolyn slowly shook her head. "You've a hard forehead,

Leah. You always have. Still, I knows I can't make you come to your wood. 'Tis not for me to wish you from your church."

Leah held her tongue. She didn't want to argue with her mother, nor did she want to continually defend her membership in the Church. "I'm hopin' for a girl," she said, trying to sway the conversation in a different direction.

Gwendolyn peered at her daughter with serious eyes. "Aye, you'll soon know what 'tis like to have your own child, to know what a mother's heart knows, to feel what a mother's heart feels." She studied the steam rising from her cup of tea. "Then you'll know for yourself how deep love really is."

Leah didn't know what to say. She reached for her mother's hand. "I'm so glad you'll be deliverin' the baby. You'll be the first one to see it, to hold it, and I'm so glad 'twill be you who does."

Gwendolyn found a doleful smile came to her lips. "Aye, and you mind me now and put those leeks 'neath your pillow."

❧

Amelia sat on the bench beside her aunt as the Saints quieted for the invocation. She lowered her head but couldn't close her eyes as they darted about the room with dubious curiosity. Was anyone staring at her? Was there a look of disgust on anyone's face at her presence? She had been welcomed to the meeting with smiles and warm handshakes, but she was just a little wary of such a congenial reception. Though she wished it to be genuine, there was still a streak of skepticism running through her mind.

She saw Jonah Reese near the front of the gathering and remembered how kind he had been to her on the day of her father's sentencing. Perhaps he was unaware of her father's horrible crime and would have treated her differently had he known. She tried to focus on what Meredith had taught her about the Lord looking on the heart and dismissed the feelings of uncertainty and inadequacy from her thoughts. She was there to continue learning about the restored gospel of Jesus Christ. She was there to find an answer to her question of baptism which seemed more and more a certainty in her mind. She was there to be spiritually fed, and that was all that really mattered.

The meeting closed and Amelia smiled. *I'm ready*, she thought, *I finally know*. She grabbed her aunt's hand and pulled her toward her Uncle Richard. "Come on," she urged with excitement.

Leah's face twisted into a bemused look of curiosity. "What is it, Amelia?"

Amelia's visage glowed as she came to a stop between her aunt and uncle. She looked at the pair with anticipation as the words blurted from her mouth: "I want to be baptized!"

Leah clapped her hands together and then pulled Amelia into her arms. "Oh, *cariad*, bless you for this answered prayer."

Richard took his turn to hug his niece with a joy-filled heart. "Amelia, how wonderful!"

She gazed up into her uncle's handsome face. "Will you baptize me, Uncle Richard?"

He chuckled and gave her another squeeze. "Just try and stop me," he murmured against her ear.

Amelia suddenly broke free of her family and darted toward Meredith. She called her name and grabbed Meredith's forearm. "I'm going to be baptized!" she exclaimed with glee.

Meredith's eyes widened with delight. "Oh, Amelia! I couldn't be happier! What a day for the King!"

Amelia lowered her tone, and tears welled up in her eyes. "You'll never know how much you've helped me, Meredith. Will you come to my baptism?"

Meredith found her own tears creeping toward her lashes. She could only manage a nod as she took the young girl into her arms.

By now the word had spread through the remaining congregation, and Amelia found herself on the receiving end of heartfelt congratulations and words of encouragement. For the first time in months, perhaps years, she knew what it was like to experience happiness. The ugly darkness of the past began to lift, and its penetrating grip on her soul began to lessen.

Jonah waited for his turn to come forward and speak with Amelia. He unexpectedly found his heart pounding in his chest with a twinge of nervousness. She was even prettier when she smiled, he decided. As the couple ahead of him departed, he extended his hand to her and smiled broadly. "I knew you was meant to be a member of the Church."

Amelia blushed as his hand tightened ever so slightly over her fingers. She could barely bring her gaze to meet his deep blue eyes. "Thank you," she managed to say with a sense of awkwardness. "I hope to be a worthy member."

He reluctantly let his grasp slip from her hand. " 'Tis a sure thing. You will be."

The clouds parted from the gray autumn skies, and a slender shaft of sunshine shone on the group of Saints gathered at the edge of a shallow pond. Richard had arrived early to break away the thin covering of ice that surfaced on the pond. He was already wet to his knees and shivering. The narrow beam of sunlight was most welcome since it provided a modest amount of comparable warmth. The Phillips, Ben, Meredith, and Leah all stood waiting with Amelia. The girl was already shivering from the cool, damp weather of Cardiff as Ben began with a prayer and then started singing "The Spirit of God," the others joining in boisterously. Richard looked upon his niece with benevolence, and although it was a chilly day, he was warmed by the Spirit and excited for the baptism to begin.

Meredith stood beside Leah. "I can't thank you enough for speakin' to Charlotte about me stayin' with her and Henry."

Leah patted Meredith's hand. "Oh, I did nothin'. Charlotte was so excited by the idea she said yes even before I could get all the words out."

"It has been a blessin' for all of us."

"When one door closes . . ."

Meredith grinned. "Aye."

Richard smiled kindly on Amelia as he reached for her hand. "Brace yourself," he warned. "The water is quite cold."

Amelia nodded willingly. "I'm ready," she said, taking her uncle's hand.

The two waded into the water. Richard was able to maintain some control of the shock to his system, but Amelia gasped loudly as they went deeper into the pond. She started trembling as her uncle pronounced the sacred ordinance and prepared to submerge her. She held her breath, and he plunged her beneath the water and pulled her up as quickly as he could. She came up sputtering and wide-eyed, gasping with the shock of going completely beneath the water.

Meredith found herself watching Ben's every move. His tall and slender build seemed to glide through his movements, unintentionally refined and fluid. His lean face still held the remnants of a summer tan from having spent so many hours outside during his missionary pursuits. He was in need of a haircut, she thought, yet she liked the way the length of his hair curled at the nape of his neck. She was especially drawn to his deep-set eyes, blue flames centered in small, darkened caves.

As Ben reached for Amelia's hand to help her onto dry ground, he caught sight of Meredith watching him. For a brief second, their eyes met. She smiled and quickly looked away, but he did not. He'd actually never really seen her before, never noticed how petite she was, or how the light played against her golden brown hair. Her hazel eyes were round and large despite her diminutive face. When Meredith happened to glance back at him, it was Ben who suddenly looked away.

Amelia's entire frame was quivering in waves of violent shivers, and her teeth chattered noisily. Leah wrapped a heavy quilt around Amelia's shoulders and pulled her close. Richard's lips were blue as he hoisted himself from the water. Claire held a welcome blanket open for him.

Ben drew near to Meredith and smiled at her. "Amelia seems quite fond of you."

Meredith momentarily flushed with his attention. "Aye, she's a love."

"How's Brother Bryant? Is he any better at all?"

Meredith's brows knitted together. "No, in fact he's worse than ever."

Ben clasped his hands behind his back as they walked toward the road. "Would he accept a blessing?"

Meredith hunched up one shoulder and let it fall back into place. "Charlotte and me, we've both asked him, and he just says there's no need for it."

Ben drew in a long breath and let it out slowly. "Well, perhaps I'll stop by and see if I can persuade him."

Meredith's lips drew into a quick smile at the thought of seeing Ben again. She hurriedly tried to cover her betraying mouth with a gloved hand, but she knew Ben had seen her instantaneous reaction and that it was too late to undo it. "Aye, maybe you can talk him into it," she said soberly.

Ben found himself stifling a grin of his own as he walked beside her. It was the first time he'd shown any interest in a woman since his wife's passing, and it surprised him. It was a strange mixture of enticement and guilt, but he was grounded enough to know he needed to move on with his life, to find happiness again. The simple fact that he was attracted to Meredith made it seem a possibility.

❦

In the weeks that passed, Meredith was happier than she'd ever been. Ben's attention had brought a level of joy to her life that surpassed her wildest imagination. He was caring and thoughtful and would stop by the Bryants' on his way home from his employment at the woolen mill just to say hello.

Sundays had become their day, one they shared together in worship. They sat together during the meetings and grew together in the gospel. He held her hand as they listened and afterward would discuss what had been taught that day. For the first time in her life, she dared to envision herself as a wife and mother. And it was Ben who brought her to that discovery through his loving understanding of the broken heart and contrite spirit she had offered the Lord. He held no judgments against her, no malevolence toward her past, and gave her only his kindness and affection.

She had also found a loving home with Charlotte and Henry, her attention to them a gift of unselfish service. She loved them as her own parents and enjoyed doting on them and seeing to their needs. With Henry's worsening condition, Meredith was worried and grateful he had finally relented to call a physician.

She stood in the corner of Henry's room as Charlotte paced nervously at the foot of the bed. The doctor concluded his examination of Henry and closed his bag. He looked at the older woman and motioned for her to follow him into the hallway. "What is it?" she breathed, her fingers clenched together in a knot.

"Your husband has a failing heart, Mrs. Bryant," he explained with a furrowed brow. "His cough is from the burden of too much fluid in his lungs, a sign that the heart is failing."

"What's to be done?" she asked, fearful of the answer.

The doctor shook his head slowly. "Nothing can be done. Make him as comfortable as possible. I'll order up a medicine from the chemist and have it delivered. See that he takes two teaspoons a day. It will help with the cough."

Charlotte clutched the doctor's arm. "Is that all?" she asked as if begging for a different answer. "That's all you can do for him?"

He gently patted the gnarled fingers dug into his coat sleeve. "I wish I could do more, Mrs. Bryant. Your husband has lived a long and good life—"

"But you don't understand," she pressed. "I've been married to that man for forty-two years, and all you can tell me is he's lived a long and good life? And I'm supposed to be satisfied with that?"

The doctor pried her fingers from his arm. "I'm sorry, Mrs. Bryant, I truly am. There is nothing else to be done for your husband. Instead of fighting the inevitable, I suggest you make the best of the time you have left with him."

He walked away from her and went downstairs as Meredith followed behind. She stopped him at the door. "How long does he have?" she asked softly.

"It's hard to say," he said, reaching for the door. "Perhaps a few days but not much more than that."

"I see," she said, her heart sinking with the confirmation.

"I'll come by tomorrow," he said, stepping through the door. "Try to keep Mrs. Bryant's spirits up. This will be much harder on her than on him."

"I will," she replied, closing the door. "Thank you, doctor."

Meredith went upstairs and found Charlotte kneeling beside the bed, praying. She hesitated to disturb her, but Henry managed that as he awoke and placed his hand on Charlotte's head. "What are you doin'?" he asked, his voice weak and thin.

She raised her face to him and tried to smudge the tears away before he could see. "How are you feelin'?" she asked as she struggled to her feet.

Meredith came forward and lifted Charlotte by the arm until she was upright. "What can I get for you, Henry?" Meredith asked with a gentle smile.

"Nothin', really," he said, "I'm just . . . tired."

"You must eat somethin'," Charlotte insisted. "You've had nothin' since breakfast, and you need to keep up your strength."

Henry was very pale, his lips tinged in blue. He held out a shaky hand to his wife and beckoned her to sit beside him. He peered at her with dim eyes and smiled gently. "Let's not fool ourselves, my dear. I'm dyin', and we both know it."

Charlotte pressed his hand to her cheek and moistened it with her tears. "Don't say that," she whispered.

"It's all right, love," he comforted tenderly. "It had to happen sooner or later. I'm only sorry that I'll be leavin' you once again, as I did so many times durin' my seafarin' days." He reached out and touched her face. "Think of it as one more sailin'—one more journey to a faraway place. I'll only be gone for a while, not forever, and then we'll be together again."

Meredith bit her lip to keep from crying out and turned to leave. Charlotte felt herself breaking in two and quickly tried to gather her unraveling emotions. "I'll make you some rarebit," she muttered, following Meredith downstairs, pushing the imagery he'd presented to the back of her mind.

The two women went to the kitchen, both aching with the anticipation of the painful loss to come, yet struggling to hold themselves together for Henry's sake and for each other. Charlotte's hands trembled as she shaved the cheese into thin slices. Meredith slowly reached for the knife and took it from her crooked fingers. "Why don't you start some tea?"

Charlotte let loose of the knife and sighed. "I don't know what I'd do without you, *cariad*," she said softly, her words filled with sincerity.

Meredith reached out and gently touched Charlotte's cheek. "That's somethin' you need never worry about. I'll always be here for you."

The old woman patted Meredith's hand. "Now don't be silly. Soon enough, you and Ben'll be paired up," she said with a wistful smile.

Meredith opened her mouth to protest, but Charlotte stopped her. "Now don't try and deny it, my dear," she said lovingly. "I think it's wonderful. You deserve the love of a good man and children of your own someday."

Meredith's eyes clouded, and she grasped Charlotte's hands in hers. "I won't ever leave you, Charlotte, no matter what. You just puts that thought to rest right now."

"You mustn't be unreasonable, Meredith. I know you mean what you say, but soon enough your attentions will be needed elsewhere," she said gently. "The last thing you need be concerned with is some old woman takin' up your time."

Meredith released Charlotte's hands and turned back to the cheese. "There's no more arguin' about this, Charlotte," she said firmly. "Whether or not Ben and me marries, or whether or not I has a dozen children, or whether or not the sun rises in the mornin', I'll be here for you. This is my home now, and you're my family. Nothin' or no one is ever goin' to change that."

Meredith slowly turned back around and took hold of the old woman's age-speckled hands as she peered into her wrinkled face. "I knows what you're sayin'. I do," she said softly, "but I wants you to know I'm not goin' anywhere. I wants to stay with you. Do you understand?"

Charlotte cupped Meredith's cheek with the palm of her hand and smiled. "Aye."

A crashing sound reverberated from upstairs. Meredith's blood ran cold as she darted from the kitchen and raced up the stairs to Henry's room. Her heart pounded in her throat as she arrived to see Henry slumped over the edge of the bed, the tray of water and medicine splashed across the carpet.

"Henry?" she breathed, reaching for his dangling arms. She pulled him back against the pillows and felt for a pulse, but the once- beating heart was still. She pressed her ear to his chest but heard nothing.

Charlotte stood in the doorway, frozen by the vision of her husband's motionless form. Meredith peered over her shoulder, the look on her face confirming Charlotte's worst fear. An overwhelming grief swelled within her until she was consumed by it. She clutched the door frame and buried her face against her arm.

As she wept, a vision came clearly to her mind. It was of Henry standing on the deck of a ship, waving and smiling to her as the ship sailed from port. He was young and handsome, strong and virile as he captained the vessel toward the unknown. "I'll return for you, sweetheart," she heard him call. "Wait for me?"

"I will," she whispered softly. "Don't be long . . ."

FIFTEEN

———— ❧ ————

As the Sunday service drew to a close, Leah once again scanned the body of the Saints. Their numbers were growing each month, in spite of the ugly attempts to thwart the work. In fact, with so much attention drawn to the Church by the ravings of Trahern and his cohorts, many attended meetings and services out of curiosity alone. Several observers were converted instantly by the strength of the Holy Ghost that was present during the meetings. Some found their curiosity growing into conviction and gradually came into the fold.

The Cardiff Branch now numbered over seventy faithful members, with new baptisms almost weekly. With the increased membership came more joyous blessings to the branch, but it also brought more responsibility to Richard with the many needs and requests imparted to him.

"Before we offer the benediction," Richard announced, "I wanted to take a moment to read to you a letter from President Brigham Young that he wrote a year ago and was included in the April edition of the *Prophet of the Jubilee*. Please let me share with you this portion. Richard held the periodical in his hands and began to read:

> "On April 14th, we, together with 143 of the brethren, began our journey toward the west. We made a new road for close to one thousand miles, until landing in the Great Basin, where we arrived in the latter part of July. We found ourselves here in an extremely beautiful valley, of some twenty by thirty miles in extent. To the east

there is a high mountain range, capped by perpetual snow. There is a beautiful line of mountains in the west, watered by showers of abounding rains. Utah Lake is on the south, hid by a range of hills, with a delightful prospect of the waters of the Great Salt Lake to the northwest as far as the eye can reach, interspersed with islands of different shapes and sizes. The valley reaches further to the north, along the eastern shores, for about sixty miles, to the mouth of the Bear River. The soil of the valley appears to be extremely fertile, although the moisture is not always sufficient to produce certain kinds of vegetation. Many streams run through it; and among others, the western Jordan (which runs from Utah Lake) at its height runs through the center of it from south to north. The climate is healthful and lovely, not too hot, rather dry and summer-like. Salt abounds at the lake. There is a variety of springs, warm, hot, and cold, coming up from the earth in several places; and there are excellent advantages with respect to streams to turn mills and machines of every kind and size. Timber is not very abundant across the valley; but plenty of box, fir, pine, and sugar maple, &c., trees may be found on the mountains, for present needs, until more can grow.

"In this splendid valley we have established a city, the name of which will be, Great Salt Lake City."

Richard smiled and folded the paper. "Brothers and sisters, as you know, President Jones is preparing to return to America one year from now and has invited any who will to join him." He scanned the attentive faces before him. "Who is ready? Who will heed the call and leave the persecution and wickedness of Babylon behind and join with the Saints in America?"

An excited undercurrent of murmurs rippled through the congregation. Wide eyes and gaping mouths were evident as the message penetrated their minds. People joined hands in solidarity of the long-awaited answer to their prayers. Now was the time. It was sanctioned and presented as a welcomed invitation.

The murmurs subsided as Richard continued. "The Lord has blessed the Saints indeed with an abundant land on which He will gather His chosen people. I urge each of you to humbly pray and consider whether your future lies in America among the Saints of Zion." Richard closed the meeting and went to his family.

A chill ran up Leah's spine. She and Richard had considered the possibility of emigration, and now she found herself enthralled by the description of the valley in America. Her desire to be counted in the presence of the prophet and apostles of the Lord fed her sense of commitment, giving her the courage to accept President Jones's invitation.

She touched her emergent belly with tender hands and smiled at the thought of her child growing up in Zion, free from the persecution and hatred they found in Wales. Leah looked at her sister, the question burning through her thoughts to Claire's. Their eyes met with intensity. As she studied her sister's face, she found relief in discerning Claire's answer to the unspoken question.

Claire looked at Samuel, and he smiled as the warmth of his own witness came fully to his bosom. He couldn't help but chuckle as he glanced at Richard. "Well, you know it would do no good to separate Leah and Claire by a continent," he said with a grin.

"Then we can go?" Claire breathed.

Samuel nodded and smiled. "Aye, the Spirit's spoken, and I'd be a fool to deny it."

"You must understand," Richard said with caution, "this may be the greatest challenge of our lives. I promise it won't be easy."

"I've come to believe that nothin' comes easy to the members of this Church," Samuel replied, his expression growing more sober. "But, I also believe we'll be blessed for it."

Amelia encircled Leah's thickened waist with her arm. "We can do it, Uncle Richard. The Lord will be with us."

"Aye, and we'll finally be free of persecution," Leah added with determination. "We'll be among the Lord's chosen people of Zion, where everyone shares the same heart."

Hearing Richard's words stirred an even greater yearning in Ben's heart to return to America. He imagined himself settled in the broad valley with a home he built of his own hands and ground he tilled with his own plow. And Meredith was there, beside him, sharing together all the rest of their days.

He looked at Meredith with loving eyes and smiled at her as they stood to leave the meeting. Ben offered his arm to Charlotte as she came to her feet. "It sounds like the valley of the Great Salt Lake is quite beautiful," he commented.

Meredith looked at him with interest. "With mountains on

either side, and the streams and rivers, it must be," she agreed.

"It may be lovely," Charlotte said with skepticism, "but it'll never be Wales."

"To be sure," Ben was quick to add. "But Wales will never be the heart of Zion."

Meredith smiled. She seemed to grasp his intention and prayed she would be a part of his plans. She slipped her hand into his as they walked into the bright sunlight. The sky was clear of clouds and brilliantly colored like that of a robin's egg despite the cold winter temperature. "Let's go for a walk," she suggested to Ben. "Do you mind, Charlotte?"

Charlotte gave her a knowing smile. "I think that's a splendid idea. I can see myself home," she said, touching Meredith's forearm. "You two enjoy yourselves."

Ben kissed the old woman's cheek and gave her a wink. "I won't keep Meredith long."

"It matters not to me how long you keep her today," she quipped, "just so's you keep her."

Meredith blushed and laughed softly. Ben linked his arm through hers as they strolled away, the slight warmth of the sun radiating across his shoulders. "She's quite something," he commented. "How is she doing, really?" Meredith gave a shake of her head. "She's miserable some days and then fine on others," she replied. "I tries to make her happy, though I don't know what her future holds."

They walked leisurely along the street for a few more steps, and then Ben stopped and faced Meredith. "And what about *your* future?" he asked, swallowing hard against her impending answer. "Would your future be a happy one spent with me as my wife?"

Meredith took in the words she'd longed to hear. Her heart skipped a beat as she contemplated an affirmative answer, and then she remembered her promise to Charlotte. Her joyous expression gradually melted, and Ben's heart sank. "Oh, Ben, I would . . . but I can't . . ."

He screwed up his face in pained confusion. "I don't understand. Why not?"

Meredith lowered her gaze, unable to bear the look of disappointment on Ben's face. "It's Charlotte," she said softly. "I promised her I'd never leave her." She looked into Ben's deep-set eyes for understanding. "She needs me, Ben. She has no one else. She took me in when no one else would. She's given me a home, and most important she gave me her love. I can't leave her, especially now that Henry's gone."

Ben was touched by Meredith's loyalty and love for the old woman. He, too, was fond of Charlotte, and he found he loved Meredith even more for her compassion. "You needn't leave her, sweetheart," he promised, taking hold of her hand. "Let me be a part of your promise to her. Let me help you fulfill that promise. We'll do it together."

Meredith found the lump in her throat choking off her words. She threw her arms around his neck and struggled to contain her tears. "Oh, Ben," she whispered, her heart bursting with happiness. *What a marvel the Lord has brought to my life,* she thought. Her wildest of dreams were coming true, and she thanked her Heavenly Father for the miracle of forgiveness.

Ben leaned down, kissed her softly, and embraced her tightly against his lean frame. He was filled with a new sense of life—of joy—something he feared he would never feel again. As he kissed her, he pressed his face against hers. "I love you," he murmured. "I love you, Meredith."

"And I love you, Ben," she answered softly, "more than you'll ever know."

Two men raced past them at a frantic pace. They were quickly followed by others. Curious about the commotion, Ben snagged one of the men by the arm, bringing him to a halt. "What's going on?"

"The church roof's collapsed," the man panted breathlessly. "People are trapped . . ."

Ben bolted into action. He found Richard still hovering near the entrance to the Tredegar Arms and watched as the branch president took on a mantle of authority. He called to the remaining Saints and shouted orders for the men to follow and the women to bring bandages and water. The membership scrambled to fulfill their directives. Richard led the men into the street and followed those headed in the direction of the disaster.

They ran three blocks and caught up with others who continued on another two streets before rounding a corner. Richard recognized the church immediately. It was Reverend Trahern's. The building was well over three centuries old, so it was no surprise that a portion of the roof had given way, the strain it had labored under for decades finally losing its battle to gravity.

A mass of people had gathered around the church, some looking helpless and useless while others tried to dig through the rubble in search of those trapped beneath. The northern third of the roof had caved into the middle of the church, exposing serrated shards of timber, splintered and ragged as they jutted upward toward the clouded November sky.

Portions of the north wall of the church had crumbled with the force of the collapsing roof, burying rows of pews of worshipers beneath stone and timber. The great wall left a gaping gash open to the street, and people crowded through the breach in search of loved ones. Cries and shouts for help emanated from beneath the debris as frantic rescuers heaved bits of wreckage toward the northern facing street. There were only two doors to the church, one on the east side and the other facing west. With the collapse of the roof, the entrances were mostly blocked. The only feasible way to reach those trapped was to dig through the ruins or attempt access through a window.

Richard assessed the situation and quickly realized the chaos of effort was doing little to accomplish rescue. It was also difficult to know how sturdy the remaining roof was now that some of its support beams had been destroyed. Richard knew it was likely that the entire roof structure would continue to give way.

"You men!" Richard yelled above the disorder. "Form a line and pass the rubble, man to man, toward the street! You there," he shouted, pointing to men standing idly by, "find something to help support the rest of the roof!"

The men obeyed without question, finding some sense of relief that someone was trying to bring order to the chaotic situation. Richard looked at Ben and Samuel. "Go through the windows to see if we can reach anyone inside." He spun toward Jonah. "Help those men find something to support the roof."

Reverend Trahern sat on the curb near the south end of the

building, his fine robes covered in dust, his spirits crushed by the collapse of his church. He sat there, stunned and unable to move, rendered impotent by the loss of his beautiful structure.

A member of his congregation hurried toward him, his eyes large with news. "Reverend!" the man called anxiously. "Reverend, Richard Kenyon is here! He's organizing men and shouting orders!"

Trahern suddenly roused to life, his face reddening as he scrambled to his feet. He stormed toward the opposite end of the church and found Richard directing the rescue efforts with competence. Trahern came up from behind and spun Richard around by the arm. "How dare you!" he charged. "Keep your filthy hands off of my church!"

Richard regarded him with a momentary look of shock that quickly turned to disgust. "There's no time for this, Trahern! I'm only here to help."

"I don't want your help!" he spewed, knotting his fists as his eyes bulged in anger. Trahern reared back his arm, ready to deliver a violent strike to Richard's face. His arm arced, forward but Richard was too quick for Trahern and seized his arm before he could deliver the blow.

Richard clutched Trahern's forearm and glared at him hotly. "Why don't you act like the leader you profess to be and help these people instead of attacking me!"

"Let him go!" shouted someone from the crowd. "He's the only one who knows what to do!"

Trahern swung about, glaring in the direction of the unrecognized voice. "Who said that?" he demanded.

Richard turned his attention back to the rescue. He saw a man's leg appear beneath the debris and raced forward. "Careful now," he shouted to the men, kneeling down to see how much more needed to be moved to free the man.

Trahern pivoted sharply and ran full force toward Richard, attacking him from behind and tackling Richard spread-eagle to the ground. Richard was pinned beneath the girth of the man and writhed to free himself as he struggled to regain the breath that had been knocked out of him. Two men ran forward and grabbed Trahern by the arms, yanking him off of Richard and to his feet.

"Get him out of here!" one of them ordered as two others came to help keep Trahern under control.

Trahern shouted wildly and cursed at Richard as he was dragged away from the scene. Richard glanced over his shoulder at the struggling reverend and then returned his full attention to the disaster.

A deafening roar of thunder rumbled through the darkening sky as the clouds suddenly unleashed a torrent of freezing rain. Undaunted by the additional assault, Richard dropped to his knees and reached beneath the stone and wood for the man's exposed leg. "Can you hear me?" he shouted into the small opening. There was no answer.

The men worked urgently to extricate the unresponsive man as the rain drenched them thoroughly and lightning pierced the sky with vengeance. Many of the useless onlookers peeled away from the scene, urged toward drier places. But the Saints were impervious to the conditions and worked with fervor to free their fellow citizens.

After hours of labor, the last victim was retrieved from the rubble. When all was said and done, they counted seventeen dead and twenty-three injured. The mourning members of the Methodist church wailed and sobbed over their loss. The Saints did their best to comfort and aid the survivors and those who had lost loved ones, but Trahern was nowhere to be found. Finally, Richard led the Saints away, their bone-weary bodies aching and frozen with cold, but satisfied they had done all they could to help.

Within a week of Ben and Meredith's marriage, they were comfortably settled in the small servant's room off of Charlotte's kitchen. They preferred the cozy room, which allowed them a measure of privacy and quiet. Meredith's happiness was so encompassing she would have lived beneath a rock if Ben had asked her to. Never in her life had she expected to experience such joy as her marriage to Ben had brought. She counted herself the most blessed woman on earth, and it showed on her face every time she looked at her husband.

Ben sat at the kitchen table with only the vague light from a candle spilling out from the tiny bedroom and a bright moon beaming through the kitchen window. He held his head in his hands and thought about America. He knew that was where his heart resided, his desire to return now a possibility with Meredith in his life. Joining with the Saints in the valley of the Great Salt Lake was becoming an overpowering angst, yet he feared Meredith's reaction should he express it.

His new wife was bound to caring for Charlotte, and Charlotte was bound to remain in Wales. He had no other recourse than to put his own plans aside until the day came when Charlotte was released from this earthly life, and he and Meredith would be free to emigrate.

Meredith peered out from the bedroom, her form blocking most of the light from the doorway. "Ben?" she called softly.

He didn't hear her. He was too lost in his thoughts. When she called him again, he raised his head toward her voice and found her standing opposite him. "What is it, love?" he answered.

She sat on the kitchen chair across from him and reached for his hand. "What's troublin' you?"

Ben was almost embarrassed. He hadn't meant for her to catch him in his thoughts. "It's nothing," he said, trying to dismiss her concern. "Let's go to bed."

Meredith squeezed his hand more tightly. "Ben," she said with meaning. "If we're to be man and wife, you must share your thoughts, even those you'd rather keep hidden."

Ben grazed his thumb across her fingers as they held hands. He didn't want his desires to become a point of contention, nor did he want to keep her from sharing in his dreams. Slowly, he formulated his thoughts and peered at her through the darkened shadows. "I want you to know I've never been happier than I am at this very moment," he said quietly.

Just for a second Meredith's heart seized in her chest. What was he about to tell her? Something horrible? Something to cause her panic? She held her breath and waited for him to continue.

"And until I met you . . . fell in love with you . . . I never imagined myself wanting to return to America."

Meredith's heart sank into the pit of her stomach. "And now you do?" she said, completing his thought.

Ben raised her hand to his lips and kissed her fingers. "And now

I do," he said. "I want us to join the Saints, to go with the Kenyons and make a new home for ourselves together where we can live in peace."

Meredith was quiet for a moment. She had sensed his need to return home since the Sunday President Kenyon read the excerpt from the Jubilee of President Young describing the Salt Lake Valley. She had hoped beyond hope then to be a part of Ben's plans, and now she was, but her promise to Charlotte kept her from emigrating.

Upstairs, Charlotte was unable to sleep and found the moonlight exceptionally bright as it penetrated her window with its ivory glow. She threw back the covers to pull the curtains and remembered there was one piece of shortbread left in the pantry. A quick trip down-stairs for a bedtime snack would do just the trick to take her mind off her sleeplessness. She ordered Captain to stay and slipped silently down the stairs, guided by the ample streams of moonlight through every window.

Low and hushed voices grew more distinguishable as she padded down the hallway toward the kitchen. She heard Ben and Meredith talking and decided not to interrupt them for her treat. As she turned to leave, her ears pricked with the mention of her name. Charlotte froze in place and strained against the quiet to hear their conversation.

"I love you for your commitment to Charlotte," Ben said with earnest, "and I would never ask you to break your promise to her, and she would never come with us, even if we asked her. Wales is her home. It's where Henry is buried. No, we'll stay in Wales for as long as it takes. Perhaps when things have changed, after she's gone . . ."

Meredith winced and squeezed his hands. "Oh, Ben, 'tisn't the answer either," she cried. "I wants to go to Zion with you . . . we can't give up on that dream. Maybe we can convince her to come with us."

Ben smiled in the softened shadows of the room. "No, sweet-heart, if we asked her to do that, she probably would, for your sake, and would that be fair to Charlotte?"

"I suppose not," she replied sadly.

"Then for now we shall keep our plans to ourselves." He kissed her hand again. "We're young enough, and our dreams can wait."

Charlotte's stomach churned as she made her way back to her room. A gnawing sadness consumed her soul at the thought of Meredith's promise to her. She lay on the bed and covered her face with a pillow. Streams of tears wet the pillowcase as she sobbed against the feathery down. She cursed herself for the burden, the stumbling block, she'd become to Meredith. It was just as she had feared it would be when Meredith had made such a binding promise. It cut Charlotte to the core knowing she was the cause of Meredith's postponed happiness. Yet she knew that even if she released Meredith fully from her promise, she would never comply. Even at the expense of Meredith's own dreams, she would remain true to her oath. Charlotte was convinced it would be pointless to insist otherwise.

Although she could not force Meredith to relinquish her allegiance, perhaps there was another way to fulfill the girl's true desires. So touched by Meredith's tenacious love for her, Charlotte contemplated the unthinkable. Could she forsake her comfort and happiness to facilitate a dream? Could she set aside her own selfish stubbornness, her reservations, her reluctance? If Meredith loved her enough to forsake Zion and remain in Wales, did she love Meredith enough to leave it?

❧

January of 1848 was bitter cold. It gnawed at the windows of Leah's bedroom. Frosted patterns of fairy's breath crusted the panes with silvery white.

Gwendolyn had everything ready for the birth of her grandchild, but she was torn between the joyous arrival of the infant and the devastating departure her daughters would be making to America. She fought a rising sense of anger that seemed to take control of her at times, causing her great anxiety and frustration. She was trapped between cursing the church that was taking them away from her and cursing her children for daring to leave.

Leah's contractions were nearing ten minutes apart, and she hated the defensive wall she sensed surrounded her mother. It pained her to feel the tension between them. "Mam," she called during a lull, "come sit with me."

Gwendolyn's face registered her stern resistance to conversation.

Reluctantly she moved closer to the bed and sat on the corner farthest from her daughter, her posture rigid with opposition. Leah reached for her hand, forcing Gwendolyn to move closer. "Mam," she said softly, *"Dw i'n dy garu di.*[3]"

Gwendolyn struggled to maintain her façade of severity but as she looked momentarily away, her defiance melted, and her expression softened. "And I loves you, *cariad.*"

"Nothin' will ever change that, Mam, nothin'."

Gwendolyn lowered her face and nodded. "I knows it."

Leah stroked the back of her mother's thin hand. "I'm not leavin' Wales to spite you."

"I knows that too, *cariad.*"

"Remember how hard you worked when we were young girls? You were determined to do whatever it took to keep us out of the coal mines or the poorhouse, remember? And it was a great sacrifice for you, Mam, a heavy price to pay to keep us together."

"Aye, but it was worth the sacrifice . . . and I'd gladly do it again if need be."

Leah beseeched her mother's hazel eyes for understanding. "Aye, you did it for your children, because you loved us."

Gwendolyn's eyes clouded with tears. Her throat constricted as she realized what her daughter was trying to tell her. It made it no easier to accept as she found her heart struggling to understand, but she knew her daughter was willing to make sacrifices for her children now too, just as most mothers do.

Leah's hand started to tighten around her mother's as another contraction gripped her body. She held her breath against the rising pain and rolled onto her side. Claire entered the bedroom with a tray and closed the door behind her. Her mother had instructed her to make a strong leek soup for Leah, which she believed would help calm the pains of childbirth. Claire placed the tray on the bureau and turned her attention to her sister.

Leah's contractions were coming more frequently, but the baby seemed to be making little progress. The hours mounted, and Leah lay drenched in sweat, her hair matted to her forehead, her body weak with fatigue. She was exhausted beyond anything she'd ever

---

3. Dw i'n dy garu di.—"I love you."

known. The piercing, wrenching pains had drained her of all her resources, and she felt herself on the brink of hysteria and collapse.

Gwendolyn was beginning to worry. She could tell the baby was not in the breach position, but protracted labor only added greater risk to the mother and child. Claire raised a cup of leek soup to her sister's lips and urged her to drink again.

Leah swung her head to the side and pushed the strong liquid from Claire's hand. "No more . . . 'tisn't helpin'."

"Just a sip," she pressed.

Leah was adamant. She shoved Claire's hand away with suprising force, causing the cup to fly across the bedroom. Claire took no notice of the aggressive act and placed a cool cloth on her sister's brow.

"One more, *cariad*," her mother encouraged. "The baban's near . . ."

She railed against her mother's order, rolling her head from side to side in rejection of the dreadful command. Her mother urged her again with greater insistence. In defiance of her own will, she drew all her remaining strength for yet another push. Claire helped Leah by supporting her shoulders from behind as she strained against the mind-numbing pain. Leah gasped and fell back against her sister. "I can't . . . I can't," she panted.

"You can," Gwendolyn ordered. "Come now, you're a Murdock. We're made of sterner stuff!"

"One more push," Claire encouraged, "and then it'll be over. You can do it, Leah."

Leah drew in a long, deep breath and prayed the horrendous ordeal would end. She gritted her teeth and pushed with all her might. A guttural growl emanated from her throat, growing to a crescendo with the increasing effort to expel the baby.

Gwendolyn's eyes grew wide. "Good, good. Keep pushin'!"

Leah summoned strength from deep within her—the last of her reserves to see this through. It was now or never, she determined, or she feared she would die in the attempt. She focused her will and commanded her body to obey.

Gwendolyn rotated the baby's shoulders with Leah's final endeavor, and the tiny infant was delivered into Gwendolyn's able hands. "That's it, Leah! You've done it!" she exclaimed, wiping the baby's face and mouth clean. "Leah, you've a daughter!"

"A girl . . . a baby girl." Leah breathed heavily as she lay back against the perspiration-soaked pillows.

Gwendolyn tied the umbilical cord in two places and cut the cord between the ties. Claire immediately swept the baby girl into a towel and began wiping her clean. The infant filled her tiny lungs with oxygen and announced herself to the world with a high-pitched cry.

"Oh, she's beautiful, Leah," Claire exclaimed as she placed her in a clean blanket and handed her to her sister.

Leah took the noisy bundle eagerly into her arms and peered at the dark haired little girl. A sudden surge of euphoria washed over her as she touched her baby's tiny reddened face with the tip of her finger and kissed her little cheek. Leah was instantly lost in an exquisite feeling of love like none she'd ever known. This was her baby, hers to love forever, she thought. "My little Seion," she whispered against her tiny face. "We've been waitin' for you."

The baby seemed to respond to her mother's gentle voice, and her cries began to subside. They had named her Seion, Welsh for Zion. Her name was fitting of the life she had chosen to lead in a time before this one. She would be the encouragement, the inspiration leading her parents toward a better life of peace nestled amid the valley of the Great Salt Lake. Leah looked at her mother and smiled. "She is beautiful, Mam. Did you see?"

Gwendolyn returned a loving smile. "Aye," she beamed, "she looks like you."

"Where's Richard?" Leah asked, casting her eyes toward the door.

"Just a bit longer," Gwendolyn urged with patience, "and then he can come in."

Claire moistened a cloth with fresh water, gently wiped Leah's face, and smoothed back her disheveled hair. "That's better," she smiled.

Gwendolyn completed her work and pulled the sheet over Leah's weary frame. "All right," she nodded at Claire. "Send him in."

Claire hurried to the bedroom door. As the handle turned in her fingers, Richard was there, both eager and nervous as he peered over her shoulder. "Come in," she greeted with a smile, "and meet your new daughter."

Richard's face lit with a loving glow as he grinned at Claire. "A girl?" he asked with a gleaming smile. She nodded. "Leah . . . is she all right?"

"See for yourself," Claire replied, stepping aside as he rushed into the room.

Leah stretched her fingers to him. "Come and see your little Seion," she implored.

Richard seized her hand and kneeled beside the bed, gazing in wonder at the blanketed bundle in Leah's arms. His heart melted as he studied Seion's small, round face. He reached out and touched her thick, dark hair and found his lashes moist with tears. Richard was enraptured as he gazed in amazement at his infant daughter. "Look at her . . . she's so tiny . . ." he marveled.

Leah caressed his face and smiled softly. Richard clasped his hand over hers and kissed her, his sense of joy bursting from every limb. He stroked her temple and kissed her again. "Thank you," he whispered, pressing the palm of her hand against his lips. "I love you so much."

The baby's delicate, bow-shaped lips stretched with a little yawn, and she opened her eyes for the first time, blinking at her astounded parents. They smiled in response to Seion's seeming awareness, instilled with love for their little girl.

Leah gazed into her baby's sweet face. A wave of contentment rippled through her being, and the sense of maternity surprised her with its depth and possession. She had never suspected she could feel such incredible and ecstatic love as she did for this child. A whole new perspective opened up to her as she began the briefest glimpse into motherhood. Her world was suddenly colored by and for this baby girl who lay so helplessly in her arms, and she knew her life would never be the same.

Richard felt as though he were floating, the impact of the ordeal finally coming into full focus. He was at last a father and never imagined himself feeling more protective than he already did of Leah, but this tiny infant made him feel as though he could stand off the world for her with his own bare fists if needed.

He was overwhelmed and worn thin from the hours spent in apprehension of Leah's labor. As he marveled at the miracle of Seion's delivery into the world, he offered a prayer of gratitude to his Father in Heaven and prayed he would know how to be a good father. He prayed for Seion, that she would grow strong in the gospel and come to love it and serve her Heavenly Father all of her days.

His heart was full, his soul content, and he realized that nothing in this world would ever surpass the way he felt at this moment. He at last knew the exquisite joy of parental love and the depth to which it could penetrate his being. He prayed to be worthy of Leah and Seion, and he vowed to dedicate his life to them always.

Richard felt an even greater sense of urgency to reach Zion, to fulfill the measure of their providence in the American West. They yet faced months of preparation, planning, saving, and sacrifice before their journey could begin, but he believed it would be accomplished. He knew the Lord would help them, and he knew his love for Leah would nourish his courage and strengthen his resolve.

He thought of his precious Seion, leaving her native land so young that she would never remember its lush, green valleys and craggy mountains, the whispering winds of her heritage, the ancient odes of time burned deep within the souls of its people. Nor would she remember the ugliness shown to so many of the Lord's Saints by her fellow Welshmen. At least he could spare her that painful memory. She was the beginning of a new generation to be raised in the shadows of Zion. She would become the beacon for generations to come, a shining light of destiny painted with the brush of the gospel of Jesus Christ.

VICKIE IS A NATIVE UTAHAN, but she spent her early years living in the states of Idaho, Colorado, Montana, and Nebraska. After many successful years in the world of business, her love of writing and penchant for history have resulted in turning a new page in her life as a novelist. She is an accomplished composer and produced playwright who enjoys spending time with her family, camping, and traveling. She loves animals, especially her cat, Katie.